It's Only Love

CITRUS PINES:
BOOK 1

Lila Dawes

It's Only Love – Citrus Pines Book 1

Dedication

To my mum, thank you for showing me how it's done…

…but please don't read this…

Contents

Chapter 1

I need a drink, a very big drink, Christy Lee sighed as she pulled her car into the parking lot of The Rusty Bucket Inn. She switched off the engine and peered up at the old building that was set back off the road, hidden away in the brush. If you didn't know it was there, you would never find it. The inn itself was a rustic style bar and restaurant that had a row of four cozy, log cabins located behind it for out-of-towners to stay in. Hell, the locals used them the most, usually after a few too many of Taylor, the owner's, lethal cocktails. Next to the first row of cabins was Taylor's private cabin.

Christy hadn't been back here for fifteen years but not much had changed. A wooden porch ran along the front of the building holding a couple of battered barstools, and there was a small, fairly new children's play area to one side. The surrounding trees swayed gently in the breeze and with the moonlight peeking through here and there, the place looked goddamn picturesque. Christy checked her reflection in the rear-view mirror. Her blond curls had gone fluffy in the heat and she already had a tinge of sunburn across her cheeks and nose.

She sighed and looked away, grabbing her purse and rummaging inside for her lipstick. Snagging the tube, she turned back to the mirror. *Pink Dynamite* was the name of it, and she was drawn to it the moment she saw it. The shade seemed like everything she wasn't; loud, bold, confident, and sexy. The second the salesgirl applied the tester, Christy was sold and she had worn it now for ten years. It was like her safety blanket and she felt naked without it.

She finished applying and dropped the tube back in her purse. Taking a deep breath, she opened her car door and headed towards the bar. The closer she got, the bigger the pit of nerves in her stomach seemed to grow, she chalked it up to seeing her friends for the first time in a year. They usually came to visit her in the city because they knew how she felt about her hometown. All this place did was remind her of grief, pain, and loneliness.

As she pushed open the doors, the sound of old school rock music washed over her, followed by a feeling of nostalgia. The scent of alcohol and cloying perfume hung heavy in the air, invading her nostrils. She glanced around the interior of the bar. Music posters of rock legends lined the walls, none of whom had ever performed here, but the bar was a hotbed for novice singers. In one corner, there was a small, wooden, curved stage with a couple of stools and a microphone.

Christy knew this was where Justine liked to perform regularly, she was a hit with the crowd, or so Christy had heard. Because she never came home, she never had the chance to see her best friend play, a wave of guilt washed over her at the thought. Hopefully, Justine would perform while she was in town and she would finally get to see her sing. Next to the stage was a corridor that led down the back of the bar and split off to the kitchen and the restrooms.

Opposite the entrance was the bar itself. Neon signs and full-length mirrors ran along the wall behind it and bottles of spirits were stacked across the back. The bar was made from rich oak with a bronze rail along the front for patrons to lean on when they weren't sitting on the worn, leather stools. The deep color and pattern of the wood made it the focal point of the room; she could see why Taylor was so proud of the place. The standard bar jukebox and pool table were also present, along with some worn leather booths that ran alongside the other end of the building.

Christy looked around, surprised at how packed the place was. Couples danced by the stage on the makeshift dance floor, and the tables surrounding it were nearly all full. A group of guys were playing pool, two people were making out in a booth, and some elderly gentlemen were propping up the bar, flirting shamelessly with Taylor. When Taylor spotted her, she screamed and came charging around the bar, throwing herself at Christy.

"Oh my God, you came!" Taylor squealed.

"Of course I did, I got here this morning," Christy replied, laughing. Taylor pulled back and looked Christy over.

"Fuck, you look gorgeous!" she exclaimed, and Christy felt herself flush. Taylor always complimented people, believing that everyone deserved to know how beautiful they were inside and out. Her compliments always made

Christy feel a little uncomfortable, but because she was working on building her self-esteem, she embraced it. Christy looked Taylor over. Her friend was a tall sarcastic redhead covered in piercings and tattoos, whose language made sailors blush.

"So do you, as always. Is that a new piercing?" Christy asked, pointing to Taylor's nose.

"Yeah, I suddenly realized the other day that I didn't have it done, and two hours later, I did! Randy, Derek, move over and give Marilyn some room," Taylor said, gesturing at the two older men at the bar. Christy rolled her eyes at the nickname; her friends had called her Marilyn for years as she had the same blond, curly bob, and curves as the infamous star. Except her curves were much curvier and her hair was much fluffier. She had no idea who started saying it first, but it had been going on for a while. Taylor pulled Christy over, put her on a stool and started making her a drink.

Christy gazed around again. "This place is amazing. Is it always this busy?" she asked.

"Are you kidding? This is a quiet night," Taylor replied, laughing. Christy could definitely see why Taylor was so attached to the place, it was cozy and inviting. As she continued looking around, she realized she wasn't the only one who thought so as her eyes landed on the couple making out in the darkened booth. Hands were roving and she was sure they steamed up the window next to them, Christy blushed at the sight.

"Maybe they should get a room?" she joked as Taylor put a drink down on the bar in front of her. *Oh goody, Sex on the Beach, my favorite!* As Christy took a sip of the cocktail, Taylor looked over and chuckled, "They probably will, he's practically our best customer."

"Who's that?" Christy asked, but Taylor had moved

away to get Randy and Derek a couple more beers. Christy turned to watch the couple again, her curious eyes drawn to them. Heat rushed through her, followed by a sense of longing. How would it feel to be wanted like that? To be so wrapped in someone that the world melts away. She'd never had that feeling before. She probably wouldn't now that she swore off ever being in a relationship again.

The couple eventually came up for air, and Christy locked eyes with the man over his partner's shoulder, his electric blue eyes flashing even in the low light of the bar. They pierced through her, pinning her in place and she held her breath, her mouth ran dry. She licked her lips, inhaled sharply, and his eyes seemed to glow at her. Her heart pounded in her chest and a prickle went down her spine. She turned away, breaking the intense eye contact. *Stop staring at the couple you pervert,* she chided herself. Just as she got her heart rate under control, she heard a shriek from behind her. She turned around as someone wrapped their arms around her. She inhaled the familiar vanilla scent and relaxed.

"Hey, Justine," she giggled. Justine squeezed her tight and then pulled back, her dark eyes alive with excitement and Christy looked her over. Where Taylor was the loud, sarcastic, porcelain redhead, Justine was the opposite. She was a calm, composed, and sweet Latina beauty.

"*Hola, Chica!* How are you? I've missed your stunning face!" Justine cupped her cheeks, her smoky voice washing over Christy, instantly relaxing her. This woman could read the damn dictionary and it would sound sexy.

"I'm fine, thanks, all things considered." A lump formed in Christy's throat. Justine flinched and put her arms around Christy, hugging her tightly again. Christy hugged her back, and after a moment, Taylor's arms came around them both from behind. They murmured their condolences in her ears and then they all collected themselves and broke apart. Taylor went back behind the bar and Justine perched on a stool next to Christy and it was like nothing had happened.

"So, how long are you in town for?" Justine asked, grabbing the shot of Patrón that Taylor had poured her and drinking it down in one. Christy sipped her cocktail, wincing slightly at how strong Taylor made it, *that woman is a menace with alcohol.*

"I don't know, maybe a couple of weeks? Just long enough for the funeral, which I need to finish planning and to clear the house now that it's listed."

Taylor poured Justine another shot of tequila and raised her eyebrows at Christy, glancing back and forth between her and her cocktail. Christy rolled her eyes and brought the drink to her lips, pausing before taking a big gulp.

"See I'm drinking it-" she started, but was cut off.

"'Scuse me little lady," a deep, southern voice interrupted. A man squeezed himself between Christy and Justine, his big body knocking Christy to the side. She squealed and tipped back, fumbling for the bronzed railing to keep from falling off her wobbling barstool. When she righted herself, she turned to the man in question, he had his back to her, leaning on the bar talking to Justine.

Christy's eyes narrowed at the wide expanse of his shoulders which were now blocking her view of her friend. She reached up and tapped him on the shoulder to get his attention but as she did, he popped his elbow out resting his hand on his hip, the action batting her hand away. *Okay, this guy is rude, barging his way into our conversation, who does he think he is?* Blocking her view of

Justine with those big, muscular, big, wide, muscular, big shoulders. *Damn, he's got nice shoulders, and back, that shirt pulled tight across them…*Christy shook herself.

"Ahem," she coughed politely, attempting to get his attention. He either didn't hear her, or he was simply ignoring her. Christy felt it was most likely the latter as he continued flirting shamelessly with Justine.

"You sure look real good tonight. When are you gonna let me take you out on the town?" he asked, oozing charm in that smoky, southern accent of his. *Ugh, do women actually fall for this routine?* She thought, rolling her eyes.

"Excuse me," Christy tried again, peering around him and catching Justine's eyes for a moment before he moved to the side and blocked her view. She started to get the impression he was doing this on purpose.

"I told you, hon, February 29th I would meet you here," Justine cooed back at him, amusement in her voice.

"Wait a minute, there ain't no February 29th," he drawled, draping an arm around Justine's shoulders, Christy's eyes moved to his back again, his shirt hugging his muscles, so tight it threatened to rip which would be ~~wonderful~~ awful.

"There is every four years," Justine replied patiently.

"Aw shucks, there is?" he chuckled.

Did he just 'aw shucks'? Who even says that these days? Christy was getting madder by the second.

"Excuse me!" Christy said loudly, her tone snooty. She finally got his attention, but Sexy Shoulders turned sharply, and he knocked her again. This time she couldn't grab hold of the railing and went sailing off her barstool. Before she managed to faceplant the wooden floor, a pair of strong arms banded around her waist and hefted her up, dumping her unceremoniously back on her barstool.

She began sputtering with indignation, but when she looked up to face him and found herself staring into the electric blue eyes belonging to the man from the booth, her words died in her throat. She thought the deep color of them had been a trick of the light but up close she could see it wasn't, they were bright and wide, sharp with a touch of amusement in them. Her stomach dropped as she realized, she had only seen eyes this amazing on one man.

Dean Campbell.

The man she spent her teenage years trying to impress, the man responsible for one of her most painful memories, the man she now couldn't *stand*, was right here in the flesh.

Christy took him in, his blond hair styled perfectly, thick black lashes framing those incredible blue eyes, high cheekbones, and a sharp-bladed nose perched above a wide, lush red mouth. That mouth she knew was framed by the cutest dimples she had ever seen on a man. Blond stubble dusted his jawline. He was even more stunning than she remembered. She opened her mouth, blowing her curls out of her eyes, ready to give him a piece of her mind but he turned away, dismissing her.

"Taylor!" he called over the music. "Get your friend some water, she's so wasted she can't even sit on her stool without falling off!" He turned back to her. "Go easy on the alcohol next time, darlin'," he patronized. He might as well have chucked her under the chin. A red mist descended over Christy and she knew she was about to detonate. He'd sent her from happy to rage-filled in ten seconds. He turned back to Justine, leaving Christy spluttering indignantly.

"Now come on, Dean, you remember Christy, don't

you?" Justine said, putting her hand on Dean's arm and turning him back towards Christy. He frowned as he looked down at Christy, his eyes drifting over her lazily from head to toe before meeting hers again. He shook his head. "Nope, can't place her."

Not that she thought it was possible, but her rage ratcheted up a notch, embarrassment now joining the party. She felt her cheeks burn; *how could he not remember me?* Dean peered down at her again, "Maybe you should go and splash some cold water on your face, you don't look so good."

Arrogant. Asshole.

She opened her mouth to unleash on him, then she spotted the wicked glint in those sharp eyes. That was exactly what he wanted. Her eyes narrowed and steel fused her spine. If that's what he wanted, she sure as hell wouldn't give him the satisfaction. She spun on her heel and stomped off towards the restrooms, muttering to herself the whole way.

"Nice to meet you, Kirsten!" he called after her. Without stopping, she raised her hand and flipped him off.

Chapter 2

Dean chuckled as Christy flipped him off, messing with her was the most fun he'd had in a long time.

"*Cabrón!*" Justine chided as she punched him on the arm. He turned to face her, rubbing the spot where she hit him.

"What?" he asked all innocent, eyes flicking back and forth between her and Taylor.

Taylor shook her head at him. "What did you do that for? Why couldn't you have been the decent guy that's hidden deep, deep, deep, deeeeep down inside?"

"Come on, she knows I'm kidding," he said, chuckling again as Christy's enraged face filled his mind.

"We're trying to keep her here, Dean. You gotta be nice to her, we want this visit to be as positive as possible, ignoring the obvious of course. Just be friendly and welcoming, make her feel at home. We want her to think about settling down here again," Justine explained. He looked at their disapproving faces and shook his head, holding up his hands in surrender.

"Fine, next time I see her, I'll apologize," he smiled sweetly at them.

"Good!" Justine said emphatically, "She'll be back in a minute."

"Ah, but I'm leaving. The usual please," he said to Taylor. She rolled her eyes and headed through the door behind the bar that led to the back office. She came back and tossed a set of keys to him over the bar.

"Are you gonna stay up all night *talking* again?" Taylor teased. He shot her a withering look. "Just be out by 10 am, stud," she added.

"Yes, Mom," he joked, dropping a friendly peck on Justine's cheek and he blew a kiss to Taylor before heading towards the door where his date was waiting. He wrapped an arm around her shoulders and grinned down at her.

"Ready?" he asked, steering her out the door and into the warm, country evening, the scent from the citrus trees wafting in the air. He guided her around the back of the bar and over to the row of cabins situated next to Taylor's private one. He headed over to the cabin at the start of the row and unlocked the door. Darcy, his date, started rubbing her hands over his shoulders and down his back. He bit the inside of his cheek to keep from cringing as her sharp nails poked him.

When she launched herself at him in the bar, forcing her tongue into his mouth, it hadn't particularly turned him on, and as their evening progressed, the idea of any intimate contact between them made him a little uncomfortable. He twisted away and grabbed her hands, maneuvering her in front of him and through the door to the cabin.

He came in behind her and flicked the light switch. The antique wall lights came to life, bathing the room in a soft, peachy glow. The log aesthetic continued inside the room with the walls and main living room furniture made from varnished wood. A log burner was located in front of the couch, and the furnishings were decorated in different colored plaid patterns creating a rustic feel. On the other side of the room was a small, modern kitchenette and the bathroom. He shut the front door and felt Darcy press herself up against his back. He side-stepped again and turned to face her, watching as she schooled her features into what she probably believed was her *come hither* look.

"I'm going to freshen up a bit," he said, stalking towards the bathroom door.

"Hurry back," she replied in a breathy voice that made him want to do the opposite. Why did he suddenly wish he were anywhere else? When he shut the door and flicked on the light, the harsh yellow beams made him squint. He took a deep breath, leaned against the sink, and looked at himself in the mirror, scrubbing a hand over his face.

Christy fricking Lee, what a blast from the past. Sure, he heard about her all the time from Taylor and Justine, but he hadn't *seen* her in over a decade. Damn that decade had been good to her, she was even more stunning than he remembered. He shook his head, *oh no, you don't! Don't even think about it, don't you remember how holier than thou she was? She always thought she was so much better than everyone else.*

Her image popped into his head, her sparkling baby blue eyes that reeled in him. Her short, blond curls flirting with her cherub cheeks and those plump lips painted hot pink. Oh, that mouth, he groaned inwardly, all the things he could do with that mouth. His cock twitched in his jeans, an unfortunate reminder that he had been celibate for years. *Stop thinking about her mouth, you idiot! Think about something else...like her body?* His brain supplied unhelpfully.

She filled his mind, her figure so dangerously curvy. Round, full breasts, a tiny nipped in waist that flowed into the wide flare of her hips. He could hold onto those hips for dear life as she rode him perfectly, moaning in his ear. His cock started lengthening beneath the denim, which he really didn't need right now. He jabbed on the faucet and splashed some water on his face trying to rid himself of her image. *It's just been a while for you, that's all, has nothing to do with Christy. Any man would feel the same,* he reasoned.

He splashed his face two more times until her image was gone and replaced with memories from his high school days. The irony of the situation wasn't lost on him. He thought back to "the incident", one of the worst memories from his stupid adolescence. He'd humiliated Christy in front of a group of his friends, had lashed out at her out of his own hurt and embarrassment, and she hadn't forgiven him. Afterwards her disdain for him had been so obvious, so visceral every time they interacted, right up until she left town. She thought he was an idiot, he had acted like one, and she treated him like one until they just avoided each other altogether.

Dean's mom married Taylor's dad when they had been fourteen years old. Their parents had been together a few years before Taylor's dad cheated and he and Dean's mom had split up. Although it wasn't a happy ending, those years were responsible for some of his best memories.

Growing up and living with Taylor, they became a family, the only time he really felt like he had one. They looked out for each other and developed a strong bond that surprised them both. He considered her his sister, still did even though there was no blood or legal ties between them. They had special dinners every couple of weeks where he had her over and would cook for her, or she would get the night off and cook for him. She would tease him about the parade of women he brought through the cabins in his quest to find Mrs. Right. Then he gave her shit about all the douchebags she continued to date, never wanting to settle down with a nice, decent guy.

He thought back to when they lived together, that fateful night when she had a sleepover with Justine and Christy. His best friend, Beau, had come round to hang out one night. They ended up talking about the girls and decided to eavesdrop on them like idiot teenage boys did. They snuck down the hall and hovered outside Taylor's room, careful to be quiet as the door was slightly ajar. He peeked in and saw Taylor and Justine sitting on the floor, thumbing through magazines. Christy was bent forward at the waist brushing her blond curls forward. She bolted upright, flipping them back and as they fell around her face, she reminded him of one of the most iconic women of all time. The name came to him and he whispered it as he watched her.

"What did you say?" Beau hissed. Dean waved at him to be quiet, his cheeks flushing from embarrassment and turned his attention back to the conversation the girls were having.

"What do you think about Beau, Justine?" Christy asked, Justine giggled.

"He's cute and seems super sweet," she said shyly.

"No, you don't want to get involved, trust me," Taylor interrupted sharply.

"Why, you jealous?" Justine teased.

"Oh please," Taylor muttered, rolling her eyes. "Bobby is so much better than him, why would I even bother with Beau when I've got the sexiest, most popular guy in school?"

Dean flinched hearing Taylor talk about his best friend that way, it really wasn't like her. He flicked his gaze over to Beau, whose ears had turned red, and he wouldn't meet Deans eyes.

"Fine, Christy what about you?" Justine asked, "Let me guess, who could you like?"

"What about Dean? He's cool and he's single," Taylor said quietly, Dean's stomach flipped. He'd had a crush on Christy forever, but she intimidated him and whenever he tried to talk to her, he always said something stupid.

"Are you serious?" Christy spluttered. "He's an idiot, I would like someone with some intelligence or at the very least someone able to hold a normal conversation. He clearly got brawn instead of brains. If I need someone to burp the alphabet, I'll give him a call." Disdain dripped from her words.

"Don't be a bitch, that's not like you. He's really smart, you know, and has some great qualities," Taylor defended. A spark of brotherly affection for her filled him, replacing the embarrassment he felt at Christy's cold dismissal.

"I'm not being a bitch, how is that worse than what you said about Beau? I'm just saying Dean sort of reminds me of the Scarecrow from the *Wizard of Oz*," Christy laughed.

"Christy, that's harsh!" Justine scolded, but giggled.

"Let's change the subject, shall we?" Taylor said, and they started talking about Ryan Reynolds, which was boring, he motioned to Beau to leave. They didn't talk about what they heard on the way back to Dean's room, maybe they should've never eavesdropped. Thanks to instant karma, he was pretty sure neither of them came away from that feeling good about themselves.

To be honest it wasn't anything Dean hadn't heard before. Being called stupid was something his old man used to say and was normally followed by a slap. He was actually happy when his dad had done a runner and left them. Taylor's dad hadn't been much better, they never bonded. He shouted and was a mean sonofabitch, but he never hit him.

After that night, every time he saw Christy, he was reminded of his humiliation. Reminded that she didn't find him attractive, she just thought he was stupid. Which is why he said what he said later on, as a childish act of revenge for her insulting him. He instantly regretted that he tried to show off to the guys, behaving like someone he wasn't, and she overheard him.

Since then, she never wanted to talk to him, even avoided eye contact. When they were involved in the same conversations, she spit barbs of venom at him, insulted him, and talked down to him. He knew she was hurt by what he said, like he had been before, but when he tried to apologize, she wouldn't listen.

So, he started trying to purposefully wind her up. *Like I did tonight, I guess I've not grown up much after all.* The idea sobered him, pulling him out of the memories from all those years ago and back into the present. He turned off the still running faucet and dried his face on the soft towels hanging on the wall.

He wasn't sure how long he had been in the bathroom. He went back out ready to face Darcy to see if she had the potential to become his future partner. He knew the town gossiped, most of the people thought he brought women back to the cabin for sex, but he actually just wanted to get to know them. Dean wanted to settle down and start a family soon. He had visions of the partnership he could have with someone, something he never witnessed before but was convinced was out there. His mission was to find his match, his soulmate. The mother of his children and he wouldn't settle for anything less than forever.

He didn't want to take these women back to his home, it was his sanctuary. He never felt like he had a home when he was growing up so he was very protective over his now. Only Taylor and Beau, the people closest to him, had ever seen it. He needed to know he was letting the right person in and so far, he didn't think he met anyone who came close.

Darcy was perched on the end of the bed and smiled when she saw him, patting the spot next to her on the mattress.

"Want a drink?" he asked, avoiding her bedroom eyes and heading over to the minibar.

"Uh, sure." she replied, sounding a little disappointed.

"Something to eat?" he asked over his shoulder.

"Something to eat?" she repeated back, confused.

"Yeah, some chips? Chocolate?"

"Got any nuts?" she asked, and he cringed at her tone. He didn't think she meant cashews. He grabbed two beers and a bag of chips. He handed a beer to her. She tried to grab his hand as well as her beer, and she huffed in annoyance as he darted out of her reach.

"Wanna watch TV?" he asked, heading over to turn it on and sitting on the couch, dropping the bag of chips on the coffee table.

"Surprisingly, no, I don't want to watch TV, Dean. I want to get back to what we were doing in the bar and see what happens next," she pouted, and came around to stand in front of him.

Dean sighed. He was upfront with the women he dated, they knew he was looking for something serious and not to jump into bed. They knew when he brought them here it was to get to know them without the whole town watching, butting in and spreading gossip.

"Darcy, this is what happens next. I want to get to know your mind first, not just your body because you're not a piece of meat."

"I'm honestly fine if you want to get to know my body, I definitely want to get to know yours." She sat down next to him and placed her hand on his thigh and squeezed.

"Well, I'm not a piece of meat either. Don't you want to see if this could really go somewhere?"

Darcy had a strong start, but she looked defeated. She sighed, reaching down and pulling off her heels. He grabbed the chips and opened them; he offered her the bag as he pulled her into his side.

"Now then, tell me about your family."

Chapter 3

The next morning, the sound of groaning woke Christy. She pried her eyelids apart, squinting against the bright morning sun that was attacking her through a crack in the blinds. She tried to sit up, but the heavy arm draped across her stomach held her down. Which was just as well because the moment she tried to move, her head began to pound and her stomach flipped dramatically. She brought her hands to her temple, gritting her teeth against the throbbing pain. She clamped her lips shut to stop from moaning and vomiting as the wave of nausea increased.

God, I think I'm dying. After a few minutes, her body began to get used to being awake, and the pain and nausea ebbed away. She heard another groan and turned her head, coming face to face with Taylor who was practically sprawled on her. Taylor's red hair was matted all around her face, her mouth hanging open with a bit of drool leaking out. Christy snickered, the action waking Taylor. One of her emerald eyes popped open and glanced around, then settled on Christy.

"You're much prettier than most of the guys I usually wake up to," Taylor rasped, rolling over and instantly groaning again. "God, I think something died in my mouth."

"I know," Christy chuckled. "What time did we get back last night? And why did we drink so much?" She began to slowly sit up, not wanting to move too quickly and bring back the headache and nausea.

"5 am and because we were celebrating your return home." Taylor heaved herself out of bed, tripped over her shoes from the night before but kept herself upright, avoiding cracking her head on the open bedroom door.

"First win of the day!" she cheered, fist-pumping the air. Christy shushed her gently, not able to cope with loud noises just yet. She leaned back against the pillows, not ready to actually get up. As she heard Taylor turn on the shower in the adjoining bathroom, she looked around the bedroom of Taylor's cabin.

The room was light and airy. The bed, wardrobe, and dressing table were all cream wood, everything else was a soft baby pink. Throw cushions and blankets dotted the floor, discarded from the bed in order to fit them both in. Big, floral canvases lined the walls along with photo collages of the girls and some of Taylor and Dean. The room was surprisingly girly in contrast to the hard ass that was its owner, but not many people realized Taylor was a secret princess.

Christy focused on a photo of Taylor and Dean. They were in a field, her arms wrapped around his waist and he was ruffling her hair, both of them pulling faces at the camera. It was adorable, Christy smiled at it, her eyes fixated on Dean. He looked so happy, his expression goofy and boyish in a way she had never seen before. His t-shirt stretched tight to accommodate his muscles. The sun was shining down on them, picking up on the gold highlights in his hair, making them glow like a halo. She felt her heart stutter in her chest and forced herself to look away.

She looked at the collage of her, Taylor, and Justine, so many funny pictures. Sadness shifted through her as she thought of the time she spent away from them. She missed them terribly, but she wasn't ready to move back here. This place only brought her pain. *No, don't think about that, not when you're hungover and already emotional.* She looked out the crack in the blinds, watching the huge pine trees swaying in the breeze, her eyes drifting closed. When she opened them again, Taylor was standing in front of her fully dressed, wet hair piled on her head, holding a cell phone out to Christy.

"It rang, but I didn't get to it in time."

Christy took it from her and unlocked it. She had a missed call and a voicemail. Sitting upright she listened to the message. "Hi Miss Lee, it's Cassie from Blossom Estates, just calling to remind you of the showing this morning at 11 am. I know you said you're fine for us to go in if you aren't there, so this is just a courtesy call to let you know we'll be around. If I don't see you there, then I'll call you with feedback once it's finished, take care."

"*Shit!*"

"What is it?" Taylor called from another room.

"The realtor is showing someone around the house this morning, but the place is a mess! I meant to tidy it up first thing, but I didn't expect us to be out so late last night. What time is it?" she asked, swinging her legs over the side of the bed and swaying when she stood. Once she felt fine again, she looked down and saw she was fully clothed, just missing her shoes which she began to hunt for.

"It's nearly 10 am," Taylor replied, and Christy could hear her puttering around her little kitchen, boiling some water for coffee most likely.

"Double shit! I've gotta go." Christy found her shoes and tugged them on but was still missing her purse. She ventured out of the bedroom into Taylor's open plan living area which included the dining room and kitchen. She found her purse on the pink fabric couch and slung it over her shoulder.

"You okay to drive? You want some coffee first?" Taylor asked.

"I'm okay to drive, just feel a bit sick but I'll pull over if I need to. Raincheck on the coffee?" She hurried over to Taylor and pecked her cheek goodbye.

"Anytime, *ma cherie*, I'll message you about tonight."

"Tonight?" Christy called over her shoulder as she reached the front door.

"Yeah, I told you last night, Justine's gig?"

"Of course, can't wait. See you later, babe!" Christy flung open the door and the bright sun immediately washed over her and lit up the room, both she and Taylor groaned at the cheerful invasion. Christy rummaged in her purse for her sunglasses, shoving them on her face. She waved at Taylor and headed out.

She hurried down the weathered, wooden porch and past the row of cabins, to the parking lot. She began digging in her purse for her car keys.

"Hey, Christy!"

Her heart thudded in her chest as she recognized who

that voice belonged to. She wanted the ground to swallow her up. She was wearing yesterday's sleep rumpled clothes, was hungover as hell, probably stank of alcohol, and she hadn't brushed her teeth or hair, her curls left untamed. Thank God she was wearing sunglasses so he wouldn't see her panda eyes from the makeup she hadn't removed.

She wasn't prepared for this. Dread mounting, she slowly turned around to face Dean. He was coming towards her smiling, dimples on full display, the sun beaming down on him bouncing off the golden highlights in his hair. *Seriously, how did he look this good in the morning?* She shook her head, he wasn't *that* good looking, she had definitely seen better-looking men, she just couldn't think of any right now. He was wearing the same clothes as last night, except his weren't rumpled like hers, which meant at some point he took them off to…sleep.

As the beautiful brunette he was with last night came up behind him, she felt a rush of jealousy flood her and immediately tried to stamp it down. The brunette was groomed to perfection as well, glossy hair smooth and styled. Makeup perfectly applied, smudge-free, no panda eyes here, *thank you*, and her clothes were also crease-free. Christy's cheeks heated in humiliation at the comparison between them. The woman grabbed Dean's hand as they approached and looked up at him with such affection.

"Good morning," he said when they reached her.

"Morning, Dean," she replied, ducking her head as his eyes ran over her. *Wait, why am I feeling embarrassed, it doesn't matter what you look like. You're a beautiful, smart woman and his opinion of you doesn't matter!*

"Lovely day isn't it?" he asked nonchalantly, glancing at the sky.

"Yes, it is," she replied evenly. "Glad to see your bout

of amnesia has worn off."

He chuckled darkly, the sound washing over her, teasing her ears. He opened his mouth to reply but was cut off.

"I'm Darcy, by the way, Dean's girlfriend," the brunette said, looking annoyed that she was being ignored. She shot Christy a smug smile and tightened her hold on Dean's arm.

"Nice to meet you," Christy replied, trying to inject some enthusiasm into her voice and failing miserably.

Darcy turned to Dean, "I've got to go, make sure you call me later." She dropped her voice at the last part, trying to sound husky, but to Christy's ears, it just came out like she was an old man who smoked too many cigarettes. Darcy reached up and pulled Dean down for a passionate kiss, tilting her head, and Christy could see her push her tongue into his mouth. Christy cringed, feeling ill at the over-the-top display, she watched Dean closely to see if he was enjoying it.

At first, he seemed surprised, but he recovered quickly and met her enthusiasm with his own. Christy shifted on her feet, needing to leave and wondering if she could escape while they ate each other's faces off. After a moment, Dean broke the kiss and Darcy moaned theatrically.

"Last night was magical," she breathed before giving him another kiss and then walking away, hips swaying so much Christy was shocked she didn't fall over.

"It would have been less gross if she just peed on you," Christy said sarcastically. Dean barked out a laugh, the sound rusty and deep like he wasn't used to it. She turned to walk away, but Dean stopped her, touching her shoulder.

"She's not my girlfriend."

"I don't think she knows that," Christy said, shrugging him off and continuing on her way, he followed her.

"We've only been on one date," he said, ignoring her comment.

"And you brought her here for a quickie? And they say romance is dead," she muttered, rolling her eyes.

"Christy, look I want to apologize," he said, sighing deeply. She stopped walking and turned to face him. "I was only kidding around last night, I'm sorry. I didn't mean to upset or annoy you," he finished, smiling down at her, dimples popping, and she melted slightly before remembering who he was and her blank expression resumed.

"Apology accepted. Now excuse me I need to get back," she said tightly, turning away and continuing to her car. He uttered another protest, but she picked up the pace, eager to get away from him and back to her shower. She made it to her car, and got in. She looked up through her windshield and saw him walking towards a red pickup truck parked on the other side of the lot. She sighed with relief, put her key in the ignition and turned. The engine sputtered but didn't roar to life as expected. She tried again and the same thing happened.

"Come on, baby, don't do this now. Mama really needs you," she crooned, hoping the gentle tone would elicit some compassion from her clapped out old car. She was wrong. She turned the key again and pressed down on the accelerator hoping to rev the engine to life, but again the car just sputtered and didn't start. She caught movement out the window and looked up, Dean had stopped walking towards the truck and was watching her.

"Shit, shit! No, no, no don't come over," she moaned, ducking below the steering wheel in a ridiculous attempt to hide.

"Come on please, I'll buy you anything you want. New wiper blades, huh? How does that sound? Full service, all your nuts-and-bolts cleaning? Filters emptying? If ever there's a time to work, it's now!" Christy whined frantically, turning the key in the ignition.

A shadow fell over her and then she heard a gentle tap on her window. She sighed and looked up, meeting Dean's eyes through the glass. Pasting a smile on her face she wound the window down. Yes, that's how old her car was. He had both hands braced on the roof of the car, leaning forward with a stupid, smug smile on his stupid perfect face. *Goddamn dimples, don't they ever give up?!*

"Having some trouble?" he asked smoothly, and she instantly bristled at his tone.

"I'll be fine, just takes a moment to get her going. You can leave." He pulled her door handle and the car door popped open easily.

"You should really lock the doors once you're inside your vehicle, to stop strangers from being able to do that."

"I was going to, but I literally just sat..." She didn't bother to finish, annoyed with herself for letting him get under her skin.

"Want me to take a look and see if I can help?" he offered.

"Why? What are you going to do, poke around and then suggest taking it to a garage?" she replied tartly. She hated herself when she got like this, she felt like a teenager again constantly needling at him because he made her feel inadequate.

"You think I don't know anything about cars?" he asked, looking slightly hurt.

"I think I'll stick to asking a professional, thanks. If I need someone to kick the tires, I'll let you know."

He didn't say anything for a moment, just stared at her. The air between them growing tense, their eyes clashing together, but she refused to back down and look away first. Then his expression changed, becoming cool and impersonal.

"There's a garage in town, I'll call them for you. They'll be here in thirty minutes," he said flatly, slamming her door shut, abruptly turning and walking back to his truck. *Great, now I'm a bitch and he's Mr. Wonderful as usual.* A wave of guilt hit her, she didn't mean to be a bitch; he was just trying to help her, but she couldn't stop herself reacting to him that way. It was her defense mechanism with him.

"Uh, thank you!" she called after him, but he didn't acknowledge that he heard her. She sat back and watched him speed out of the parking lot, he didn't even look her way as he drove past.

While she waited, she started thinking about the past, which was always a minefield in one way or another. She thought back to Dean as a teenager, they spent some time together at first, with him being her best friend's stepbrother, he was always around. But then she heard what he said about her, and she didn't want to spend any more time with him. She shook her head as old humiliation suffused her and she decided that she didn't want to take the trip down memory lane after all.

She sat in her car and waited, making a mental to-do list for the funeral. A short while later, a tow truck appeared and pulled up in front of her car. A giant of a man climbed out and came over to her, he was at least 6'4" with broad shoulders and a wide chest. His dark hair was wild around his head and he had a big, bushy beard that covered a majority of his face. She could just make out his dark eyes, so pretty with thick, dark lashes. He grunted at her that his name was Bear. *Very apt,* she thought, but he seemed nice enough. He had a quick play around with her car, declared it would need to go back to the garage, and began hooking it up to the truck. She ignored the irony screaming in her face about what she said to Dean.

The sun shone down on Christy and the breeze tickled her skin gently, the scent of citrus fresh in the air, energizing her. When Bear said he was ready to go, she insisted on walking back to town as it wasn't too far, and it was a lovely day. She was too late to make it to the house viewing now anyway, so she might as well take her time. He gave her a business card for the garage in case she needed to contact them and drove off.

As she walked back along the road, her mind tried to drift back to her childhood again. This time she gave in and let it. She didn't want to focus on the time shortly after her mother died; her father's withdrawal was still too painful, so she thought back to her later years spent with Taylor and Justine. She thought about Dean and their strange history, seeing him at school and then knowing him as Taylor's stepbrother, the new stepbrother Christy had a giant crush on.

She had been so nervous around him and he always seemed so confident and sure of himself. Beautiful girls were always fawning all over him, his bedroom practically had a revolving door at one point. Christy knew how she looked compared to the other girls, she was frumpy, clumsy and awkward. She was an insecure teenager whose heart got trampled on one day by the hottest guy in school.

She had been at school late one evening, studying in the library and generally avoiding going home. Things with her father were difficult, so she tried to avoid being around him as much as possible. She needed to hand in her absence note to her gym teacher; her period had started and she had cramps so bad that swimming was a no go. Since her father was incapacitated most of the time, she had to forge his signature to make the note acceptable. The last thing she needed was another unauthorized absence for them to contact him about.

She hurried down the halls, hoping it wasn't too late to hand in the note. The gym teacher, Mr. Fitzpatrick, was also the coach for the school football team, and they usually had practice after school midweek. It should have finished half an hour ago, so hopefully, he was still around. She rounded the corner close to his office and stopped as she saw the football team, including Dean and his best friend Beau. Practice must have run over if they were still hanging around. She didn't know what to do, she needed to get past them and into Fitzpatrick's office to at least leave the note on his desk. As she stood there deciding what to do, hoping none of the boys would notice her, she overheard their conversation.

"Seriously? You wanna ask out Christy?" Dean said, disbelief dripping from his voice.

"Yeah, she's so freakin' hot, don't you think?" Beau replied. Dean scoffed.

"Hell no, you need to get better taste ASAP, dude!" Dean joked, high-fiving one of the other guys, his laugh piercing right through Christy, shattering her heart.

"Are you kidding me? Do you have eyes? Those curves, that mouth!" Beau cried. Christy couldn't feel appreciation for Beau's words, her mind reeling from what Dean was saying about her.

"Nah, man. She's what I call a 'boner killer', you feel me?" Dean laughed again, and the group of boys joined in, cackling away. Christy felt sick with humiliation, her cheeks flaming, tears stinging her eyes.

"You're a jerk, you know that?" Beau retorted. Christy didn't hear the rest of the conversation, Dean's words playing over in her mind. He found her *that* disgusting? She knew that she didn't look like the other skinny, pretty girls he dated, but she never thought he was the type of boy to think like that.

She had never felt uglier than in that moment. All the insults that ran through her mind constantly, that she worked so hard to ignore, flooded through her. She tried to hold back the tears, but they wouldn't be stopped, a sob escaping her lips. She clapped a hand over her mouth and the boys all turned to face her. Their laughter dying on their lips, the silence was deafening. Dean had the decency to look ashamed and took a step toward her, holding his hands out, palms up as though he were trying to placate a wild animal.

"Christy, I..." he started, but she didn't listen. She turned and ran, the pounding of her footsteps echoing off the walls. She ran away from the hurt she felt at his words, the mortification fusing her cheeks and pushing her on. She didn't stop until she realized she was outside her house. Her dad wasn't home, thankfully, so she went straight upstairs to her room, threw herself onto her bed, pulled the covers over her head and let the tears fall.

That was the moment that had changed her and Dean.

She could no longer be around him or talk to him normally knowing how he felt about her, he probably knew she was practically in love with him. He tried to seek her out at school, but she avoided him as much as she could. Every time she caught sight of him coming towards her, she felt sick and terrified, like a caged animal. She didn't tell anyone what happened, she definitely couldn't tell Taylor. She loved her friend and didn't want to put her in an awkward position with her brother, so she kept quiet.

She couldn't avoid him forever though, he was a huge part of Taylor's life, and she couldn't ignore him without drawing attention to herself. She would be civil but nothing more. She would show him, you didn't need beauty if you had brains. She was super smart, and she knew he was struggling in his classes. She would show him how smart she was. She became icy, detached, and borderline rude to him whenever they spoke.

Eventually, they didn't speak at all unless she was making a snooty comment. She felt guilty but couldn't get past her embarrassment and couldn't bear the thought of him thinking she was obsessing over him like some pathetic, lovestruck kid. What better way to throw him off than to act like she couldn't stand him? Then he would never know how much he had hurt her.

Christy was so lost in her thoughts that she didn't realize she made it into town. She was going to stop a passer-by to ask for directions to Iris Motors, but she spotted it as she walked through town. It was a typical small, country town. Local shops and offices lined each side of the main road. It hadn't changed from her memory; the diner was still there with the same red and white striped awning. The old police station and laundromat had been spruced up a bit. Iris Motors was new, but otherwise, everything was as it had been all those years ago.

As she walked up onto the open forecourt of the garage, she spotted Bear and headed over to him.

"Hey, Bear, thanks for getting her back so quickly."

He shrugged. "When you're a friend of the boss, we work quickly," he replied gruffly.

"The boss?" Christy didn't know anyone here. Bear

hiked his thumb over his shoulder pointing to an office in the back of the garage. She headed over to get a closer look and she really should have known karma would screw her.

Dean was sitting behind a desk inside the small office, reclined in his chair, talking on the phone. As if he sensed her, he looked up, and their eyes met through the glass. His electric blues flashing angrily at her, and her heart thudded in her chest. She remembered what she said to him this morning and her cheeks flushed in humiliation. God, she could be such a bitch sometimes. Not wanting to disturb him, she broke their eye contact and turned away, walking back over to Bear and watched him tinker with some tools.

"So, do you know what's wrong with her?" she asked.

"Your spark plugs just need changing over, been a while since your last service?" She heard from behind her. She turned to see Dean standing with his arms folded across his chest, expression unreadable.

"Oh, Dean, hi..." she started, but he interrupted her.

"But what do I know?" He smiled humorlessly at her.

"Dean, I'm sorry I was so rude. I'm tired, hungover, and..." she tried again but he turned around.

"Bear will finish her up for you," he called over his shoulder, went back into the office and slammed the door. He was really pissed; she must have really upset him. She would wait for him to calm down before she tried again. She asked Bear how much longer it would be. He offered to give her car a service, which it evidently needed, and they agreed she would come back in an hour. With a sigh, she headed over to the diner to grab a late breakfast.

Chapter 4

Christy stopped at Ruby's Diner for a late breakfast but, more importantly, coffee. After she ate, she felt slightly more human. She felt better physically but still felt bad about her run-in with Dean and how she treated him. When she went back to collect her car later, she would look for him to apologize. In the future, she would behave like an adult and not let childish feelings from her past overtake her. She was in her thirties now for God's sake, she needed to stop acting like a teenager! Christy was so deep in thought she didn't notice the elderly couple approach her table.

"Christy, honey, is that you?" the man asked, his voice gravelly with age but thick with a deep southern drawl, like her father's had been. She felt a lump form in her throat at the thought. She met his eyes, and vaguely recognized him.

"Yes, it is, Mr. uh..." she floundered for his name.

"It's Bob, Bob Ingles? And my wife, June," he rasped indicating to the woman standing next to him and her memory kicked in. Bob owned half of The Rusty Bucket Inn and Taylor owned the other half.

"Of course! How wonderful to see you again," she gushed, jumping up to embrace them both. June held on to her and cupped her face.

"My dear, you look just like your mother, you could be twins. I do miss my Janey," she said sadly, she released Christy's cheek and gripped her hand tightly.

"We were so sorry to hear about your father, weren't we, Bob?" Bob nodded in sad agreement.

"Oh, yes, very sad business. We hoped you would come home eventually before he passed, not like this though. Your father was missing you so much."

Christy frowned. *He was missing me?*

"Anyway, dear, we best be on our way. We'll see you for the funeral, if you need anything at all don't hesitate to ask." June gave her hand another tight squeeze, she had a strong grip for an old gal, and they left. Christy was mulling over their words as she grabbed her purse, paid her bill and left the diner. Could he really have missed her? Was that possible? Why didn't he ever reach out if he did? Bob and June must have been mistaken. As she stepped outside the diner and onto the street she looked up and down, surveying the town. She spotted another familiar face coming out of the laundromat and hurried over.

"Rebelle!" she called, waving her arm. The woman struggling with her bag of laundry turned, her eyes wide with alarm. Her expression softened slightly when she saw Christy. She slung her bag of clothes over her shoulder, swaying slightly from the weight. As Christy took her in, she was surprised to see how little Rebelle had changed since school. She had the same short brown hair that fluttered about her delicate, pixie face, same warm brown doe eyes. She was still very delicate and petite but looked a little too thin.

"Hey, Christy," Rebelle said, sounding slightly nervous.

"How are you? It's been so long since I've seen you!" She always liked Rebelle, they had been friends as teenagers. Their bond had stemmed from tragedy as both their mothers had passed away around the same time. At school, they were subjected to pitying looks from the teachers and other students. One particular day Christy had escaped to the bathroom for a break from the constant outpouring of sympathy which she found smothering, and found Rebelle already hiding in there.

They talked and felt a freedom that came from having someone understand what they were going through. Rebelle had a twin sister, who was her only surviving family since Christy had heard her father passed away a few years ago. Christy wasn't sure what had happened to the sisters since school but heard from Taylor that Rebelle married a few years back, soon after her father passed away.

"Yes, it has. What's brought you back home?" Rebelle asked, avoiding Christy's question.

"My father passed away," Christy replied, and Rebelle blanched.

"I'm so sorry. How are you coping?"

"A bit hit and miss. We had such a complicated relationship so it feels a bit strange, like I'm not sure how I should be feeling." Rebelle was one of the very few people who knew all about Christy's relationship with her father and one of the few who would understand the emotions.

"I would love to catch up with you and talk. I could come round sometime?" Christy asked, eager to spend time with her old friend. Rebelle looked at her, slightly wary. Christy realized she put Rebelle on the spot, they hadn't spoken for over fifteen years and she just invited herself around.

"Or, I'm going to be at the Bucket tonight if you want to join me for a drink?" she tried again, Rebelle was silent for a moment.

"Yeah, okay, I'll see you later then," she replied with a small smile and turned to leave.

"It really is great to see you," Christy called after her.

Rebelle turned back and nodded. "You too, Christy."

Then she was gone. Christy felt a bit weird after their encounter, maybe too much water had passed under the bridge and Rebelle wasn't interested in catching up. Maybe she's just shy? Either way, Christy would find out later tonight. She turned and headed off to the general store to pick up a few things and then went back to the garage feeling a sense of trepidation about seeing Dean again. Underneath the trepidation was a sliver of excitement that she tried to ignore.

When she arrived, she saw her car parked in the lot at the front of the garage. She walked past it, headed inside and found Bear under the hood of another car. She glanced back to the office where Dean had previously been, but it was empty. She moved her gaze around the rest of the garage, trying to be subtle yet failing miserably.

"He's not here," Bear gruffed out, now facing her.

"Oh, uh, I was looking for you," she lied, smiling at him sweetly. He stared at her for a moment, then wandered over to the office and went inside. He came back out a minute later and held out her keys.

"She's all ready to go," he said, she took the keys from his giant paw.

"Amazing, thank you so much for fixing her and giving her a service."

Bear shrugged, "The boss ended up doing the work."

Dean worked on it himself? How...sweet. "How much do I owe?" she asked, rummaging in her purse.

"No charge." Bear disappeared back under the hood, his husky voice echoing slightly.

"No, really, how much?"

"Boss said there's no charge, just let us know if you have any more troubles." He popped out from under the hood again and grabbed some more tools. He gave her what she imagined he thought was a smile but it looked a bit like a grimace. She thanked him and headed over to her car. When she got inside, she locked the doors immediately, thinking of Dean's comment earlier. She noticed her seat was still in the same position, Dean must have put it back after he moved it into the lot, no way would his long legs fit in this tiny gap. *That was thoughtful,* she sighed, feeling worse about earlier.

The scent of pine needles and sandalwood enveloped her. Dean's scent, she remembered it well. She closed her eyes, breathing it in. He smelled like the forest, wild and earthy. It was intoxicating, making her sigh as she imagined burying her face in his neck and breathing in deep, running her mouth along his skin, tasting. Deep in her daydream, she accidentally leaned on the steering wheel, beeping her horn, startling herself out of the fantasy. When she looked up, Bear was watching her with a quizzical look on his face. Her cheeks flushed, she waved at him then started her car, and drove off wondering where the hell that fantasy came from.

The closer to home she got, the bigger the pit in her stomach became. She wasn't used to being back in that house yet and certainly didn't like being there alone. Each room held memories. Some sad, some happy, but all of them painful. She tried to spend as little time as possible there. Maybe she needed a distraction while she was in town, to keep her busy, something to give her focus so she didn't have to keep worrying about spending time alone here.

In the meantime, she would get ready, head back out, and see if Justine wanted to hang out before her gig later. Christy could help her get ready and then go to the bar together. She pulled up outside the weathered, two-story farmhouse and switched off the engine. As she got out of her vehicle and walked up the stone path she took in the house. The wraparound porch was peeling white paint but was pretty sturdy. The hedges and bushes in the front yard needed pruning, badly, the weeds pulled up, and grass cut. The list of jobs was growing by the minute.

She let herself into the house, the front door opening straight into the living room. Old, faded floral wallpaper decorated the walls, starting to peel from some corners, and a few pieces curled up on the hardwood floor. The gray couch and matching armchair were worn but still in pretty good condition, as was the glass coffee table. There was a wooden bookcase in one corner that held paperbacks and ornaments, and an aging plant stood in the other corner. A cream archway led to the hall where the stairs to the second floor and entrance to the kitchen were. Christy didn't linger, she went straight upstairs to the shower.

After her shower, she went into the spare room where she was staying and dried her hair, trying to tame her short, insistent curls but they weren't having any of it. She rummaged in her two suitcases for something to wear and selected a hot pink sleeveless sundress and white sandals.

While she was applying her makeup, her thoughts drifted back to Dean. She wondered what he thought of her now. Did he know much about her life from Taylor? Did he know what Douchebag Alfie had done to her, what he had taken from her? How many girlfriends had Dean had? *Whoa, where did that one come from?* His love life wasn't her business, she didn't even care anyway. She wondered if he would be at Justine's gig tonight. She hoped he would be, but only so she could thank him for his kindness with her car. Her cell rang, distracting her from her thoughts.

"Hello?"

"Hi Christy, it's Cassie from Blossom Estates, how are you?" Cassie's soft voice came through the phone.

"Good thanks, and you?"

"Yes, good thank you. I just wanted to let you know the potential buyer we showed around earlier was quite interested in the property, so fingers crossed we'll have some good news for you very soon."

"That's fantastic, thank you!" Christy said, Cassie promised to call her once she heard anything and they hung up. Christy felt a little better. Hopefully, this buyer would want to take the property as soon as possible. Although it needed some work to freshen it up, Christy just wanted this all finished so she could hurry up and leave town again. She applied *Pink Dynamite*, loving how perfectly the color matched her sundress, she tried to smooth her hair down again but gave up. She grabbed her purse, and keys and left the house.

Chapter 5

That evening Dean sat in a booth at The Rusty Bucket Inn across from Beau. He stared at his best friend who had turned up on his doorstep with a six-pack and a suitcase. Something had happened, this wasn't like Beau, Dean didn't know what and he didn't want to pry. He was just glad his friend was back in town.

Beau had moved to L.A. about fourteen years ago, he became a hugely successful personal trainer, and started his own gym company called *Beau's Bodies*. He mainly worked with actors, keeping them in shape, helping them bulk up or slim down for new movie roles. When Beau was a teenager, he had his own body and fitness battles which he had worked hard to overcome. Dean was so proud of everything his friend had achieved.

Dean and Beau used to visit each other regularly, but it

had been a while due to how busy they both were. He was happy to see Beau at his door, no matter the reasons for his return, Dean was thrilled to have him stay as long as possible.

Beau took a swig of his beer. "You and Tay still doing your dinners?" he asked.

Dean nodded. "Yeah, not quite every week but often enough." As the song on the jukebox ended and quiet descended over the bar, Taylor's dark chuckle echoed around the building. He watched as Beau's eyes flicked over to her. His gaze tracking her body and his face flushing before looking away.

"Anything new with her?" Beau asked, sounding bored, but Dean knew better.

"Nope, no boyfriend if that's what you're asking."

"It wasn't." Beau rolled his eyes. "Seriously, we gonna do this again? I'm not interested, okay? We can't stand each other," he finished, his eyes finding Taylor again and lingering in a way that made Dean feel like he needed to be her protective older brother. He grabbed a handful of nuts from the bowl on the table and tossed them at Beau.

"If you say so, bro."

"Real mature," Beau muttered, brushing them onto the floor.

Dean chuckled but got distracted as the door to the bar opened and Justine came in carrying her guitar, followed by Christy. A bolt of lust punched Dean straight in the chest as he took Christy in. *Fuck, she looked good.*

The ends of her curls teasing her neck and bare shoulders. The lush tops of her breasts peeking out over the edge of her silly little pink sundress. The dress nipped in at her waist and flared out over the curve of her rounded hips before stopping mid-thigh, her creamy skin on display. Little white sandals wrapped around her feet.

Dean's mouth ran dry and his pants started to tighten.

"You okay, buddy?" Beau asked, drawing his attention.

"Huh? Uh, yeah," Dean replied, voice slightly husky. Beau smirked at him.

"Who's got you looking like you need a cold shower, or fifty?" Beau glanced around the bar and spotted Justine who was standing in front of Christy, shielding her from view.

"Ah, you're still trying to date Justine, huh?"

"Justine? Oh yeah, um, she's still turning me down," Dean replied, trying to inject some disappointment into his tone. They both looked back over as Justine moved, and Christy came back into view. Beau whistled low.

"Damn, who's the blond?"

Dean's stomach dipped slightly; this is what he had been afraid of.

"It's Christy Lee," he gritted out.

"No shit! Christy?"

As though she heard them, Christy turned in their direction, spotting Dean, she headed over. As she walked towards them her eyes moved to Beau and widened, her step faltered slightly and the pit in Dean's stomach grew. Shit, he needed to get Christy away from Beau as quickly as possible before the inevitable happened and Beau asked her out. His friend was clearly going through something and the last thing he needed was a brief romance with Christy that was sure to end in heartache. Dean was just trying to do his friend a favor that's all, he was good like that.

"Beau, is that you?" Christy gasped when she reached them, ignoring Dean completely. He watched as her baby blues roved over Beau, she looked like she was ready to start panting. Dean bit the inside of his cheek in annoyance.

"Is that me?! Is that *you*, Christy? You look amazing!" Beau gushed, standing up to greet her. Beau towered over her, making Dean realize just how petite she was. Beau bent down and gave her a lingering kiss on the cheek and Dean noticed twin spots of pink brighten her cheeks which made him feel—*nothing.*

"Oh, you charmer!" she chided lightly smacking Beau's solid chest. "What are you doing here? Aren't you supposed to be training all those gorgeous movie stars in L.A.?"

"Well, I've got to give them a break sometime, don't want to work them too hard," he replied smoothly, winking at her. Christy giggled and Dean rolled his eyes, muttering under his breath. He finally caught her attention.

"Hey, Dean," she said quietly. The flirty smile disappeared as she took in his frown, which annoyed him, did he not deserve her flirty smiles too? Out the corner of his eye he saw Beau check her out, which ticked him off even more. He needed to get rid of her quickly before Beau could make a move.

"I just wanted to say thank you for fixing my car and not charging me, you didn't have to do that, especially after the way I behaved earlier today." Her eyes shifted away like she didn't want to face him.

"Don't mention it," he said abruptly, needing her gone.

"No, really, you didn't deserve that and I..."

"Seriously, don't mention it," he interrupted, panic rising in his chest. Beau shot him a questioning look.

"Oh, well thanks anyway," she said quietly, and he felt like a jackass. She shifted from one foot to the other. Beau continued to stare at him as if he grew another head.

"Well, see you around. Was real nice to see you again, Beau," she offered him a shy smile.

"You too, sweetheart," Beau drawled as she walked away. Dean breathed a sigh of relief as they managed to avoid Beau asking her out.

"Asshole!" Beau hissed, punching his arm.

"Ouch, what was that for?" he asked, rubbing his arm where it started to burn.

"Were you actually just rude to that beautiful woman for no reason whatsoever?"

"She's not *that* beautiful," Dean mumbled, instantly regretting the lie.

"Are you kidding me? You blind as well as stupid? She's beautiful." Beau looked over at Christy as she joined Justine and Taylor at the bar. Dean saw a gleam in Beau's eye and his heart sank.

"In fact, I'm feeling thirsty. I'll get us some more beers, you sit tight." Beau flashed him a shit-eating grin as he got up and swaggered over to the women.

*

"He's gorgeous," Christy sighed to Justine and Taylor.

"He's not *that* gorgeous," Taylor muttered tartly.

"Who shit in your shoes this morning?" Christy asked, and Justine snorted, both women staring at her.

"What? It's an expression from the city," she shrugged, patting her curls demurely. She glanced over her shoulder back at Dean and Beau, feeling slightly breathless at the sight of them together. Beau was stunning to look at, but she would be on her deathbed before she admitted to anyone that Dean was gorgeous, maybe not even then. The man, judging by his behavior just now, clearly still thought very little of her. He was rude and completely embarrassed her in front of Beau.

Her eyes shifted to Beau; he had certainly changed

since she last saw him. He had a growth spurt, was likely 6'3" now. Gone was the baby fat that she found made him so adorable, hard muscle had taken its place. His dark hair was just long enough to see a faint curl forming. He had high cheekbones, with a hard square jawline that was dusted with faint stubble. A straight nose and full, wide lips, but the pièce de résistance were his eyes. They were dark, wide pools that curved upward at the edges with thick lashes. On any other male they would have looked feminine, but they softened his angular features.

"He's definitely changed while he's been away," Justine said, also staring at him.

"Still got that boring, goody, goody personality though. No amount of sexy can make up for that," Taylor grumbled.

"Oh, so now he's sexy?" Christy teased, and Justine spun around to face them.

"Ssh! He's coming over!" she hissed. She and Christy pretended they were deep in conversation while Taylor just ignored him.

"Ladies, looking beautiful this evening," Beau said pleasantly looking at Justine and Christy before turning his attention to the bar.

"Oh, Taylor, I didn't see you there," he continued, Christy watched Justine smother a laugh behind her hand and Taylor smiled sharply at Beau.

"Can I get a couple of drinks?" he asked Taylor while smiling down at Christy.

"Of what?" Taylor snapped.

"You're the bartender, surprise me," he said, still looking at Christy. She thought she heard Taylor mutter *asshole* under her breath as she turned away to start making the drinks, but she could be mistaken.

"So, Beau, are you in town for long?" Christy asked,

she glanced around him and saw Dean scowling in their direction. *He probably still thinks I'm not good enough for Beau, after all this time.*

"Hopefully long enough to take you out," he replied, Christy blinked in surprise.

"Damn, that was smooth," Justine whispered loudly.

"You wanna take me out?" Christy squeaked. Could he still be interested in her after all this time? She started doubting herself, and then remembered she wasn't meant to do that anymore. *Of course, he wants to take you out, you're a smart, gorgeous woman, remember?!* Beau leaned in towards her slightly, bringing her out of her thoughts.

"I do, and I've been waiting a really long time to ask you," he dropped his voice so only she could hear. She stared into those soulful eyes and realized that although she didn't want to have a relationship ever again, nothing was stopping her from having a little fun. Perfect, she found exactly what she was looking for. *Christy, meet your new, sexy distraction!*

"Hello ladies, you sure are looking mighty fine this evening," Dean's deep, southern voice interrupted. Beau leaned away from Christy and stepped to the side, Dean came into view and clapped Beau on the back.

"Yeah, we've already heard that Dean, but more eloquently put," Justine said sarcastically, hopping down off her barstool and grabbing her guitar case.

"I'm gonna go get set up. I'll be ready in five, Taylor," she called over her shoulder.

"Where are those drinks, buddy?" Dean asked. Although he appeared casual, the tightness of his jaw and the tension Christy spotted in his shoulders suggested otherwise.

"What can I say? The service here is slow," Beau sneered, and Christy thought she heard another muffled curse from Taylor. She turned and eyed Dean again, he had his hard gaze fixed on her. Why was he so tense and angry looking and why was he trying to rush Beau? Then it clicked; he was trying to get Beau away from her, he knew Beau was still interested despite Dean's efforts to dissuade him in the past. Christy felt anger and steely resolve fuse her spine.

"I would love to go out with you, Beau." She put her hand on his arm. She noticed Dean gave no reaction, just turned away.

Beau smiled down at her. "Great, tomorrow night?" he asked. "I'll pick you up at six?"

Christy smiled at him. "Perfect, can't wait."

"Your drinks, Beau; two *Blowjobs*," Taylor said, innocence dripping from her tone. Christy watched as she pushed two small glasses of the shot across the bar. Dean chuckled but Beau just smiled at her. He picked one up, licked the cream off the top and downed it, then did the same with the other, moaning.

"Thank you, they're my favorite," he said in a way that made Christy wonder if he was talking about something else entirely. Taylor's eyes flashed and she moved away.

Beau turned back to Christy. "See you tomorrow night," he said, dropping a kiss on her cheek then he and Dean walked away. Her eyes met Dean's as he passed, she shivered at the intensity in their depths as they moved over her.

That was weird.

"I made you one too, I figured as soon as you saw it you would want one," Taylor sighed, placing the shot in front of her. Christy squealed, she did love whipped cream.

"Yay, I was so jealous when I saw them," she said excitedly, swiping her finger through the cream and licking it off. After savoring the sweet taste, she downed the shot, the cool Irish cream sliding down her throat. She turned to face the stage where Justine was now sitting on a stool with her guitar perched on her lap. She nodded over at Taylor signaling she was ready to start. Taylor grabbed a microphone from under the bar and turned down the lights so that the only lighting came from the candles flickering on each table. The bar felt cozy, and Christy felt a warm haze settle over her from the atmosphere and her shot.

"Good evening, ladies and gentlemen! We've got a very special treat for you, the radiant Justine is performing for us again." The crowd interrupted with cheers, "You will pay attention to her. You will not talk during her performance. Anyone caught talking will be removed forcefully by myself. Everyone is encouraged to dance but no dirty dancing under any circumstances, that is only reserved for me." Chuckles sounded throughout the bar as though everyone had witnessed Taylor's dancing before. "There will be a break after half an hour to get more refreshments, but don't bother trying to get anything before then as I'll ignore you. Now give it up for Justine!"

Christy cheered along with the crowd and Taylor put her fingers in her mouth, whistling loudly. Christy hopped down off her stool, then she and Taylor moved towards the stage. Justine began to strum the opening notes on her guitar and the crowd fell silent, all watching her. She opened her mouth and began singing a soulful ballad, her voice exquisite and heart-breaking. Goosebumps covered Christy from head to toe and tingles ran up her spine. It was the most beautiful song she ever heard and it ended far too quickly.

The crowd erupted with cheers and she glanced

around to see if anyone else was as affected as she had been and saw Beau and Dean on the other side of the stage. Dean was staring at her, his gaze deep and intense again, she shivered as a wave of arousal moved through her, surprising her. *What's wrong with me and what's his problem?*

Justine started up a new song and Taylor pulled Christy away to dance to the upbeat tune. The pop song had Taylor throwing her hands in the air and wiggling her hips, the crowd was doing the same, everyone moving to the beat Justine created. Taylor whooped, and Christy laughed as she bumped her hips against Christy trying to get her to join in. Normally Christy felt clumsy and self-conscious, why wobble all your wobbly bits even more? But she was trying to become more confident and there was no one better to learn from than Taylor.

The alcohol combined with Taylor's insistence made her give in and she swung her hips and shimmied her shoulders. Taylor spun her around and she laughed, then the song changed to a lazy, dirtier beat and she moved her hips slower, morphing into a sensual bump and grind. She closed her eyes and let the music control her body.

*

Dean was dying, he was burning up, but he couldn't tear his eyes away. He watched Christy shake and shimmy like no one was watching. Except he was watching, his eyes drinking in the sight of her. He tried not to, but she drew him like no one else. He felt flames licking him from head to toe as he watched her breasts bounce with her movements, his mouth drying. She was wild, sexy, carefree and he could no longer deny his attraction to her, he wanted her.

She swayed her hips in a slow bump, bump, griiiind, running her hands over her body.

"*Jesus*," he muttered as his cock hardened beneath the fly of his jeans, aching to get to her. Sweat beaded on his brow and he wiped it away, shifting his stance to hide his arousal. As if she knew his thoughts, she peeked at him over her shoulder. Her cheeks flushed, blond curls dancing around her face, mouth open slightly as if part way through a moan. She batted her lashes at him, and he cursed. He needed to get out of here before he did something silly, like storm over there, grab her, shove her against the wall and really make her moan.

He leaned into Beau; "Shit, man, I just remembered I've got your hotshot friend coming to pick up his Mercedes in the morning and I need to finish working on it. I'm gonna head over to the garage, you good here?" he asked, raising his voice over Justine's singing, earning a glare from Taylor.

"Yeah, don't worry I'll make my way back," Beau replied. Dean clapped him on the back and walked over to the door. He turned back to wave 'bye to Taylor but saw Beau had made his way over to the women and had begun dancing with Christy. He bit his cheek, jealousy lashing at him, as Beau slipped his hands around Christy's dainty waist. It took all his willpower not to storm over there and tear them apart. Instead, he banged out the door and into the humid night.

Chapter 6

The next evening, Christy was at her house frantically rushing around for the right outfit to wear on her date with Beau. She was nervous, she hadn't been out on a proper date since Douchebag Alfie. Her stomach was in knots and she felt so sick that going out to dinner probably wasn't the best start. She hoped the feeling went away after they settled into the evening. She finally decided on a khaki blouse tucked into a leather skirt with black ankle boots. She added a gold chain and earrings to finish off the look. She looked good, if she did say so herself, but the longer she looked at her reflection the more she started to see flaws and the old thoughts crept in. *No, there's nothing wrong with thinking I look nice when I've made an effort.*

She'd just finished her makeup when there was a knock at the door. Dang it, he's early! She smoothed her hair, grabbed her purse and went down to greet Beau.

She opened the door and found him waiting on the porch, he looked gorgeous. He had his dark khaki shirt tucked into black slacks and finished off with shining black oxfords. He smiled when he saw her, giving her a quick once over.

"We're matching tonight," he said, dropping a kiss on her cheek and gesturing to her outfit.

"Great minds and all that," she joked. He smiled again and held out his hand to her. She slid her palm into his warm grip and they walked down to his sleek, black sports car. She laughed as she saw her beat-up old car parked a few feet ahead, the two cars together looked like a before and after photo.

"Sorry if I'm a bit early, I was eager," he said with a chuckle. "You look amazing by the way." She flushed at his compliment and didn't immediately try to dismiss it, which was progress.

"Thank you, so do you." When they reached his car, he opened the door for her and helped her inside like a gentleman.

"I was thinking we could go to that Italian restaurant in Bakersville," he said when he got in. He started the engine and pulled away from the curb.

"That sounds great, as long as you don't mind the drive though, it's about an hour away isn't it?"

He flashed her a quick smile, "I'm sure the time will fly by once you start telling me all about what you've been doing for the last fifteen years."

It was a lovely evening for a drive, warm but not humid, she sent a prayer up to the hair gods to keep the weather like this. Beau was right, as soon as she started telling him about her writing, the journey flew by and in no time, they were pulling up outside the restaurant.

"That's amazing, I don't think I could ever come up with a mystery interesting enough to engage people. I can't believe you do it all yourself!" he said excitedly, shutting off the engine and getting out of the car. By the time she unbuckled her seatbelt and grabbed her purse, he was opening the door for her.

"Sometimes it is hard self-publishing and that's not even the main challenge. Writer's block, which I'm battling at the moment, is the devil. I also worry that the mystery isn't…mysterious enough," she finished lamely.

"I'm sure you make them plenty mysterious," he said, a cheeky gleam in his eye. He took her hand and they walked inside the restaurant. When they were inside, she glanced around. It was decorated in a vintage Tuscan villa-style with lots of plants dotted around the room, and olive branches hanging low from the ceiling. Decorative plates lined the walls and bottles of wine were grouped together in wooden cabinets. Each table was covered in a red checkered linen cloth and had a candle flickering romantically in the center.

A waiter greeted them and led them to a quiet table in the corner of the room. Beau pulled out her chair for her and once they both were seated and had ordered their food, they were left alone.

"Now I've talked about myself plenty so tell me about you," she said sipping her wine, she noted he seemed to look nervous for the first time all evening.

"Well, when I left Citrus Pines, I moved to L.A. and studied sports nutrition. While I was studying, I had a part-time job in a gym. I watched people training, I studied hard and I became fascinated with the psychology behind people's behavior towards food and diets. I had my own food and weight issues as a kid, so once I graduated, I worked to become a trainer to help people.

The more clients I worked with, the more my passion for helping people developed. I went to a couple of investors, managed to get the money to start my own business, and happened to stumble onto the right clients, I guess. I'm sorry this must be so boring for you," he said shyly, looking embarrassed.

"Don't be silly, it's not boring at all! You've built a hugely successful business from the ground up, that's fascinating. It's taken hard work, determination, and intelligence to get where you are, don't ever put yourself down!" she said passionately. The waiter appeared with their food and once he left, she gestured for Beau to continue. Beau picked up his fork and began digging into his pasta and she noted he had lovely table manners.

"So then one day this woman comes into my tiny gym telling me she's an actress and needs help training for a movie role, she was unknown at the time and-"

"Which one?" Christy interrupted.

"I can't say, I have non-disclosure agreements with all my clients," he said regretfully, then she caught that gleam in his eye again. "But let's just say she won the Academy Award last year for Best Actress." Christy cast her mind back and sucked in a breath when she realized who it was.

"No way! That body is all you?"

He nodded, laughing at her reaction. "Then she passed my details to a friend and the rest is history."

"That's amazing, I need to get you to train me if I can end up looking like her," she muttered, forking in another mouthful of penne.

"I think you look fantastic, but I'm always up for a one on one," he said, his voice deepening slightly, and she smiled shyly at him. *Oh my God, he's flirting with you, be cool!*

They chatted throughout the rest of their meal and all through dessert which he insisted on having. Before she knew it, the restaurant was closing and the check was on their table. He paid for the meal, shushing her protests and telling her she could pay for the next one, her mind filing the comment away to hyperventilate over later. As they drove back to Citrus Pines, he told her stories of his clients, her favorite one being when he got caught up in a tabloid scandal. He was accused of being a homewrecker to a famous elderly gay couple who everyone knew had been together for years.

She enjoyed listening to him talk and was reminded of her brief conversations with him when they were younger. He had been so kind and funny, it was a shame they hadn't done this years ago, her joy diminishing slightly when she remembered why. She wondered if Beau remembered the incident too.

When they pulled up outside her house she glanced at the clock in the car and saw it was after midnight. Beau got out and came around to open her door, taking her hand in his as they walked up to her front door. As they got closer, the butterflies in her stomach started fluttering more and more at the thought that he might kiss her goodnight. When they reached the door, they faced each other, and she began to rummage in her purse for her keys.

"I had a really nice time tonight," he said softly, reaching up to tuck a strand of hair behind her ear. She met his eyes and his hand lingered on her cheek.

"Yes, I did too."

As he bent his head, she sucked in a breath; their lips met in a gentle, sweet kiss. His lips were soft, the light pressure was nice, he wasn't forcing his way in like she hated some men doing but before she knew it, the kiss was over.

"Would you like to go out again?" he asked, his voice

even and unaffected.

"Yes, I would love to."

"Great, I'll call you." He gave her hand a squeeze, she said goodnight and watched him leave, he waved as he drove off. As she got ready for bed, she analyzed the kiss. It had been nice, good but chaste. She knew he was a nice guy, had always been nice, not arrogant and overbearing. She didn't need to worry about him stealing her money and going on the run like Alfie had done.

It was a nice kiss but there wasn't any heat. Beau seemed fairly unaffected by it, not exactly swept away with passion. She wasn't swept away by the moment either. *Calm down, it takes time to get to know someone, to learn what they like and to push their buttons. Just give it time, you're not looking for 'forever' just a distraction until you leave again*, she reminded herself. She got into bed feeling calmer and relaxed. But as usual, the nightmares plagued her. Except this time they were interspersed with dreams of a blond-haired, blue-eyed devil which left her panting and needy when she awoke in the morning.

*

Christy didn't think the bar would have been busy on a Sunday at lunchtime, but she was wrong. The bar seemed to be packed all the time, which was great for Taylor. She met Justine and Taylor for lunch, they couldn't really go anywhere else as it was Taylor's shift and she was training a new girl.

"So..." Justine said when they were all seated in a booth. "Tell us how your date went and don't spare any of the dirty details." She waggled her eyebrows.

"Spare me the dirty details, I'm about to eat thank you," Taylor replied dryly. "Actually you were out with Beau so nothing exciting would have happened anyway," she added, Justine rolled her eyes.

"What is your deal with him?" Justine asked.

"Nothing," Taylor shrugged, when she said nothing more, Justine turned back to Christy.

"Well, I want dirty details, I need them. You probably had sex this morning." She nodded towards Taylor. Justine was still a virgin which was rare these days for someone of her age, but she believed in true love and wasn't willing to settle for anything less. She was saving herself for Mr. Right. *She's probably the only person sitting in this booth who still believes in true love.* Justine went on a lot of dates, determined to do her bit to find him but he was elusive and so far, nada. Taylor grinned at Justine,

"Oh, I had sex this morning, with myself," she said, waving her fingers in Justine's face.

"Gross," Justine chuckled, batting Taylor's hand away.

"Hey, you asked!" Taylor griped.

"No, I speculated. Correctly as it turns out," Justine retorted, and they were laughing as the new barmaid, Kayleigh, appeared at the table with their food. After they had taken their plates, Kayleigh stayed in place, shuffling her feet nervously.

"Everything okay?" Taylor asked between clenched teeth.

"I'm sorry to interrupt, but the oven is making that banging noise again," Kayleigh replied softly.

"You remember what I told you? Open the door, bang the top three times in quick succession, kick the side twice and then close the door *gently*. That should stop it."

"Okay, thank you," Kayleigh replied, bobbing slightly and hurried away.

"You need a new oven," Justine commented.

"Did she just curtsy?" Taylor asked.

"I think so," Christy giggled. As they ate their food she told them about her date with Beau. Justine sighed periodically and gushed over everything Beau did while Taylor scoffed, tutted and criticized everything he did.

"He just gave you a quick kiss before leaving you all alone? Didn't even put any effort into it? Lazy that's what he is!" Taylor said heatedly. Christy looked at Justine who was smothering a laugh behind her napkin. When they finished their food, Taylor started gathering their plates together.

"Well *chica's*, this was fun, but I've got to get back as I have a client," Justine said, grabbing her purse.

"Is it the peeper?" Taylor joked.

Justine sighed "No, it's his wife."

"I'm going to hang here for a bit, I don't really like being at the house on my own," Christy said, and Justine gave her a sympathetic look. "I've got calls to make and a funeral to finish arranging anyway."

Justine leaned over, kissed her cheek, and said, "If you need any help then I'm right here." Christy thanked her and waved goodbye. When Justine had left, Taylor turned back to her.

"Would you like me to bring you an adult beverage?"

"Hmm, I don't think getting wasted will help with this planning, maybe just a coffee?"

"Okay coming right up, don't worry about paying for lunch, it's our treat," Taylor threw over her shoulder as she headed back to the bar.

"I can afford lunch!" Christy shouted after her, but Taylor waved her away. Christy's heart clenched slightly in her chest, *they're so good to me.* She felt guilty, but guilt soon morphed into anger when she thought about Douchebag Alfie and put the blame with him.

She'd met Alfie at a library and he seemed nice, sweet and unassuming; at first. But then he changed, he became aloof and distant, and she got the feeling he wasn't interested in her, that he didn't even like her sometimes. Turns out, she was right.

She woke up one morning with no boyfriend and no money. He took it all, leaving her nearly bankrupt. She reported it to the police, but unfortunately, there was no way to prove he emptied her accounts. She let down her guard with him, desperate to have a deeper connection and build a foundation with someone. He often stayed at her apartment while she went out to write, she loved to sit in coffee shops and people watch in New York. She thought he was being supportive and giving her space to write. In actual fact, he was rifling through her belongings, trying to find all her bank accounts. *Asshole.*

She would never trust a man again, not with her money and certainly not with her heart. She would never let anyone get close to touching it, casual dating only, and she would get out if she started to feel too much. She pushed her thoughts aside, she had plenty going on this week without making herself feel like shit.

She got her notebook and pen out of her purse and started working through her super long list. She already booked the crematorium and invited everyone from the town. She didn't know if her father had any friends so figured a blanket invite would be best. The crematorium had a sweet-looking chapel where the ceremony would take place. She just needed to check there was enough room for everyone, organize for the flowers to be dropped off in the morning, and find somewhere to host a last-minute wake.

She rang the florist to check the order and gave them the address of the crematorium and the time to deliver. Then she checked the list of attendees and rang the crematorium to update them on the number, seating arrangements, and the flowers. Lastly, she rang around all the bars and local venues in the area, struggling to find somewhere to host the wake. It was her own fault but with the news of her father's death, the Alfie situation, and coming back to town, she had forgotten to organize it. She begged, cajoled, and threatened but no one had anything available.

Christy dropped her phone on the table and sighed. She noticed there were now three empty coffee cups in front of her. *How long have I been here?* She looked out the windows and could see the evening sun was setting through the trees. The door to the bar swung open and she spotted Beau entering and smiled. Dean came in behind him and her stomach dipped, immediately her brain filled with flashes of the dreams she had last night.

Beau glanced her way and flashed her his beautiful smile as they headed over to the bar to get a drink. It made her smile back but didn't quicken her pulse the way just looking at Dean suddenly did. Which irritated her, especially as Dean also looked over but couldn't so much as muster a smile. Their eyes clashed; his brow furrowed in anger, he seemed permanently angry at the moment. And yet something stirred as he held her gaze, awareness prickled through her, making her feel hot and...uncomfortable. He reluctantly lifted his arm in a wave and she waved back. *Well at least he acknowledged me,* she thought sarcastically. As she watched Beau give their order to Kayleigh, Dean headed over to her. Her stomach fluttering increased.

"Hey Christy, mind if we join you?" Dean asked, his deep voice washing over her.

"Uh, sure," she replied and began clearing the table of her debris as he eased into the booth opposite her. When he settled himself, his knee brushed against hers under the table and she jolted at the contact, banging her knee on the underside.

"Ouch, shit!" she cried, reaching down to rub her throbbing knee.

"Are you okay? That sounded painful," he said, concern furrowing his brow, turning him from broody sexy to adorable sweetie pie in the blink of an eye. Heat suffused her cheeks as embarrassment over her clumsiness washed over her. Also, annoyance at his stupid, big, sexy – uh – body taking up all the room and encroaching on her space.

"Yeah, your knee hit mine and jolted me," she snapped accusingly, instantly regretting her show of temper. Why did Dean always bring out her bitchy side? Dean frowned at her again looking annoyed but before he could open his mouth, Beau appeared with the drinks.

"Hey beautiful, how are you today?" Beau asked, leaning down to kiss her briefly on the mouth. As he eased in next to her, she looked across at Dean who, *shock*, looked angry again.

"Hey, Beau, fine thank you."

"And what have you been up to?" he asked.

"Not much really, met the girls here for lunch, and I've been trying to organize a few bits for the funeral but I'm not having much luck," she said and all of a sudden, completely out of nowhere, she got choked up.

*

As Dean watched Beau drop his head to kiss Christy, white-hot jealousy consumed him. This was ridiculous, he wasn't jealous of Beau and he didn't have any designs on Christy. He was just getting worried for Beau, yeah that's it, his friend was going through a tough time and getting involved with Christy would only lead to heartbreak. He was trying to do the noble thing and get Beau to realize what a mistake this was, he was *such* a good friend.

Not all heroes wear capes.

It certainly didn't have anything to do with how much he kept thinking about the curvaceous, blond sitting opposite him whose mouth he couldn't stop fantasizing about. He watched as Beau asked her a question but then immediately turned his attention to the bar, watching Taylor and Kayleigh. He wasn't even listening to Christy's response. If it was him she was talking to, then he wouldn't be able to take his eyes off her mouth, because – uh – that's what a good listener he was.

"...organize the funeral but I'm not having much luck," Christy's words registered with him. Oh God, her father's funeral was at the end of the week. As his gaze moved to her eyes, he saw them fill up with tears and she bit her bottom lip looking away out the window. His heart ached for her, in that moment she looked so vulnerable that he just wanted to wrap her in his arms and comfort her, but he couldn't. He looked at Beau who hadn't even noticed what was happening.

"Beau!" he hissed, but saw Christy stiffen. She looked uncomfortable and he spotted a single tear slide down her cheek, Beau turned to him and Dean nodded towards the bar.

"Christy needs another coffee," he said quietly, and Beau jumped up eagerly.

"Sure thing! One coffee coming right up," he said and left. Dean looked at Christy, but she wouldn't meet his eyes. She sniffled quietly, and it just about broke his heart. She had no family left that he knew of, except for Taylor and Justine. Her dickhead ex had stolen all her money and her father had just died. She's having a really tough time and he suddenly felt even worse about acting like a jerk to her. Another tear slid down her cheek, and he watched as it collected in the corner of her pink mouth, soon followed by another.

"I'm sorry, I'm sure it'll stop in a minute," she said softly.

"Don't worry about a thing, it's only you and me here, no one else. Take your time," he replied gently, trying to use a soothing tone. He must have said something wrong because more tears fell, quicker and fatter than the first. Her shoulders began to shake and he ached to comfort her. He didn't want to draw attention to her though, thinking she would be embarrassed by it, despite there being nothing wrong with crying. Dean reached under the table and placed his hand on her knee. It was bare, warm, and soft and he pushed aside the zing he felt at the contact. *Get your mind out of the gutter, she needs comforting, not pawing!*

He was going to pull his hand away, worried it was making her feel awkward, but after a moment he noticed she seemed to relax slightly so he left it right where it was. He rubbed his thumb back and forth gently, hoping the touch would calm her. She took a few shuddering breaths and after another moment, the tears stopped, and she hiccupped. He rummaged in his back pocket with his free hand looking for the clean rag he usually kept there for wiping his hands on when he was fixing a car. He pulled it out, inspecting it discreetly before offering it to Christy. She took it hesitantly.

"Thank you," she croaked, her voice thick with tears. As he continued to stroke her knee he said, "If you ever need anything or if you want to talk, just let me know." She smiled at him and his heart thudded in his chest. Her cheeks all red and splotchy from crying, her eyes wide and shining, staring up at him like polished blue Topaz. Damn, she was beautiful.

"Thank you, I'm sorry, again. I think everything just

hit me right then. Especially having spent all afternoon arranging the funeral details, well as much as I could anyway. I still can't find anywhere to host the wake," she said. His brow furrowed.

"Could we not host it here?" he asked, her eyes widened and he hoped she didn't notice his use of we.

"Oh my God, I didn't even think of that, what's wrong with me?" she groaned. "I'll go and check with Taylor," she started to get up, but he tightened his grip on her knee. As she moved to the side to get out of the booth, his hand slipped to rest on the inside of her thigh. She slid her eyes to him, and time seemed to slow. When their eyes met, something hot and unknown moved between them. He stroked over her thigh once with his thumb, unable to stop himself and her eyes, which had only moments ago been sad, seemed to heat as he stared at her. He felt a prickle along the back of his neck and his blood stirred in his veins. In the background, he heard Taylor cackle and the spell was broken.

"I'll go speak to Tay, you stay here and just take a minute for yourself," he said, letting go of her thigh and sliding out of the booth. He didn't wait to hear her reply, just headed straight to the bar feeling slightly scandalized for stroking her thigh in public. When he got to the bar, Taylor was gone.

"What's taking so long?" he asked Beau.

"No idea, Taylor refused to serve me, so Kayleigh is doing it but she can't find the filters," Beau replied sulkily. Dean chuckled, *sounds about right.*

"Is she in the back?" he asked. Beau nodded and Dean headed around the bar and opened the door to the back office where Taylor was sitting at her desk, punching numbers aggressively into a calculator.

"Hey, sis," he called, leaning casually against the door

frame. She snapped her sharp, emerald eyes up to him and waved him inside. He came in and shut the door to give them some privacy.

"You don't need to call me that you know. Our parents got a divorce, any responsibility ended then," she said this to him regularly as if giving him an out of their relationship and any responsibility, each time he ignored her.

"That's bullshit; you'll always be my little sister," he said fiercely, she gave him a shy smile.

"What's up?" she asked, changing the subject quickly. She always did that, keeping her emotional armor in place at all times. Impenetrable, even with him. He explained about Christy and needing the bar for the wake, Taylor slapped her palm to her forehead.

"Jesus, I didn't even think to offer, I'm such a shitty friend! Of course, she can."

"Thanks and, uh, I'll cover it," he said sheepishly. She eyed him closely, pursing her lips.

"Why?"

"Because I can be a nice guy sometimes," he said defensively, she scoffed.

"I know that, but why *this*?" She continued to stare at him unblinking, and he could feel himself getting ready to crack under the intensity. *She would make a good interrogator,* he thought randomly.

"Are you trying to sleep with her?" she asked, her voice held a deadly undertone, *message received.*

"Hell no, and you know I don't do that anymore. I overheard you and Justine talking about her asshole ex, I know she's broke and this is the last thing she needs to worry about paying for."

"You're a little old to still be eavesdropping on our girl chats," she teased, he gave her a scornful stare and she sighed.

"Fine, cover the food. Me and Justine will cover the rest," she said. He blew her a kiss.

"Thanks, sis."

She smiled at him and that was his cue to leave. As he turned away, he heard her say softly, "You're welcome, bro." His step faltered slightly and damn if he didn't get a lump in his throat. He kept walking, but when he reached the door she had gotten up as well.

"Actually, I need to check on Kayleigh," she muttered and came out with him. Dean saw that Beau was back with Christy and making her laugh. The jealousy gnawed at him again, but he was glad she was smiling, even if it wasn't him making her smile.

He slid back into the booth, when Christy looked at him, he nodded ever so slightly. She visibly relaxed and mouthed a *thank you*. His chest puffed up with happiness at solving this problem for her. He enjoyed the time he'd spent with her this evening, tears aside obviously. He loved getting to offer her comfort and support and didn't want it to end.

"...should take you to that new seafood restaurant that's opened up on the lake on Saturday night." Beau was saying. Beau was organizing another date together so soon? His brain screamed *don't*, but his mouth said, *fuck you, brain* and did it anyway.

"Sounds great! Where are we going then?" Both Beau and Christy turned to stare at him like he'd sprouted horns.

"Oh, I meant for me and Christy's next date," Beau said motioning at Dean to *shut the fuck up*.

Dean ignored him. "Great, I can bring Taylor and we can double, that'll be fun."

"You wanna double date with your sister?" Christy

asked, arching her eyebrow at him.

"Yeah, why not? Hey Taylor!" he called. Taylor was showing Kayleigh how to stack glasses, she glanced over and saw Dean beckoning to her. She huffed and stomped over to them.

"What?"

"We're double dating with Beau and Christy."

"Gross," she said and then glared at Beau, "I'm busy anyway."

"It's your Saturday off this weekend, I know your shift pattern," Dean replied with a smug smile. She huffed some more then rolled her eyes.

"Fine, but you're paying." And then she stomped back to Kayleigh. He chuckled at her enthusiasm, or lack of. Beau watched her leave, suddenly seeming more interested.

"Sounds great!" he enthused, echoing Dean from moments before. Dean felt Christy's gaze boring into him but refused to meet it. He couldn't work out whether this was the best idea he ever had or the biggest mistake he ever made.

Chapter 7

Christy spent the rest of the week finalizing the funeral plans, walking around the woods trying to come up with new mysteries to write, and spending time at the bar with Taylor. Generally avoiding being in the house on her own and trying not to think about the side of Dean that she witnessed during her meltdown at the bar. The side she hadn't known existed, and why would she? She only knew adolescent Dean who hurt and humiliated her with his cruel, flippant words.

The way he stroked his thumb over her knee still had her shivering, what would he think if he knew her thoughts? That a moment of friendliness on his part had turned into one of the most erotic moments of her life. She groaned and dropped her head on the bar. He would probably pity her, thinking how sad she was that a little knee foreplay had affected her so much, inflating his already massive ego at the same time. She forced herself to turn her thoughts to Beau and their upcoming date on Saturday night. Their double date. With Dean. Her heart rate sped up and she groaned again.

"Oh my God, stop!" she exclaimed to herself.

"Stop what?" Taylor asked, appearing at her side.

"Oh, nothing, ha. You ready?" she asked. She was spending the night at Taylor's and was waiting for her to finish locking up the bar. The funeral was tomorrow and the pit in her stomach tightened at the thought of what she would be facing. So far, she tried to ignore the approaching day, even while she was organizing it. The planning helped to distract her from looking at her feelings too closely but now she couldn't avoid it. She hadn't wanted to wake up in that house on her own tomorrow morning and spend the hours beforehand getting ready in silent contemplation.

Christy's mind flashed back to the last time she considered that house a home. She was fifteen, her mother had just passed away and she assumed that grieving together would bring her and her father closer. But her father had been consumed with the grief of losing his wife and his grief changed him.

He became cold and inattentive, wanting little to do with his only daughter who had begun to look too much like her mother, avoiding her where possible. His rejection in the midst of her grief shattered her. She tried harder to reach him, wanting to spend time with him, her only parent and he rebuffed all her attempts. He began to drink, some nights getting so drunk he just sobbed uncontrollably. Other nights he would rage at her if she tried to help him. She would shut herself in her room and listen out for his movements, terrified. Trying to determine where he was in the house and make herself small enough to escape his notice. Would he come upstairs and start screaming at her again? When would he turn back into the dad he was before her mom died? Would he ever love her again?

She began to hate the way she looked, so similar to her mother, which she should've cherished but instead despised. She had it thrown in her face constantly as a reason her father couldn't stand to be around her. She reminded him too much of his lost love, he would never recover while Christy was there, taunting him every day with what he lost. One night, just as she turned eighteen, he came to her, drunk again, apologizing and begging her forgiveness. She rejoiced, this would be it, the pain was finally leaving him, and they could rebuild their relationship, it wasn't too late.

Moments later he began to rant and rave again, working himself up so much he had screamed that it should've been her who died. Once the words had left his mouth a look of shock had crossed his face, he flung himself away from her, running down the stairs and out of the house. Her heart shattered and a black chasm filled its place. He would never love her and she couldn't live like this anymore.

She took a suitcase and started packing her things, throwing clothes into it, not caring what she grabbed. She left the house and went to Taylor's. When Taylor opened the door and saw Christy standing there with a suitcase, she reached out to grab it and bring it into the house.

"I'm leaving." Christy had said quietly, her throat clogged with tears.

Taylor shook her head. "No, you can stay here; you don't need to leave!" she cried, but Christy was adamant.

"I can't be here anymore, I think it's killing me."

Christy's voice cracked, she turned away.

"Please don't go, don't leave me too," Taylor begged, but Christy no longer had any energy, she was drained.

"Come with me then."

"You know I can't leave Dad." Christy knew that Taylor's dad had become ill and needed care.

"I can't stay, Taylor, I won't make it. I'm sorry, I don't want to leave you but I have to go. I'll let you know when I'm safe." She threw herself at Taylor in a fierce hug. She understood her friend would be devastated and would have come with her if she could. But Christy couldn't stay in this town anymore, it was too full of bad memories that haunted her.

"I love you, Tay," she said, and Taylor started crying. They hugged for a long time before Christy pulled away, she grabbed her suitcase and left without looking back.

That night she got a bus to the next town over and stayed in a motel before deciding her next move. She contacted Taylor to let her know she was alright and also Justine, who had been extremely hurt when she heard Christy left without saying goodbye to her. She stayed at the motel a few days before she bought another bus ticket to New York. She thought about reaching out to her father to see if he was okay, but every time she lifted the phone to call him, his last words played through her mind and she slammed the receiver back down.

So she went to New York and worked in diners, department stores, and as a tour guide, trying to scrape together money for English and creative writing classes to help her develop her writing skills. When she graduated from her classes, she managed to get a job writing articles for various magazines and blogs. She tried to become a published author, but it was a tough world. She had issues with rejection which stemmed from her relationship with her father, and that fateful afternoon in the hallway with Dean. After a few attempts and no success, she decided to publish her novels on her own.

She stayed close with Taylor and Justine who visited whenever they could. At first, she and Justine struggled to get back to normal with Justine still upset about the way Christy had left, it had taken them a long time to move on. She often paid for them to visit, feeling guilty they always made the trip to see her as she would never return to her hometown. The pain too real, and the fear of seeing her father kept her away. She never heard from him and never wanted to, over the years the hurt and sadness had morphed into anger and bitterness. She forbade Taylor and Justine from giving her any information about what he was doing, so she had no idea what his life was like.

Her success as a self-published author was enough to get by and pay the bills, she was lucky she could make enough money doing what she loved. She was finally happy and she felt the only thing missing was a romantic relationship. When she met Alfie, she fell in love with him, at least she thought she had. She trusted him completely, the first man she had trusted to love her since her father. And he had broken her trust and left her unable to pay her rent, bills or even afford food.

Christy had done some research since, wondering what had made Alfie choose her as his next scam. Apparently, easy targets were people who were alone, cut off from close family. Downtrodden was a word that came up, weak was another. Insecure, timid, lacking confidence, and self-esteem—check, check, and checkmate.

That was what drove her to make a change to stop putting herself down, she needed to build herself up. Look what mentally browbeating herself had gotten her, nothing, literally! She might never want to have another relationship again, but she could be strong and love herself enough for two. And just when things couldn't get worse, she received a call from a hospital near Citrus Pines informing her that her father had passed away from a heart attack.

"All done, lets go!" Taylor called, jolting Christy out of her memories and back to the present. She slid off her barstool, then they locked up and walked around the back of the bar to Taylor's cabin. Taylor moaned about their double date all the way there. When they got in, Christy changed into her pajamas while Taylor made some popcorn. When Christy came back into the room, Taylor was starting to make some drinks.

"Let me make you a drink for a change," Christy said, pushing Taylor out of the kitchen. Taylor spluttered but went off to put her pajamas on and Justine was already wearing hers when she arrived a few minutes later. Christy made them all cocktails and they sat in the living room with their snacks and drinks and watched horror movies. *The perfect distraction.* They spent the evening trying to scare each other, laughing hysterically, and eventually they all fell asleep in a heap on the floor.

When Christy woke the next morning, the reality of the day immediately hit her. She couldn't explain how she felt, just very mixed—sad, angry, heartbroken, regretful. She tried to push the thoughts away and focus on a routine. As she made coffee, her movements woke Justine and Taylor, both were bleary-eyed as they came into the kitchen.

"Morning ladies," she said, pasting a smile on her face and handing them a mug each.

"How're you feeling?" Justine asked, her voice extra raspy from lack of use. Her soulful eyes bored into

Christy.

"Weird, very mixed. Don't analyze me though please, I need to keep it together."

"I won't unless you want me to," Justine replied, and Christy gave her a small smile. They drank their coffees and then both women helped her get ready. She went through the motions almost mechanically. Putting on her black dress and shoes, Taylor did her hair while Justine helped her with her makeup before getting ready themselves. Taylor drove them all to the crematorium and when they arrived, she noticed a lot of the mourners were gathered around outside the building, waiting to go inside and pay their respects.

Taylor parked on the opposite side of the road and they all got out. Christy was instantly surrounded by the familiar faces of the people she grew up around. They crowded around her, offering condolences, and grabbing at her, trying to hug and kiss her. She had no space to breathe and panic rose inside her as she was mobbed.

"Okay, everyone, why don't you all make your way back towards the building ready to go inside. I'm sure you'll all have a chance to catch up with Christy afterwards," Taylor called out, she began guiding Christy around them as Justine fended people off, acting like her bodyguard. Christy had the bizarre thought that she felt like a celebrity and bit back the urge to laugh.

As they approached the doors, the celebrant came out to greet her. He took her hand gently and talked to her in hushed, quiet tones.

"My condolences on your loss, Christy. I'm sure your father is now at peace and in the arms of the Lord. The pallbearers are going to bring the coffin in and place it inside. Then everyone will be able to come in and take their seats ready for the service to begin. I'll say a few words, just what we've already agreed, did you wish to speak at all?"

Christy shook her head, feeling slightly dazed.

"Not a problem. We'll then read some passages from the Bible and sing the hymns you've selected, say a prayer, and then invite everyone to come and say goodbye," he finished. Christy's throat tightened when he said *goodbye* and it took her a moment to respond.

"Great, thank you," she murmured. He squeezed her hands then gestured for her to stand to one side.

"Can everyone please stand back for a moment of silence?" he called, and a hush fell over the crowd.

Christy turned to see the pallbearers, all dressed in their dark suits and top hats, raise the coffin that held her father onto their shoulders. Their hands clasped tightly together in front of them, and they moved forward as one. *They're not even holding it, what if it tips and falls? What if it opens and the body comes out?* Her brain panicked and her breathing sped up as they moved, but the coffin stayed in place and her fears subsided.

They passed by her and moved into the building and once they were inside, the celebrant signaled for her to go in. Justine and Taylor had their arms around her, but her legs locked in place like she couldn't walk. They gently pushed her forward and her feet slowly began to move. The room was furnished in light wood and sage green furniture, it was brightly lit with windows running along the top of the walls. The dias was in the center of the room, chairs fanned out from here and filled the room with a plinth placed in the center at the front.

Christy sat in the front row with Justine and Taylor taking seats either side of her. Everyone came in and sat behind her. She was surprised but pleased that so many people had turned up, some people she recognized from the town, some she didn't. As she glanced around, she spotted Dean in the front row on the other side of the aisle, he turned to look in her direction and offered her a small smile. She hadn't thought he would turn up, but she was glad he was here. After the way he was with her in the bar, she took comfort in his presence.

The celebrant began the ceremony, she tried to pay attention to what he was saying, but her eyes kept getting drawn to the coffin. Her father's body was so close, this was the closest they had been to each other in nearly fifteen years which was a horrible thought. A lump formed in her throat and tears stung the back of her eyes. She felt like her autopilot had been disengaged and now she was feeling everything, the emotions she held at bay beginning to sink in.

As the celebrant's words washed over them, she heard sniffles throughout the room, her own emotions growing to a suffocating level and she felt something close to panic rise up inside her. She darted her eyes around the room, trying to latch on to something to ground her, but all she could see was grief. Her eyes landed on Dean and he was already watching her, worry etched on his face. As they stared at one another she noted the rhythmic rise and fall of his chest and tried to focus on matching the pace. She started to calm and after a moment he nodded at her slightly, as if he were saying, *you can do this* and her panic subsided.

The speech ended. The hymns were sung. A prayer was said, and then it was time for everyone to say goodbye. There was a table to one side with a large vase of roses placed on top. Each person was to take a rose and place it on the coffin as they said farewell.

This was the part Christy was dreading. The last moment, the final goodbye. They started with the back rows and moved forward which meant Christy would be last. The wait was agony, and she once again felt the panic rise up inside as one by one everyone became more upset and distressed. When it was finally her turn, she struggled to take deep breaths, her hands shaking. Justine and Taylor moved to collect their roses. Taylor went first and said goodbye, then Justine. They stood either side of the coffin, waiting for Christy.

Christy couldn't catch her breath, she looked at Justine and Taylor as they watched her, nodding in encouragement. But she couldn't move, she stared back panicked. She was afraid, she couldn't move her feet, couldn't accept this final moment, couldn't walk up there alone, but couldn't open her mouth to tell them, afraid the sob of hysteria she was holding in would escape. As she stood there gazing around in terror, she felt heat against her back and a solid arm wrapped around her waist holding her up. A warm, firm hand slid into hers, clasping her palm.

"We'll do it together, you don't have to go alone," his voice murmured in her ear, she looked up and her eyes connected with Dean's. Those bright blue eyes shining down at her, calming her. He moved his other hand to cover the one that was clasping the rose, so they held it together. She opened her mouth to tell him she couldn't go but a small sob escaped.

"It's okay, you're not alone. We're going to do this together, I've got you," he soothed, his southern timbre drifting over her. He squeezed her hand and urged her forward. She placed one foot in front of the other and in no time, stood in front of the coffin. Dean moved behind her, she felt him against her back and was strengthened by his presence. A calmness enveloped her, it was time to say goodbye to the pain, time to move on and to finally be at peace. After a moment's hesitation she stepped forward, moving closer for privacy, Dean's heat no longer encasing her and she took a steadying breath.

"You may not have known how to love me, but I did love you and I think no matter what, I always will."

Dean released his grip as she raised her hand and placed her rose with the others. She kept her hand in place, flattening it on the cool wood of the coffin, lingering. She felt Dean's hand, still clasping the one at her side, tighten and his thumb stroked over the skin, comforting her again.

"Rest in peace, Daddy," she whispered and then the tears fell. She felt arms envelop her and Justine and Taylor's soothing words in her ears. When they finally pulled away, she realized Dean was gone.

Chapter 8

Taylor drove Christy and Justine back to the bar, together they went inside and started putting out the food the caterer had delivered.

"Christy, you don't need to help," Taylor said over her shoulder.

Christy shrugged, "I know, but I need to do something. I feel all…itchy. I need to keep myself occupied."

"In that case, you can occupy yourself with getting me a drink!"

"Oh, me too, please!" Justine called after her. Christy chuckled to herself as grabbed three beers from the fridge. She twisted the tops off and slid them across the bar to Justine and Taylor. Just as Christy raised the bottle to her lips, Taylor cleared her throat.

"To Thomas," she said quietly, raising her bottle slightly in the air. Justine lifted hers too and repeated the sentiment. Christy felt a lump rise in her throat, she raised her bottle and then swiftly brought it to her lips and took a large gulp, the liquid burning as she forced it passed the lump that had formed.

They finished putting the food out, both women scolding her and swatting at her as she tried to help. Then everyone started to arrive and some gentle music began playing in the background.

Christy glanced towards the door every time it opened and each time it wasn't Dean that entered, she felt a flare of disappointment. *Seriously? It's your father's funeral and you're man hunting? That's gotta be a new kind of low.* But she couldn't help it, ever since Dean had comforted her she was beginning to, how could she put it, dislike him less?

Twice now, he was there for her during emotional moments, she found herself confused as to why, after all their history. He had changed, there was no doubt about it. She was starting to see signs that he was someone who could be counted on and she was beginning to trust him, something she found very difficult. But she was still guarded, she had been burned before, badly and was still stamping out the charred remains of that experience. She scowled and shook her head, clearing her thoughts. She needed a distraction, so she began mingling with those that she vaguely recognized.

As she spoke to each person, and they all said variations of the same thing, she became more and more emotional.

"What a wonderful person your father was."

"He missed you so much, how come you never visited?"

"He loved you so much, it's a shame you didn't come back and see him more."

Christy wanted to cry and scream, *"I'm not the villain here!"*

She'd had to leave, he couldn't love her and her breaking heart couldn't take it anymore. All these protests rose up in her throat, choking her and begging to be let free. But looking around this crowd and seeing the love they had for her father, she knew they wouldn't understand.

She swallowed her pride and decided there was only one way to get through this; alcohol. She went to the bar and ordered a double whiskey from Kayleigh, she downed the drink immediately and asked for another, then followed that with a shot of tequila.

*

Dean entered the bar and his gaze immediately sought out Christy. He spotted her talking to an elderly couple and instantly felt at ease. Ever since he left the crematorium, he was worrying about her. He had to swing by the garage as he had been working on a car of some fancy politician Beau knew and the guy wanted to collect it now, now, now! The asshole had been late and then given Dean shit about how much he charged so he had been longer than he planned. When he saw she was doing fine, he went to the bar to get a drink.

"Hey Kayleigh, how ya doing?" he asked, the timid girl looked up at him with wide eyes.

"Fine thanks, you?" He nodded in lieu of a reply and looked around for Taylor but couldn't see her.

"Taylor in the back?" he asked. Kayleigh nodded and then scurried off to find her. He looked over to Christy again and as he watched her, he noticed her cheeks were flushed, her eyes appeared a little glassy and she had a wan smile on her face. *Was she swaying?* Just then, Taylor appeared looking flustered.

"I've been trying to call you," she huffed.

"Well hello to you too, sis," he joked, and she rolled her eyes.

"Yeah, yeah. Listen I need you to take Christy home, like, right this second."

"What, why?"

"Because this one here doesn't know when to cut someone off yet!" she said, hiking her thumb at Kayleigh who hung her head in shame. Taylor grabbed his arm and pulled him to the end of the bar for some privacy.

"Christy is trashed and needs to go home pronto. I've got to stay here with Kayleigh and Justine has been drinking too."

"Nothing wrong with a little alcohol, puts the fun into *funeral*," he teased.

"No, you don't understand. Christy is dangerously close to losing it and we need to get her away from these people, okay?"

"What are you talking about, what's the big deal?"

Taylor sighed, "Just trust me, if we don't get her out of here then all these nice people are going to find out what Thomas was *really* like."

Dean felt his blood run cold. His stomach twisted, a thousand thoughts zooming through his mind, each one worse than the previous.

"What did he do to her? Why did she run away?" he gritted out; his tone deadly. Taylor frowned at him, surprised.

"We can talk about this later, just get her out of here and take her home, please?"

"Yeah, okay," he said and went over to Christy, placing his hand on her shoulder.

"Hey Christy, you ready to go home now?" he asked gently. She slowly slid her glassy eyes to his, the color reminding him of a frozen lake.

"Dean, you made it." Her words were slightly slurred, but she sounded relieved to see him and didn't that just butter his cracker. As she held his eyes, the pale blue pools melted and drowned him in sorrow as they filled with tears.

"They all love him so much," she whispered, her voice cracking and his heart ached for her. He turned her away from the elderly couple who looked very concerned.

"I know, darlin', let's get you home and put you to bed." He tried to maneuver her towards the door, but for such a small woman, she sure was strong.

"No!" she shouted, "Everyone needs to know, I'm not the bad guy here!" she slurred loudly, glaring at him. He looked over her head, back towards the bar where Taylor was watching them. Taylor gestured to the door then held up a knife, motioning violently at him. *Message received, get her out now.*

"Hold on, darlin'," he said and put his shoulder into her stomach and upended her. She squealed, then groaned as if in pain.

"I don't feel too good."

"Yeah I bet, it's all that nasty alcohol. Excuse us, folks."

He moved towards the door with her bouncing on his shoulder, his hand wrapped around her firm thigh for support, he was trying not to notice how lush and warm it felt under his grip. He managed to get them out of the bar and over to his truck. As he stopped to rummage for his keys, he felt her hand brush over his back, leaving a trail of heat in its wake.

"You okay back there?" he asked through clenched teeth. He could not deal with her getting handsy right now, because he would let her.

"So strong," she murmured before hiccupping. He felt himself puff up with pride at her comment and he resisted the urge to pound his chest like a neanderthal. He snagged his keys and unlocked his truck. Bending down, he placed her on the passenger seat as gently as possible. He leaned across her to buckle her seatbelt and inhaled her scent. Fuck, she smelled delicious, like berries and candy floss, and his mouth watered. *Did she taste like it?* The thought had heat rushing to his groin and a moan nearly slipped out from his lips but he clamped them shut. He could feel her watching him but refused to make eye contact, not trusting himself. He pulled away, shut the door, went around to the driver's side.

He started the engine and headed towards her father's house. After a moment of silence, she leaned across the seat and rested her head on his shoulder. He stiffened, not daring to move and jolt her. He glanced down and saw her eyelids flutter closed, more of that tantalizing scent invading his nostrils, making his mouth water for a taste. His cock started to harden in his pants. He gritted his teeth as they went over a bump in the road which tightened the material against his arousal, creating a delicious friction. It also pressed her lush breasts into his arm and he tried to ignore the heat of them, scalding him through his shirt.

Although it wasn't far to the house it felt like the longest journey of his life. She didn't stir the whole time until he tried to get out of the truck without moving her which didn't work and resulted in her waking.

"Where am I?" she asked, voice thick with sleep and alcohol.

"You're home, darlin'," he replied.

"In New York?" she asked, her voice filled with hope.

"Nope, Citrus Pines." He came around and helped her

out of his truck. "Let's get you inside."

"I can walk, you know!" she huffed and shoved away from him, stumbling immediately and he smothered a laugh.

"Sure you can."

"I just require ass…assis…*help* from time to time," she slurred. He put his arm around her and this time she didn't try to remove it. He walked them towards the front door and helped her find the keys in her purse. He unlocked the door and let them in. She stumbled inside and felt along the wall for the light switch, flicked it on and he saw they were in the living room. She dropped her purse on the couch and turned to him.

"Are we going to bed now?" she asked, peering up at him with those innocent eyes and that damn sexy mouth of hers. His erection kicked in his pants because, yep it was still there. He swallowed thickly,

"I'm going to *help* you to bed and then I'll *leave*," he said. She looked upset and flung herself at him, wrapping her arms around him.

"No! Please don't go! Please stay with me, I don't want to be here on my own," she begged. Having her body pressed against him, her soft curves fitting him perfectly, only ratcheted up his desire. She was soft to his hard, molding to him until they became one. She ran her hands up his chest and he tensed as her lower body rubbed over his erection, a flare of heat flashed in her eyes. He knew it wasn't real though, just the effects of the alcohol.

"I can't stay," he choked out as she rubbed against him again.

"Please, Dean?" She buried her face in the hollow of his throat, her hot tongue licking up his neck. His hands found their way into her hair and he tangled them, fisting the soft strands. She moved her head back and looked up at him. She pulled his head down to meet her, her eyelashes fluttering closed. She wanted to kiss him, his heart pounded, and excitement rushed through his veins. *No!* his brain screamed. *Stop this before you regret it, you're taking advantage of her!*

He stopped her when she was a heartbeat away from his mouth. Hot tension passed between them, he wanted her, badly. But not like this, he couldn't take advantage of her when she was drunk and grieving, what sort of man did that? He reluctantly pulled back and her eyes popped open, hurt and betrayal clouding them before she masked the emotions and her features grew cold.

"Thank you for bringing me home, you can leave now."

"Christy, I can stay down here if you don't want to be alone?" he offered.

"No, I'm fine. You can go now, thanks," she said, and turned away, dismissing him. She went over to the staircase and went upstairs, not turning back. She muttered to herself, stumbled a few times, and then she was gone.

He sighed and tunneled a hand through his hair. *Shit.* That didn't go well, it was the right call though. He hunted for some painkillers in a kitchen drawer and grabbed a glass from the side, filling it with tap water and went in search of her upstairs. He stood on the landing, unsure of which room was hers so he started opening doors.

The first door on the left looked like it had been her father's room, she wasn't in there. He moved to the door on the right. He turned on the light and saw it was a teenage girl's room, it must have been Christy's when she was younger. Nothing appeared to have been changed, the room preserved, but empty. The next room was the bathroom, so he opened the last door on the left. As he went inside, he immediately saw her form splayed on the bed in the center of the room. Her heavy breathing suggested she was already asleep.

He looked around, it seemed like the guest bedroom, why would she stay here and not in her old room? He saw her suitcases lined up along the wall, clothes trying to escape the confines, makeup and shoes littering the floor. He walked over to the nightstand and put the glass of water and painkillers down, she was going to need those tomorrow.

He turned and looked down at her, face turned to one side, a blond curl twisted across her cheek. Her pink lips parted slightly. He stroked her cheek gently, brushing the silky curl to one side. He smiled softly as even in her sleep, she frowned at his touch. He moved to take her shoes off, and she didn't stir once. He looked down at her again, struck by how tiny she was, especially in comparison to him and remembered how perfectly she fit against him. He had an overwhelming urge to protect this dainty firecracker from whatever came her way.

"Goodnight, darlin'," he whispered and left the room. Back downstairs he switched off the lights, grabbed the door keys she dumped, and he left the house. He locked the door and pushed the keys back through the letterbox, happy she was safe. On the drive home, he replayed over and over in his mind what would have happened if he let her kiss him and vowed to himself if he ever got the chance again, he was going to go for it.

Chapter 9

Christy woke the next morning feeling extremely fragile. She lay in bed, with her eyes still closed trying to remember what happened. It had been the funeral, and as she said goodbye to her father, she felt like she released some of the pain she had been holding inside all these years.

Afterwards, she went to the bar with Justine and Taylor to sort out the food and then everyone arrived. She remembered hearing more and more stories about how wonderful her father had been which was...confusing. Her memory of him was tainted obviously, but what had he been like with other people? Had he been the man she vaguely remembered from before her mother died? A memory came to mind, one of the last times the three of them had been together.

Christy had walked into the kitchen one evening to get a drink and she found her mom and dad in there slow-dancing to a song playing on the radio. She watched as they stared into each other's eyes, their love filling up the room. As she stood in the doorway watching them, the song came to an end, changing to an upbeat number. Her mom had spotted her then and grabbed Christy's arm, pulling her between them, insisting they all dance together. Christy and her dad went nuts, pulling crazy moves, each one more ridiculous than the last, both trying to make her mom laugh the loudest. Christy took a shuddering breath as the memory faded. That was the last time she remembered her dad as he was, a couple of weeks later, her mom died.

She pushed the remaining thoughts away, not wanting to dwell on them. She made her peace with her father yesterday and wanted to keep it that way. But the more she tried to focus on remembering last night, the hazier her memory became and the harder her temples throbbed. She forced herself to keep going, she had been talking to various people about her father, then Dean appeared and...

"Oh, shit!" she shouted, bolting upright in bed, immediately groaning as her temples throbbed angrily and her stomach roiled at the sudden movement. Her mind replayed the night, he brought her home, she tried to kiss him, tried to *sleep* with him, and *he rejected her*. She couldn't believe she'd done that, what had she been thinking? And he rejected her! She tried to brush off the feelings of hurt that came over her. Why had she done that when she knew what he thought of her?

She. Was. Mortified. Especially now he would think she wanted him, and wouldn't that just inflate his ego even more? She was drunk and grieving, it would have been a massive mistake and she would have thrown herself at anybody. *Right?*

"Oh God, what is wrong with me?" she groaned. Her mouth was drier than the Sahara. She needed a drink and something to stop her head from pounding. She pulled back the duvet and sat up, moving her legs over the side of the bed, gently. She was still fully clothed, her shoes neatly placed on the floor.

On the nightstand was a glass of water and some painkillers, *drink me is the best!* Snatching them up she swallowed the pills with a mouthful of water. She glanced at the clock and realized it was still early. After the events of yesterday she just wanted to stay in bed, so that's exactly what she did. She snuggled back under the duvet, convinced that when she woke up later, she would feel better and would have forgotten all about yesterday.

But she hadn't. She slept like the dead and when she finally woke up again, she felt better but still remembered everything. She sat up, rubbing the sleep out of her eyes. She remembered tilting her face up to Dean, trying to pull him down to kiss her, closing her eyes, and then nothing. She felt him pull away and when she opened her eyes, she saw his expression. Uncomfortable. The image flashed behind her eyes every time she blinked, torturing her.

Had she sexually assaulted him? Her horror increased at the thought, could it be classed as that? She tried to kiss him, rubbed her body against him without permission, it could be? An image of him trying to defend his well-worn honor had her trying not to laugh. *This isn't funny,* her brain scolded. She couldn't face him again. She was far too embarrassed, and he would be all smug knowing she threw herself at him and he turned her down. And then her bitchy side would come out like it always did with him.

Would he tell everyone? Of course he would, she was stupid to start trusting him. The idea of him betraying her now hurt a little. The more she thought about it, the more she couldn't just explain it away as a drunken and grief-stricken mistake. It was borne from years of wanting him and never feeling confident enough to go for it because she knew how he felt about her. She forced herself to get up and stop thinking about it. No headache and no stomachache, the extra nap had worked miracles.

She was in desperate need of a shower, so she padded into the bathroom and stripped off the clothes from yesterday. She stood under the hot spray for at least half an hour before washing her hair and body. She reluctantly got out, wrapping a towel around herself and went downstairs in search of her cell. She spotted her keys on the doormat of the living room. Bending to collect them, she stared at them quizzically before dropping them on the coffee table. Her heart did a silly little flutter when she realized that Dean must have locked up when he left. She ignored the feeling and grabbed her purse, digging through it and fishing out her cell. The screen flashed; a voicemail and one new message. She opened her message first and saw it was from Beau.

Hope you're okay! If you want to talk then I'm here for you. Can't wait to see you tonight. xx

Christy groaned and threw herself down on the couch, burying her face in the cushions. She'd forgotten all about the double date, with Dean. She certainly couldn't go now, couldn't sit across the table from him all night, accidentally brushing against his knees and him shooting her smug, dimpled glances. But she couldn't cancel on Beau. Sweet, gentle, *un-smug* Beau. She looked at the time and saw it was midday, she had plenty of time to get ready. She closed the message and played her voicemail.

"Christy, hi it's Cassie from Blossom Estates, I have some great news! We've received an offer on the house and its full asking price! I figured you would be very happy to go ahead with that, but please call us back to confirm so we can begin."

Christy didn't bother listening to the rest of the message, just dialed straight back.

"Yes, please go ahead!" she said as soon as Cassie answered, she heard Cassie chuckle on the other end.

"I figured that would be the case but just needed to check first. It's someone looking to move into the area-"

Christy cut her off, "It's okay, I don't need the details. Did they even ask for a reduction?"

"No, they didn't, they said it would be worth every cent."

"How strange, not that I'm complaining." Christy hastened to add.

"Yes, that doesn't happen often, best not to query it. We'll go ahead and get the ball rolling. We'll be in touch when we need you. Take care now!"

Christy thanked her and hung up, she went to put her cell down, but it beeped another message alert. She swiped up and saw a message from Taylor had come through.

Hey Guuuurl! How's your head? Cocktail emoji, vomit emoji.

Christy smiled and her fingers typed out a reply.

It was pounding but drugs saved the day. xx

Goooood! Didn't want you bailing on tonight and leaving me with Mr. Snoozefest.

No guesses who she was referring to. Christy felt a pang of guilt at her earlier thoughts of canceling, she definitely couldn't back out now.

No, I can't wait! Kiss emoji.

That makes one of us, can't wait to spend the night with Boring

Beau...NOT. Haaaaaa, I'm so bad! Devil emoji.

Christy snorted and put her cell away again. She didn't know why Taylor disliked Beau so much. They had gotten on great as kids, were thick as thieves at one point. Christy got up and looked out the window. The sun was shining, it was a glorious day, so she decided to get dressed and after a very late breakfast, went for a walk to clear the cobwebs. She was gone for a while, re-exploring the forest and enjoying the fresh air. When she came back to the house, she didn't have quite the same feeling of dread as she felt previously. Maybe the funeral had exorcised more demons than she originally thought.

She decided to treat herself to a mini pamper session in preparation for the date, she wanted to look her best for ~~Dean~~ Beau. She went upstairs into the guest room and began rummaging in her suitcases. Luckily, she packed quite a few things, not knowing how long she would be in town. She gave herself a mani-pedi, did a facemask and began to get ready for the date.

Christy was ready by the time Beau arrived. She answered the door and looked him over. He looked good in his baby blue button-down shirt tucked into light gray slacks. As she looked him over, appreciating the beauty before her, she waited for a spark to ignite inside her. Any heat? A shiver? Some sign of arousal? But no, her pulse remained steady. Sometimes attraction can be a slow burner, taking time to build up. It comes from getting to know a person and learning about them, their likes and dislikes. This could also be slower to flare inside her as she didn't have much experience with men, her issues would take a lot for someone to overcome.

Christy pasted a big smile on her face. "You look wonderful!" she gushed.

"So do you," he replied, giving her a once over that

lingered slightly. She smoothed her hands over the fabric of her bardot summer dress. Its navy-blue skirt ended just above her knees and the top was red and white striped, very nautical themed. She wore white, open toed sandals on her feet which showcased her cheeky red toenails. She also wore a navy-blue ribbon choker that had a gold anchor charm dangling delicately from the center.

Beau offered her his arm and dropped a kiss on her cheek, and they headed down to where his car was parked. He helped her inside and as they drove off, he said, "I'm so sorry I couldn't be there yesterday; I feel terrible that I wasn't around for you."

"Oh, don't be silly!" she replied.

"I had some business back in L.A. which had to be dealt with right away."

"Really Beau, it's fine."

"Did it, uh, go well?" he asked nervously. "Is that even the right thing to ask?"

She laughed gently at his awkwardness. "Yes, it did thank you." She was trying not to think about how the night ended, she was already nervous enough about seeing Dean again without remembering what a fool she had been.

"That's good, if you want to talk about it at all, I'm here." He glanced over at her quickly before turning his eyes back to the road. She appreciated his sweet offer, but she didn't get the urge to discuss it with him. Opening up required trust, which had to be earned and they didn't know each other well enough for that. She thanked him again and decided to change the subject.

"So, what are your plans? Are you just visiting for a little while?"

"I'm thinking about that at the moment, I'm definitely at a crossroads where I've got to make a decision. I just don't know what that is yet, I'm hoping some time away will help," he explained, an air of mystery about him.

"Well, if you ever want to talk, I'm here," she echoed brightly. He flashed her a dazzling smile and reached over and patted her knee, letting his hand rest there. It was a nice gesture, his hand was strong and firm and his palm heated her knee, but again there was no spark at his touch. When she had been at the bar and Dean had accidentally touched her with his knee, she practically leapt out the booth, let alone when he purposefully stroked her knee. Warmth flowed through her at the memory and she shivered. *Stop it, forget about Dean, he doesn't want you, focus on Beau!* Turning to smile at Beau, she placed her hand over his and they rode the rest of the way in comfortable silence.

The closer they got to the restaurant the bigger the pit in her stomach grew. Would Dean mention what happened last night in front of everyone? Would he tease her about throwing herself at him? What would Beau think if he heard that? What would *Taylor* think? They pulled into the parking lot of the restaurant and Beau helped her out of the car. Just as Beau shut her door, Dean's truck pulled into the lot. They waited for him to park up and when Dean got out, her heart stuttered in her chest as she took in his charcoal gray shirt and neat, black slacks.

His shirt fitted snugly against his torso, molding to the rows of muscle that cut across his chest and abdomen. She longed to see the view from behind, his shirt pulled tight across his toned back and shoulders, his pert ass flexing as he walked. Was he walking in slow motion? That's not a real thing, right? Damn, he looked good in formal wear. When Dean lifted his head and smiled, a dimple popped on each side of his mouth and she felt a sudden throb deep in her core. The feeling took her by surprise and she stumbled slightly. Beau reached for her,

"Did you trip?" he asked, she nodded, her cheeks flushing. He took hold of her hand in his, trying to steady her. As Dean walked towards them, Taylor was still sat in the truck, and when she saw Dean wasn't coming round to open the door for her, she threw her hands up in the air and then let herself out.

"Come on, Taylor, hurry up. We're all waiting for you!" Dean called over his shoulder, Christy bit back a laugh as Taylor flipped him off. Beau's hand clenched around hers, she looked up and his expression was furrowed. *Note to self, don't swear at Beau's friends,* he looked hella angry.

"Christy, Beau, great to see you," Dean said as he reached them. She said hello and noticed his eyes lingered on her, running over her body. When he finished, he scowled and looked away. *What's his problem? He's probably wondering what on earth the 'boner killer' is doing with Beau,* her confidence momentarily taking a knock. But she squared her shoulders remembering she was supposed to be building her confidence, not tearing it down. She didn't care what he thought, she was a pretty great person and deserved whoever she wanted.

Taylor finally tottered over to them. Looking stunning as usual in a black, fitted bandeau dress that was cut to mid-thigh and hugged all her curves perfectly. Her long, slender legs were bare and tapered down to trim ankles, and she wore strappy black sandals. She piled her long, red hair on top of her head in a messy knot, but a few rebellious tendrils had escaped and were blowing gently in the breeze. She felt Beau shiver beside her.

"Cold?" she asked him innocently.

He gave a sharp nod. "Let's go in," he said tersely and

turned, pulling Christy along behind him.

Inside the restaurant, Christy looked around in awe at the beautiful decoration. The tables and chairs were all white with navy blue tablecloths and seat cushions. The tables themselves each held a mason jar with a white, tealight candle flickering inside and delicate string lights draped from the ceiling creating a soft, romantic atmosphere. Painted life rings, starfish fossils and seashells decorated the walls, she felt like she was at a restaurant on the beach instead of on a lake outside a small town.

The waiter greeted them and led them out the glass double doors, onto the deck overlooking the lake. The warm evening air caressed her skin, the breeze carrying a hint of citrus from the trees. The table and chairs decor continued outside and more lights were wound around the railing of the deck and twinkled in the reflection of the water.

They reached their table and Beau pulled out her chair for her, she smiled at him as she sat down. Dean, spotting what Beau had done, did the same for Taylor who was seated opposite Christy. As Christy sat down her dress tightened across her chest, pushing her breasts up slightly, plumping her cleavage. Taylor spotted straight away and winked at her; Christy smothered a giggle as she tried to pull her dress up a bit to contain them. The waiter gave them the drinks menu and hovered to one side giving them time to look it over.

After a moment, Taylor said, "I'll have a Nautical But Nice, please." Fixing Beau with a sharp smile as she did.

"I'll have Sex On The Beach," Beau ordered, staring Taylor down, and Christy noticed her smile faltered slightly. *What's with these two?* she thought, glancing at Dean to see what he would order but he was already staring at her, he gestured for her to go first.

"I also like Sex On The Beach," she said and Taylor laughed. Christy looked at her and then at Dean whose intense gaze was making her feel all flustered. He raised an eyebrow at her and she flushed hotly. "I mean, I would also like one of those, thanks," she added, ducking her head back into her menu.

"I'll have a glass of your local Pinot Noir, thanks," Dean said, surprising her. He seemed like a beer and chips kind of guy, not a wine drinker. As they all looked at their menus, silence settled around them. Dean hadn't said anything about last night, yet. Was he going to? She felt nervous but risked a peek at him over the top of her menu, she slowly raised her eyes and met his immediately. The lights surrounding them reflected in his blue eyes, making them appear alive with heat and possibly desire? No, must be the trick of the light. She couldn't see the rest of his face, his menu obscured him so she couldn't tell what expression he held. She felt awareness prickle the back of her neck and looked back down at her menu, breaking the spell.

They all ordered and as the waiter left, Christy began to mentally work out how much this would cost. She was serious when she said to Beau that she would pay the next time they went out. That reminded her, Taylor never told her how much hiring the bar for the funeral yesterday would cost. She would pick it up with her separately though, not wanting to bring up the funeral now and dampen the mood or risk a comment from Dean.

"I, uh, got an offer on the house," she said tentatively as their drinks were placed on the table.

"That's amazing, congratulations!" Taylor beamed and lifted her glass to toast. "Although, that means you'll be going home soon, right?" she added, pouting. Christy felt all three pairs of eyes stare at her, Dean's gaze boring into her the most.

"Well, I still need to get it cleared and tidied up. There's the garden to fix and some repairs that need doing so it will probably take a couple of weeks yet," she replied. "I'll need to rent a truck to move most of the stuff out too."

"You don't need to do that; you can just borrow Dean's," Taylor offered.

"Oh, no it's fine honestly!" Christy rushed out.

"I don't mind," Dean replied. "I was about to offer but Taylor got in there first. I can help you, if you like?" She turned to face him, but his expression was unreadable.

"I can help too." Beau added.

"Oh, both of you, that's really sweet but-" she started but Dean interrupted.

"It's no problem, I want to help you." She studied him again, but his features were schooled, what was his angle here? Beau nodded in agreement with Dean and she felt like she couldn't protest without seeming unreasonable.

"That's very nice of you, thank you," she said reluctantly.

"No problem, we're nice guys you know, just give us a chance," Beau joked and Christy saw Taylor roll her eyes.

They chatted a bit more about small town life, the bar, the people and the scandals. Dean made them laugh with stories of the pranks he pulled on Taylor over the years. Christy listened with rapt attention being a huge fan of pranks herself. Every time they all laughed, she met his eyes and felt a connection bouncing between them, deepening.

More drinks came and soon she felt a warm buzz descending and everything was a little bit funnier than it had been earlier. Until Taylor mentioned that the previous town sheriff died not too long ago and a replacement would probably be appointed soon. Christy knew he had been married to Rebelle and realized she hadn't shown up at the bar the other night as agreed. She was sad, not only that Rebelle hadn't come, but that Christy hadn't noticed either. She vowed to make more effort to reach out to her, especially if her husband recently passed away, she must be going through such a tough time.

"So, tell me, have you two done it yet?" Taylor asked mischievously. Beau choked on his drink.

"Done what?" Christy asked innocently.

"You know...*it*!"

Christy blushed as she realized what she meant. "Taylor!" she scolded, embarrassed to have been asked, especially in front of Dean and guilt about last night hit her once more.

"What? We're all friends here!"

"I don't think we..." Beau started, but Taylor interrupted him.

"Oh, come on, it's surely just a yes or no kinda answer?"

"It's not something to discuss in polite conversation," Beau replied, sounding uncomfortable and putting an arm around Christy's shoulders protectively.

"Come on, Christy, woman to woman? Is he a dud as I suspect?" Taylor joked.

"That's enough, Taylor," Dean said, steel coating his words. Christy flicked her eyes to him and his eyes no longer looked alive, they were cold, hard, and unfriendly. She realized then that Dean would never want her and Beau to be together. He had an issue with it from the start and now the thought of them getting closer made him angry. He still thought Beau was too good for her.

Well, fuck him!

Christy put her hand on Beau's firm thigh. "We'll just have to see what happens tonight," she replied, squeezing Beau's leg. Christy leveled her hard stare at Dean, *challenge accepted*. His eyes flashed, burning anew. He opened his mouth to reply, but the waiter turned up with their food.

As they ate the general chit chat from before resumed, Taylor and Beau sniping at each other occasionally. As Dean watched her with his hardened stare, she could tell he was plotting something, his expression was too contemplative.

"Say, Beau," Dean said, "Someone called Cassandra rang the house for you earlier." His tone was so calm and conversational that Christy watched him suspiciously. She felt Beau tense beside her.

"Is she one of your girlfriends from the city?" Dean continued. *Aaaand there it is.*

"As if you still have a house phone," Taylor mocked.

"What? No, she's uh, a client," Beau replied, and Christy could already tell he was lying.

"So, not one of your *many* girlfriends from the city then?" Dean asked with a hard glint in his eye.

Beau shook his head. "Nope."

"Oh, okay. I know you were seeing a few women before so I wasn't sure," Dean said with a smug grin.

"I wasn't seeing that many!" Beau replied hotly.

Dean chuckled. "Come on man, no need to be shy. We all know you're a ladies' man. I used to love hearing about all your conquests. Wasn't there this one time with a set of famous twins..."

Taylor nudged him, "Dude, shut up!" she hissed theatrically. It was Christy's turn to raise an eyebrow at Dean. *You wanna try and psych me out by talking about all his girlfriends? Go ahead buddy, we've all got a past.* After a moment, the conversation started again with Beau telling stories of ridiculous things his clients did. Taylor was talking about all the new music acts she signed up and said that Justine was singing again next Saturday.

"If you're sticking around a bit longer, you'll be able to come?" Taylor asked and the hope in her voice made Christy's heart squeeze.

"Yeah, sounds great."

"Wouldn't miss it," Beau and Dean chorused. Desserts came and went, and coffees were ordered. She watched the camaraderie between Dean and Taylor, they were adorable. As she watched them tease each other she was grateful that Taylor had him, she'd worried about leaving Taylor alone all those years ago. She felt herself beginning to soften towards Dean as she thought about all the ways he would have looked out for Taylor and protected her. *No, don't soften now, his behavior earlier was appalling!* She felt so confused, her mind warring with her emotions.

When the check finally came, she leaned over to Beau and whispered, "Don't even reach for that wallet of yours, you said I could pay for the next one." Beau started to protest as she reached out to snag the check, but Dean snatched it up first.

"My idea, my treat," he said, not even glancing at the slip of paper. She mentally worked out the total in preparation for paying. She wasn't by any means a snob, but Dean was the manager of a garage in a small town. He couldn't be making enough money that he could cover their total bill on a whim. Beau tried to take it off him.

"Pretty sure this was my idea, buddy," he said, but Dean held it out of reach.

"No way, I'm going in," Dean said, getting up and

heading inside the restaurant. Beau followed him and they squabbled as they went. When they disappeared inside, Christy eyed Taylor.

"What's the deal with you and Beau?"

"There's no deal. I should be asking you that," Taylor replied, shifting nervously.

"You used to be such good friends and now you can't stand each other, what happened?" she prodded again.

"Nothing happened. People change and grow apart, it's no biggie." Taylor avoided her eyes.

"He's certainly changed. Are you okay with me seeing him?"

"What? Of course, I'm not *jealous*!" Taylor scoffed.

"I didn't say you were, I meant if you don't like him are you okay with me seeing him?"

"Of course, babe! You do you, just don't expect it to be an exciting affair."

"Oh my God, he's so *not* boring!" Christy cried.

"Well, he certainly ain't exciting!" Taylor shot back.

"Just because he's well groomed, has manners, communicates with words instead of grunts, and doesn't ride a motorcycle like all your other boyfriends, doesn't mean he's not interesting."

"Eh." Taylor shrugged, and Christy laughed at her. The men returned back to the table.

"We were thinking we could head back to the bar for a drink or two? It's still pretty early," Beau said, helping Christy to her feet.

"Yeah, sounds great, if that's okay with you Taylor, as it's technically your night off. Do you want to go to work for socializing?" Christy asked. Dean snorted as he helped Taylor up.

"Can't keep her away normally," he said.

"Yeah, that's cool with me, it's been at least a day since

I whipped your ass at pool," Taylor teased him. Dean gestured for Christy and Beau to lead the way, Beau took her hand and started walking ahead. She followed Beau but felt heat at her back.

"Will be interesting to see what we're all like with some more drinks in us," Dean whispered softly, warm breath fanning her ear and a tremor moved through her. She gasped and looked over her shoulder, but Dean was busy talking to Taylor. She thought she was hearing things but then he looked at her and winked, a sly smile playing across his lips. She narrowed her eyes at him, he was just trying to get in her head and she wouldn't let him.

On the drive back to the bar she noticed Beau kept glancing over at her.

"Everything okay?" she asked when he did it for the fifth time.

"Just, that stuff Dean was saying, it's not true. I don't even know why he brought it up. I really don't do this...go out with loads of women. I don't have much experience. I mean, I am experienced, just not as much as he made out. God, I'm making this worse," he groaned, and she laughed.

"It's fine, it doesn't bother me." Why would she be bothered, she didn't care how many women he'd been with as she wasn't looking for anything serious. He seemed to relax a bit.

"I just don't know why he would say that is all."

I do, she thought. "Maybe he thought he was being funny or just teasing you."

"Yeah, maybe. He is a funny guy, he's a great guy actually, never met anyone better than Dean. I tried to pay for dinner, but he wouldn't let me, he's too kind sometimes. I can't complain I guess, that's paid off for me in the past. I honestly don't know where I would be without him," he gushed.

"What makes you say that?" she asked quizzically, suddenly desperate to hear the end of that story.

"Ah, we're here. They beat us back," he said, ignoring her question. Beau parked the car, and they went inside the bar. It was busy again, being a Saturday night, but she guessed that was no surprise. There were lots of couples sitting and chatting or dancing to the music blaring from the jukebox. She saw Taylor at the bar and led Beau over.

"Dean went to the bathroom, but he's ordered you a root beer," Taylor said to Beau and then turned away sharply, dismissing him.

"I'm gonna go choose some songs, anything you wanna hear?" Beau asked, she shook her head.

"I'm good with whatever you choose," she replied, he smiled at her and walked off. She turned back to Taylor.

"Before I forget, how much do I owe you for yesterday?" she asked. Kayleigh put Taylor's drink in front of her and Taylor snatched it up, slurping noisily from the straw instead of answering. Christy stared at her until she finished.

"Don't worry about it." Taylor shrugged.

"I don't think so Tay, I owe for the space, the food, and the bar staff at least. Let alone any money you lost not having your normal customers in!"

"Are you kidding? There were loads of people here, I didn't lose money. Anyway, it's fine, it's been taken care of," Taylor said, not meeting her eye.

"Well as sweet as that is, I'm not having you and Justine pay for it. It's not your place to. So, tell me how much and I'll split it between you, assuming you went halves?"

"Um, we didn't pay for it. Not for all of it anyway, just

some," Taylor hedged. Christy had a sinking feeling inside and she already knew the answer to her question before she asked it.

"Well then who did?"

*

Dean dried his hands and wandered out of the bathroom whistling. He started walking down the narrow corridor back out to the bar but stopped short when he saw Christy stomping towards him. She sure did look mad, her hands fisted at her side, glare on her face. Pretty pink lips pinched in anger, her little blond curls bouncing adorably with each furious step. Her lush breasts bounced, threatening to spill over the top of her sexy dress, like they had all *damn* evening. He flicked his eyes back to her face before he started drooling, and before she caught him and detonated.

"Hey Christy, what's up?" he called, making sure his smile was wide enough to pop his dimples. He figured she liked them, he caught her staring at them before.

"You bastard!" she spat. *Wait, what?* He looked behind him in case there was someone else she was talking to. There was no one there, he turned back to face her, confused. Was she mad at him? He expected her to slow down the closer she got to him, but she didn't, she kept going and backed him into the wall, the brick scraping his shoulders through his thin shirt.

"Whoa, what's the matter darlin'?" he asked, holding up his hands in mock surrender. She stood on tiptoes, getting in his face and jabbed her finger into his chest.

"Don't call me that! I didn't need you to pay for yesterday. He was my *father*, my responsibility, and no one asked you to do that!" she shouted, her eyes flashing angrily.

"Damnit, Taylor," he muttered. Christy poked his

chest again, her sharp nail digging in. It wasn't hurting but there was definite pressure there, not that he was complaining.

"Don't blame her, I'm glad she mentioned it. I won't be indebted to anyone, I'm not your charity case and I didn't need you to pay for dinner either!"

"Look, I was just trying to be nice, alright? You're having a tough time at the moment and I just wanted to help you, any way I could," he said gently putting a hand on her shoulder, she shrugged him off.

"Oh, *now* you're being nice to me? I'm surprised you know how!" she snapped.

"Hey! That hurts darlin', how many times have I tried to apologize for being an idiot to you?" He smiled down at her, hoping to charm and disarm her. He grabbed hold of the hand that was still jabbing his chest and brought it down to her side but didn't let go. He took a step towards her. She moved back, still fuming at him. He wondered how big her bluster really was and how quickly he could coax her out of it. He took another step forward, a bigger one and she stepped back again, frowning up at him. He did it again and this time when she moved back, she bumped into the wall on the other side. His torso now pressed up against hers, her softness giving way beneath the wall of his chest. She glared up at him.

"I don't need your charity; I can handle things myself," she huffed; he could see she was starting to run out of steam. He was a little disappointed, he couldn't deny he liked seeing her all worked up. Her cheeks flushed with anger, eyes flashing, chest heaving. She was stunning, his little firecracker.

"And whatever you're trying to do to me and Beau, stop it." As she spoke, she flattened her hand to his chest to push him away, but she couldn't budge him. The warmth of her palm seeped through the material of his shirt and heated the skin beneath. Her breath was coming in shallow pants now, brushing her breasts against his chest and then moving them away with each exhale. When he didn't move away from her, she stared up at him, her icy blue eyes melting the longer they stared.

He felt the air get thick and hot with tension; his breathing became as shallow as hers as desire spread through him. Did she want him? She ran her tongue over her lips, and her eyelids dipped slightly, hooding with arousal. Oh yes, she did but her body tensed as she fought against it.

He had wondered if it was just the alcohol last night or the stress of the day that had made her try to kiss him. God, he thought about that only about a thousand times. What would have happened if he gave in and tasted those lush lips. He had hardly thought about anything else since last night, his dreams filled with what could have happened. He needed to know, was dying to know what she felt. He bent his head down to her ear.

"Shall we talk about last night?" he rasped, his voice thick with need. He heard her sharp intake of breath and smiled to himself. He nuzzled against her ear, the sweet berry scent of her hair enveloping him. "Did you want to kiss me, Christy?" He watched goosebumps spread across her neck and pulled back to see her. Her eyelids had drifted closed, her mouth parted slightly. A rush of heat flared in his groin and he felt himself hardening.

"I was drunk, not thinking," she replied, sounding sluggish. He moved his mouth back to her ear.

"That's not what I asked you, Christy," he admonished, slowly laving the shell of her ear with his tongue. She gasped and fisted her hand in his shirt, pulling him closer. He nibbled on her lobe and she whimpered. Oh yes, he had her, he just needed her to admit it.

"Say it."

She pressed her lips together, refusing to let the words tumble out and free them both.

"Say it, Christy."

"Yes, I wanted to kiss you," she rushed out, breathing heavily. He rewarded her admission, tracing a line of kisses down her neck. She sighed and leaned into him, relaxing her body against him. He tangled a hand in her curls and kissed his way back up and along her jaw.

"Wait, what are you doing?" she asked, pulling out of the moment, but he was too far gone, he couldn't let her walk away without tasting her. He grabbed her hand and pinned it over her head, the movement arching her back and mashing her breasts into his chest. Feeling her hard nipples abrading him, evidence of her arousal, he hissed at the contact. He rubbed his lower body against her, the moment she felt his erection, her eyes widened and she moaned at the contact.

He dropped his head and slanted his lips over hers, her mouth was soft and hot. She moaned again, and her tongue swept into his mouth. He tilted his head for deeper contact and stroked his tongue over hers. A punch of lust hit him low in the stomach as their tongues touched, tingles scattering through him.

She tasted like strawberries, sweet and irresistible, and he licked into her mouth again her taste branding him. His free hand moved down to cup her breast, unable to help himself, she arched her back again pressing herself into his palm more firmly. This wasn't like any kiss he had before; it was hot and sweet, wild and passionate. She matched him pace for pace, lick for lick. She sucked on his tongue, hard, and his thoughts strayed to what else she could wrap her delectable mouth around and suck.

The kiss spiraled out of control, becoming carnal and dirty. He ground his pelvis into her, needing release. She moaned into his mouth again, sending vibrations through him, and rubbed herself against him, just as desperate for relief. Was she wet and ready for him? His cock pulsed at the thought of sliding into her wet heat.

All of a sudden as fast as it started, it stopped. She pulled herself away from him, her cheeks flushed, that sexy mouth all swollen from his kisses.

"Beau," she murmured, not meeting his gaze. She swiped her hand across her mouth, wiping his taste away.

"Shit," he replied. What had he been thinking? How could he do that to Beau? It didn't matter that she and Beau weren't serious yet. What sort of guy did that to his best friend? He needed to get away from her, now, but he couldn't while sporting wood. She shoved passed him and went down the corridor, back out into the main bar area. He leaned against the wall, trying to get control of his emotions. He went back into the bathroom to splash some water on his face and when his body had calmed, he went back out to the bar.

Chapter 10

Christy woke up feeling a little out of sorts. She lay in bed, refusing to move from the cozy domain, this was where she belonged now. She replayed the memory of her kiss with Dean, and ran her fingers over her lips as though she could still feel his there.

Their kiss had seared her, her body still humming with arousal, and ready to pick up where they left off. She had been furious with him, humiliated by him once again, and ready to unleash fiery hell on him. But the longer she was in his presence, backed up against the wall with his heat enveloping her, his hard, muscular chest against hers, the fuzzier her brain had become. His closeness and teasing scent had awakened urges in her that she hadn't felt in so long, if ever. When he caged her in, he felt on edge and tension had radiated from him, if he hadn't kissed her, she certainly would have kissed him.

But why did he? He didn't like her, she knew what he *really* thought of her and he'd rejected her the previous night when she threw herself at him. He also spent most of last night glaring at her when he wasn't trying to drive a wedge between her and Beau. Wait, was that what he was trying to do? Get her to cheat on Beau and ruin his trust? Yes! That was it, it made more sense now. Hurt speared through her chest at the thought of Dean doing such a low thing. He was already trying to split them up, and he was definitely ready to play dirty to do it.

But his kiss had been so convincing. Especially as she felt his arousal, had rubbed up against it, needy and desperate. She had been desperate for him, the kiss had been raw and carnal, like nothing she ever experienced before. Beau's kisses hadn't been like that. They were sweet, not down and dirty. It made her question her feelings for Beau. He was kind, caring, and so beautiful but he didn't make her heart pound. Didn't make her lose her breath when he so much as glanced in her direction; which she guessed was fine because she didn't want more than a bit of fun anyway, but she didn't want to lead him on.

At least if we call it quits then Dean will be pleased and he can stop invading my thoughts, dreams and general life, she thought bitterly. Or maybe Dean would tell Beau about what happened and Beau would end it with her first. She couldn't believe Dean would be that mean, the image so at odds with the man who comforted her so readily, not once but twice. Maybe that was him easing his guilt? Maybe that's why he paid for the use of the bar too? To lull her into a false sense of security. She shook her head not wanting to think about it anymore.

She forced herself to get up, have a shower and get

dressed. She started to go downstairs but stopped outside her father's bedroom. She hadn't been able to go in there since she came back to town. Before the funeral it had been because she hadn't wanted to open up her pain and anger again by seeing his things. But now, she felt some semblance of peace and wasn't sure if she was ready to upset that just yet by seeing his belongings. Would she recognize anything in there? Would the familiar scent of his clothes bring forth any memories? No, she would leave it for now. She knew she had to go in and clear the room at some point, but she wanted to keep hold of her newfound peace a little longer.

She went downstairs and began moving around the kitchen making a much-needed coffee and heard a knock on the door. When she opened it, she saw Beau on the porch, smiling down at her.

"Morning, gorgeous," he said, ducking his head and kissing her cheek.

"Hey, you," she said nervously. *Crap, did he know?* Is that why he was here? To confront her and end things? Judging from his expression, he didn't seem very mad.

"I was thinking we could go for a late breakfast and then have a little walk," he said, coming into the house.

"That sounds great," she replied.

"Cool, I could drive us to the bar so you can grab your car as well? Then I know a great place that does pancakes, if you're game?"

Definitely doesn't know what happened if he's being this nice. Maybe spending the day with him and having more time one on one would help solidify her feelings. Get to know him a bit more before dismissing the fling potential. Passion wasn't everything, right? She liked him, so she would love to keep getting to know him, even if it was just platonic.

"Perfect, let me just grab my purse and shoes," she said over her shoulder, already hurrying off. She stumbled up the stairs, *really need some coffee*, and rummaged for the right pair of shoes in her suitcases. When she came back down, he was staring intently at the door frame.

"Everything okay?" she asked.

"The door sticks a little. I know you're selling the place, but I would like to fix this if that's okay? I don't want you to have any trouble with it while you're still here?"

"It was sweet of you to offer to help out last night, but you really don't need to."

"No, I don't mind. I told you I would help out and I meant it. I want to do it, I love this stuff. I'll come back tomorrow and fix this and look at the rest of the place if you like?"

"I'll feel bad, you spending all this time helping me," she whined.

"Don't be silly, guys love this stuff. Working with their hands, helping out a beautiful woman, you'll be doing me a favor, trust me," he said.

After a moment she caved. "That would be amazing, thank you."

They left the house and Beau drove them to the bar. "Did you speak to Dean last night at all?" she asked, trying to sound as casual as possible.

Beau turned to her, smiling quizzically. "Yeah? You were there for most of it," he laughed.

"Oh yeah, I meant afterwards. You know, back at his place? Did you guys sit up all night in your pj's talking about girls?" she teased.

"Pretty much. He's been telling me about the women he's been seeing and I, uh, talked about you."

"But nothing else?" she pushed, and he stared at her

again.

"Did I talk about anything else but you? Not really."

Relief flooded her, followed by guilt. "I'm sorry, that was rude."

He shrugged. "Want to know what I said?"

"Sure."

"That I'm a huge idiot for not asking you out when we were younger."

She sucked in a breath as her mind flashed back to that afternoon in the school hallway all those years ago. Would he bring up the elephant in the car? No, of course he wouldn't, it's not like he would come out and say, *yeah, I was into you, but Dean thought you were a boner killer sooo*....get a grip woman!

Beau continued, "I was young and immature. I was overweight, had zero confidence, and you were so gorgeous there was no way you would have gone out with me." He rushed out the last part. And last night, she had kissed his best friend. Even though she and Beau weren't official it was still a shitty thing to do, she felt like a snake.

"Well you seem pretty confident now, and much, much older," she joked, he gave her a mock glare. "And I liked you too," she finished.

"You did? Well, shit," he chuckled. They sat in comfortable silence for the rest of the journey and when they arrived at the bar, he pulled up next to her car. She unbuckled her seatbelt but before she got out, he said, "Oh, and Dean told me about last night by the way, if that's what you were wondering about."

Her stomach dropped and she stared at him. "What?"

"Yeah, he said he had too much to drink and that he laid one on you, but you pushed him away."

"He...he told you about that?"

"Yep. I chewed him out about it, but we're cool. It's

not like me and you are official but he still shouldn't have done it."

"Oh, okay," she mumbled, still in shock, her mind trying to process the information. It was technically true, but she had kissed him back, should she tell Beau that?

"So, I'll meet you back at yours and we can go for breakfast, I'm starving," he said, changing the subject. She nodded and grabbed her purse, getting out of the car. She got in hers, it took a moment to start up as she hadn't driven it since before the funeral. She set off with Beau right behind her and all the way back to the house, her mind was racing. Dean had told Beau about the kiss; this she had suspected, but not that he took the blame for himself and left her out of it. That was the opposite of what she thought he would do and she didn't understand why. What kind of game was he playing? It made no sense and she didn't trust it.

When she arrived back at the house, she put the incident with Dean out of her mind. She wanted to focus solely on her and Beau today, to see if she could make sense of how she felt about him. She left her car and got back into Beau's.

"Ready for breakfast, although now it's probably brunch?" she asked brightly.

"Definitely," he replied, pulling away from the curb. "You know your exhaust looks like it's hanging a little low under your car, maybe you should get Dean to take a look?"

She waved a hand dismissively. "I'm sure it's fine, it's an old car so that's probably why it looks so low."

They spent the day together, talking and laughing through brunchfast and then went for a walk by the lake. They talked and got to know each other better, had a bit of light flirting, and when he dropped her home later that evening, he walked her to the door.

"I've had a really nice time with you today," he said, she nudged his shoulder as they walked.

"Yeah, I did too. Thanks for letting me pay," she teased.

He snorted. "Are you kidding? I thought you were going to rip my hand off when I reached for my wallet."

"Ah see, look how well you know me now, I was *definitely* going to," she replied, and he barked out a laugh.

As they reached the front door they lapsed into silence. She felt a bit awkward, was she supposed to wait or go straight in? He took her hand in his and stepped closer, with his other hand he cupped her cheek, stroking it with his thumb and tilted her head back. He leaned down and covered her mouth lightly with his. His lips were soft, gently pressing against her, she opened her mouth to welcome him in and he tasted like mint. He pulled back and then placed another quick kiss to her mouth. She opened her eyes and found him looking down at her, a confused expression on his face. He blanked his features quickly, but she saw it.

"I'll be back tomorrow and you can tell me what you want to do to the house," he said, brushing her hair behind her ear. The fluffy curls immediately rebelled and popped back out to fall over her cheek. He squeezed her hand and then left, waving as he drove off. She sat in the old wicker chair on the porch, staring after him.

Beau was great. She had gotten to know him more, he was witty, so smart and genuinely nice, not boring at all like Taylor thought. Despite all of his amazing qualities, his muscles being right at the top of the list, there was still no spark. There was no heat in his gaze, no lingering touches, no electricity when they accidentally brushed against each other. His kiss, although very good, hadn't left her begging for more like it had with De-, she clenched her teeth, cutting off the thought.

Did she want to sleep with Beau? Not really, she didn't feel any sexual chemistry between them. It wouldn't be right to lead him on and when he came by tomorrow, she would tell him straight away and give him the out so he didn't help her out of obligation. She didn't want him to think she was using him to fix the house. Heaving a deep sigh, she got up from the chair and went inside. Although it was still quite early, Christy was bone tired and went straight to bed, ignoring her father's bedroom and went into the guest room.

The next day when Beau arrived, Christy was a bag of nerves. She had never broken up with someone before, they usually left her so she didn't know the best way to start the conversation. She didn't know how Beau felt and didn't want to hurt him. She opened the door to him and as usual he smiled down at her and ducked his head to kiss her cheek, but today she felt like he seemed reserved.

She stepped back to let him inside and as he walked past, she looked him over. He looked gorgeous, his navy t-shirt stretched tight across his rippling muscles, there was no denying it, hell she had eyes! But while she appreciated his looks, and his ass in those faded blue jeans, there definitely wasn't a spark. She decided to just jump straight in.

"Can we talk?" she asked, motioning for him to take a seat on the couch. He looked a bit apprehensive but sat down. She paced in front of him, wringing her hands, unsure how to start.

"Everything okay?" he asked. She stopped in front of him and faced him. She decided as painful as this could be, honesty was definitely the way forward if she wanted to salvage any type of friendship with him. She squeezed her eyes shut and blurted out,

"Idon'tthinkweshouldseeeachotherromanticallyanymore."

After a moment of silence, she cracked open one eye to peer down at him and saw him smothering a grin.

"What?" she asked defensively.

"Nothing, I'm just...is *relieved* the right word?" he laughed, she opened her other eye and her shoulders relaxed.

"Relieved?"

"Oh, gosh sorry! No, I didn't mean it like that, it's just that after last night, we kissed, and..." he trailed off, she slumped down next to him.

"No spark?" she supplied, he nodded.

"Yep. I really wanted there to be one. You're a beautiful woman and I had such a crush on you for so long. When I saw you again after nearly fifteen years, I thought it was fate but then we kissed..."

She laughed. "It wasn't that bad!" she cried, and at his horrified expression she laughed again. "It's fine, I know what you mean, it wasn't right. I'm so glad, I was so worried last night."

"Same," he said laughing. He stood up and pulled her to her feet and wrapped her in a big hug.

"I do, however, think we could become very good friends. And that's always a win," she said, muffled against his chest.

He chuckled. "Sounds good to me."

When they pulled apart, he started looking around the room.

"You really don't have to help me with the house, you know," she said.

"Can I tell you something if you promise not to be mad?" he asked, looking sheepish.

"I guess?"

"It's me that's buying the house." He bit his lip, looking anxious.

"It is? That's amazing!" She threw herself at him for another hug.

"You don't mind?"

"Why would I mind? It's perfect! Do what you want with the place."

"I was hoping you would say that."

They headed into the kitchen as she fetched them some drinks from the fridge. She tossed him a Coke, and then something occurred to her.

"I bet Dean is so happy," she said, feeling herself blush like a teenager as she said his name.

"Well, I haven't actually told anyone else yet. I wanted to wait until it was all confirmed and the sale closed. Do you mind keeping it to yourself for now?"

"Of course, my lips are sealed."

They went back through the house and out onto the porch to sit in the wicker chairs in the shade. The warm breeze tickled Christy's cheeks, the smell of citrus gliding through the air, there for a fleeting moment and then gone. She listened as he told her of his plans to turn the house and land into a fitness and rehabilitation retreat. He wanted to get back to helping people with their quality of life rather than just getting a budding starlet to drop a few pounds. He wanted to help people who had injuries and the elderly, offering physical therapy. His passion as he spoke was infectious.

The more they talked the more he really began to open up and he told her the reason he wanted to move back home. He loved L.A. but he also saw how detrimental the lifestyle was. He had been seeing a woman, Tracy, for almost a year, she started out as a client and they began dating. She became obsessive about her looks, her weight, and demanded he help her lose more and more weight. He could see what she was doing and refused to help her become unhealthy.

Unfortunately, she had taken it to mean he was no longer interested in her and thought he was seeing someone else behind her back. She began following him, accusing him of cheating on her constantly with other clients, even the woman who served him coffee every morning. It became too much and he decided to end it. But she must have known what he was planning because when he tried to end it, she attempted to kill herself. Christy felt sick.

"That's horrific," she said, putting a hand on his arm.

"Yeah, she locked herself in the bathroom and swallowed a bunch of pills. At first I thought she was just having a tantrum and locked herself in, but after a while I realized her silence wasn't right." He dropped his head. "I should've known what she was doing. By the time I figured it out and busted down the door, she was unconscious. I called for an ambulance and managed to bring her around, sticking my fingers down her throat to get her to throw the pills up."

Christy began rubbing his arm, trying to comfort him. She could tell from his voice he was still shaken by the incident.

"I should've known; I took too long to figure it out." He shook his head, frustrated.

"It wasn't your fault, she clearly needed help and that isn't something that you could have provided. At least you managed to bring her around and she's alive because of you."

"But she nearly wasn't and that was because of me too!"

"No, it was because of her," Christy replied vehemently. "You're not responsible for other people's actions, remember that."

"She's tried to contact me a few times since, she wanted to talk but after the incident, I fell out of love with L.A. and wanted to get away from the toxicity of it. That's why I'm moving home. I want to help people. I'll always be grateful for the work I did before, it got me the knowledge and the financial stability to be able to do it. I still want to help people, but in the right way." He nodded as if driving his point home.

"That's also why I want to keep it quiet about the house. I'm worried Tracy will follow me here and I want to get away without her finding out."

"Don't worry, I'll keep it to myself," she replied. They fell into comfortable silence and watched the trees blowing in the breeze. After a while he stood up and held out a hand to help her up.

"Wanna show me what you want doing to the house?" he asked.

"Well, what do you want to do? It's going to be yours soon."

"I think we'll just focus on fixing and redecorating for now. I don't want to do any massive renovations to the house itself, it's more the land I want to develop."

She took him around the house and pointed out various areas of improvement in every room, he followed her making notes on his phone. As they went upstairs, they stopped outside her father's old room. Her heart thudded in her chest as Beau reached for the door handle.

"Wait!" she yelled, and he let go of the handle like it was radioactive. He stared at her.

"I can't go in there yet. Can we leave that one for now?"

She watched as understanding dawned on him. "Sure thing, have you been in there at all since you came back?"

She shook her head.

"Okay then, it's off limits," he said easily, and moved to the room opposite. He rested his hand on the doorknob and paused, looking at her for permission. She nodded and he opened the door and immediately started laughing.

"I guess you were a big fan of the color pink and boybands?" he asked, his tone teasing. She went into her childhood bedroom and looked around, nostalgia washing over her. She waited for the sting of pain that usually accompanied the feeling, but this time it wasn't nearly as sharp as it used to be. She walked around, looking at her things, the room was exactly as she left it. Double bed with flower duvet, pink butterfly throw that she had since she was a kid, stuffed toys lined up along the bed. Pink curtains, pink rug, and pink wallpaper. Posters of various boybands lined the walls, the epitome of a teen girl's room. Beau whistled low as he looked about the room.

"Man, finally in Christy Lee's bedroom, the dream of most of the guys at school."

Christy choked, "What? You're crazy!"

"Come on, Christy. The boys at school always had such a thing for you," he said. She didn't believe him, no one had ever approached her. She wasn't one of the slim, beautiful, popular girls. Which was fine because she was herself and there was no one else she would rather be.

"Well, not everyone," she muttered, thinking of Dean.

Beau faced her and folded his arms over his impressive chest, raising an eyebrow at her. "Anyone in particular you're thinking of?"

She turned away before he saw the blush creeping over

her cheeks. She shook her head and started to leave the room.

"Remember Christy, boys are stupid and just because they're mean, that doesn't mean they don't like you," he said, as though he knew where her mind had wandered, replaying the scene. He walked past her and went off down the hall, leaving her staring after him.

They finished inside and went outside to look at the land around the house. It didn't need quite as much doing to it. Just a lot of weeding, the trees and bushes needed pruning, and the grass definitely needed to be cut.

Once they finished, she realized it was actually getting quite late. Christy was due to spend the evening with Taylor and Justine, and Beau was off to meet Dean for dinner. They said goodbye with Beau promising to come back the next day to start work on the house. As he left, he kissed her on the cheek in an affectionate familial way, and she felt lighter than she had in a while.

Chapter 11

Dean walked into The Rusty Bucket Inn and had a cursory look around for Beau, but he hadn't arrived yet. He made his way over to the bar, perched on a stool, and watched Taylor serve a couple of her regulars. He frowned, noticing the dark circles under her eyes. She looked like she hadn't slept, although he hadn't slept much either. Every time he drifted off, a blond haired, cherub cheeked vixen invaded his dreams and did things to him that left him hard and aching when he awoke.

He couldn't get that kiss out of his mind, could still taste her sweet flavor in his mouth and was dying for another hit. Her delectable curves pressed up against him, rubbing him just right as he swallowed her moans. He shifted uncomfortably on his stool.

She had wanted him; she just hadn't *wanted* to want

him. He had watched as she fought her urges. He smiled to himself as he remembered the look that crossed her face before she surrendered to him. That had been the best kiss of his life and he was desperate to do it again. Dean sobered at the thought, reminding himself that she was seeing Beau so it couldn't happen again.

He put her in an unfair situation and, swamped by guilt, he told Beau straight away. He felt like a creep doing that to his friend. What had surprised him was, although Beau seemed annoyed and had laid into him, there hadn't really been any heat to his words. Dean's own temper had risen just seeing the looks that other men in the bar had given Christy that night, let alone if any of them had tried anything.

"Hey, Dimples," Taylor called, and leaned over the bar offering Dean her cheek which he leant forward to kiss.

"Evening, Trouble. You look tired," he said, and she rolled her eyes.

"Has anyone ever told you that you're too charming?" she asked dryly, but avoided his gaze, he knew her too well.

"All the time, what's going on?"

She continued to bustle around the bar, fetching him a beer he hadn't ordered yet and putting glasses away.

"Tay, what's going on?" he pushed, concern furrowing his brow. He knew she wouldn't lie to him, but he would have to press her for the info.

"I'm gonna keep asking until you fess up."

After a moment she huffed and turned to face him.

"Just my ex, Dale. He isn't happy about being my ex and wants to get back together. He showed up after the bar closed last night, wanting to talk and I couldn't get him to leave."

"What?!" Dean exploded. "Did he try to hurt you?"

"No, I was home. He tried to get in, but I locked the doors already. I threatened to call the cops and he left, it's fine." She shrugged like it was no biggie, but it was.

"You know I don't like you living out here all alone and this is exactly why!" Dean was practically shouting, getting some looks from the other patrons in the bar but he couldn't help it.

"This is the first time something has happened, Dean!" she replied, the volume of her voice rising to match his. She would never be outdone in an argument.

"I want you to come and stay with me, okay? Pack a bag and I'll pick you up after your shift. You know I've got plenty of room at the house."

"I'm not leaving, and you have Beau staying with you already."

"Exactly, we'll be one big happy family."

"No, Dean. I can take care of myself," she said firmly.

He was torn, he knew how stubborn she was and he wouldn't be able to force her. He didn't want to force her, didn't want to drive a wedge between them, he was just worried about her.

"Fine," he grumbled reluctantly. "But if this asshole shows up again you immediately call the police and then me, you hear me?"

"Sure thing, bro." She grinned at him. "You just stopped by for a visit?"

"Nah, I'm meeting Beau. He should be here soon, probably just got held up at Christy's."

He took a swig of his beer and she fixed him with a hard stare.

"What?"

"I saw you. The other night, down the hallway, with her." she said.

Dean swallowed audibly and felt himself blush, feeling

like he'd been caught red-handed by his mom.

"What're you doing? Don't mess around with Christy. You're looking for something serious and she's only sticking around for a couple of weeks at the most. There's no point in getting anything started and I love you but if you hurt her, I'll never forgive you. She's been treated badly by men her whole life," Taylor said quietly.

Now he felt like he was being told off by his mom, and he immediately went on the defensive.

"It was a mistake, it's nothing serious and I was so drunk that night-" he started, but she interrupted him.

"No, you weren't."

He pursed his lips shut before another lie slipped out. He could feel himself getting hot under her stare.

"It was just a stupid moment and I *had* been drinking. It was a mistake, she pushed me away and I've already told Beau about it and apologized," he explained. She nodded, seeming satisfied with this.

"She pushed you away? Interesting." She smirked.

"Yeah, yeah laugh it up, I got rejected." He took another swig of his beer.

"Good." She lifted her stare to focus on something over his shoulder. He watched her face brighten briefly before her expression blanked and she turned away. A moment later a large hand clapped him on the shoulder, and he turned to see Beau easing down onto the stool next to him.

"Hey, man."

"Sorry I'm late, I got held up at Christy's," Beau replied, trying to get Taylor's attention to order a drink but every time he waved at her, she turned away and conveniently didn't see him.

"No worries, is she good?" he asked. He felt weird asking Beau about Christy, but he wanted to show he was supportive of their budding relationship, even though it killed him.

"Yeah, we decided to just be friends though."

A frisson of excitement rushed through Dean at the news. Now she was unattached, free which meant...*nothing*. His eyes flicked over to Taylor as he remembered what she said. He couldn't get involved with Christy even if he wanted to. He clenched his teeth in frustration. Christy was officially off limits. He took a swig of his beer, trying to act nonchalant.

"Oh yeah? That's a shame buddy, what happened? Shit, did I mess things up between you?" he asked, guilt pouring from his words.

"Nah, we just work better as friends. I was pretty gutted to be honest. I had a crush on her for so long and when I saw her again, I really thought it meant something for us. But we kissed and there was just no spark, it felt like kissing my sister," he sighed.

Dean choked on his beer. *No spark? No fucking spark?!* Christy's kiss damn near sent him up in flames. She was passion incarnate; she kissed him with her whole body, nothing held back. He shook his head as his jeans tightened against his crotch.

Don't think about that now. He wiped his hand over his mouth.

"Aw that sucks, man, sorry to hear that. Was she upset when you ended things?"

"Me? Oh no, it was her, she said she felt nothing either. It's the darndest thing," Beau chuckled to himself. Dean was lost in thought as Taylor came over.

"Taylor, so glad you finally noticed you had a customer," Beau said dryly.

"I noticed, I just didn't care," she smiled at him tightly.

"There's that five star customer service I keep hearing

about," Beau deadpanned.

"What can I get you?"

"How about a smile?"

"I'll smile non-stop as soon as you leave."

"Do you know what's funny?" Beau asked.

"Your dating history?" Taylor shot back, fire crackling in her eyes. Beau chuckled darkly then raised his eyes to meet hers.

"I thought I saw someone from school earlier. What's his name again, oh yeah, Bobby Bryson. Didn't you used to date him, Taylor?"

Dean felt the air between them thicken with tension. Taylor blinked, momentarily shocked. She just stared at Beau and then grabbed a beer, slamming it down in front of him, suds flying, and stormed off. *What the hell was that?* Dean thought, staring at Beau as he calmly lifted his beer to his mouth. After a beat Beau turned to him.

"Anyway, there's a lot to do at Christy's house. I'm gonna need an extra hand if you're up for it? I know you offered the other day but if the garage needs you, that's cool."

Dean could feel someone staring at him, he looked up to see Taylor at the other end of the bar glaring down at them. It's true, he had offered to help but that was before Taylor's warning. But he didn't want to rescind his offer as that was just downright dickish behavior.

"Sounds good," he smiled. "When do we start?"

*

Christy was up and dressed early, ready for her and Beau to start working on the house. She was actually quite excited about it, she loved having a project to throw herself into and God knows her writer's block wasn't going anywhere. Maybe some physical labor would work something loose. There was quite a bit of renovating to do and Beau was fine for it to be done. She thought that he wouldn't want her to do anything considering he was buying the place, but he was so laid back. It was only cosmetic work; just stuff he would need to do anyway. She knew she didn't need to do it, but she wanted to, she felt like it was the way for her to leave her final mark on the house. But there were a few basics that needed fixing first.

"Like this goddamn garbage disposal!" she hissed as she bent over the sink wrestling with it. She heard the front door open and Beau call out.

"Christy?"

"I'm in here," she grunted, flicking the switch again and growling when nothing happened.

"This damn thing won't work!" There was a beat and then she heard an all too familiar southern drawl.

"Well then I guess I know what my first job is."

She turned her head to the side, heart pounding in her chest and saw Dean casually leaning against the doorway. His arms folded over his wide chest, big ol' panty melting smile stretched across his face. He looked cheeky and boyish in his blue t-shirt and faded denim jeans, blond hair all mussed, a light shadow of stubble dusting his jaw. He looked her up and down, eyes lingering on her ass which was sticking out as she bent over the kitchen counter. She flushed brighter than the red playsuit she was wearing and swiftly straightened.

"Dean, what are you doing here?" she asked. *Is that breathy tone really mine?* She cleared her throat to repeat the question as Beau came in with a toolbox and set it on the counter next to her.

"He's my muscle," Beau smirked, nodding towards Dean. Then he leaned down and dropped a now customary kiss on Christy's cheek. Dean watched the action and when Beau moved back out of the way, he also came over to Christy, crowding her against the counter with his large body.

"Exactly, I'm the muscle," he rumbled as he bent his head, brushing his lips softly against her cheek. The gentle rasp of his stubble against her skin had her eyelids fluttering closed in bliss. He lingered a moment and then pulled away and she had to clamp her mouth shut to keep from moaning at the loss of him. She met his eyes as he pulled back and she thought she detected a sparkle of amusement in those electric depths. Clearly, he was up to his tricks again, trying to move her attention away from Beau. *I've got news for ya buddy, we've called it quits, so there!* Then she remembered Beau was still in the room. She turned to face him, worried he picked up on the tension between her and Dean, but he was busy rummaging around in the toolbox he brought.

"Want me to start with sorting this out?" Dean asked, gesturing to the evil garbage disposal. She could feel his gaze boring into her but she couldn't meet his eyes, afraid he would be able to read her expression.

"Um, yeah, sounds good. Beau, you know what needs doing so just go ahead and start wherever you like. I'm going outside to start the garden," she muttered. She turned around to grab the secateurs from the counter, but something pulled her back against the cupboards. She turned to look behind her and saw the belt loop from her playsuit was hooked around a cupboard door handle. She tried to unhook it but couldn't quite reach without pulling her suit and it wouldn't budge on its own.

"Here, let me," Dean said, coming forward.

"No, it's fine!" she protested rather loudly, wanting to keep as much space between them as possible. She held up her hand to ward him off, but he'd already moved in front of her and her palm flattened over his chest, his firm pec jumping under her touch.

"Sorry," she muttered all flustered. She could feel heat rising in her cheeks and he chuckled darkly in her ear as he bent down, the sound spreading warmth throughout her body. He put his hands on either side of her hips and pushed her back against the counter roughly, and pressed his hard body against her. Her breath left her in a huff and she peered up at him through her lashes, her core heating at his aggressive move. He was peering down at her, a strange look on his face. His nostrils flared and he closed his eyes. When he opened them again all traces of amusement were gone and replaced by something she didn't entirely recognize.

He pulled her to the left and reached behind her, his hand at her back. He leaned into her, bending down to look over her shoulder. The sun-kissed skin of his neck inches from her mouth, tantalizing her. What she wouldn't give to lean into him and run her tongue over the pulse she could see thumping beneath his skin. His delicious musky pine scent invaded her nose, creating a heady sensation that made her want to rub herself up against him, she just wanted to touch him. Suddenly she was popped free, and all his delicious heat disappeared as he moved over to Beau and turned his back on her.

"Uh, thanks," she said, but didn't get a reply. She turned away to grab her gardening equipment and unfortunately, uh, *thankfully* didn't get stuck again. She went out the kitchen door and onto the rear porch, scolding herself profusely as she went.

Stop acting like a horny teenager! Especially around that man in particular. In fact, with any other man, feel free to act like a nun who's just been released from a convent, but not with him. She stood on the porch, taking a few deep breaths, trying to get her body under control.

The sun was already high in the sky and the temperature was beginning to rise. Soon it would be too hot to work outside. She took another deep breath then headed over to the biggest patch of weeds. After an hour of bending, leaning and squatting her knees, thighs and ass were aching. She pushed herself to keep going while it was still cool enough. It was better to be out here on her own than in the house watching Dean do manly things that made all his glorious muscles flex and ripple. Maybe he would accidentally hit one of the water pipes and burst it, then water would spray out, soaking his shirt and plastering the material against his skin. Then he would have to remove it, obviously, and his muscles would...

"Stop!" she yelled at herself, grateful she was alone in the garden. She really needed to stop wasting her thoughts on a man who only kissed her to try and get his friend to dump her. She got mad all over again thinking about that and used her rage to power through the weeding.

*

Was she trying to kill him? Was there such a thing as being aroused to death? Surely there had to be, especially if all his blood was focused in one area in particular. Was this his penance for branding her so harshly in high school, because karma was being a massive bitch.

If he had to watch her squat, bend, or stretch one more time he was going to...well he was going to shove her into the grass and show her just how worked up she got him. The round, creamy globes of her ass playing havoc with his mind as they peeked out the bottom of the shorts on that ridiculously cute outfit every time she bent over. He panted, sweated, cursed nonstop, and now he was trying to avoid looking everywhere but out the kitchen window. How could weeding be so fucking sexy? *Christy Lee, that's how…*

This was a mistake, hell, he knew it as soon as he walked in and saw her bent over the kitchen worktop like she was bent over his – he growled in frustration, shoving the rest of that thought from his mind. It was his own fault, he shouldn't have kissed her cheek and he certainly shouldn't have pressed himself up against her when she got caught on the worktop, but he couldn't help himself. The innocent way she peered up at him through her lashes had him fighting a groan. Why was he playing with fire? Because it burned so *good.*

He knew he needed to stay away from her. There was no future for them and his relationship with Taylor was far too important to mess up. No matter how edible Christy looked in that adorable outfit. His traitorous eyes found her again, his pulse speeding up. She was making it very difficult to look anywhere else, not that she realized.

He watched as she stood up straight and looked around, wiping the back of her arm across her forehead and then turned towards the house. He quickly rearranged himself so she didn't think tinkering with the garbage disposal was his kink. She came in and dumped her stuff on the side and moved over to him.

"Still broken?" she asked, leaning over to have a look and accidentally brushing her breast across his forearm.

"Yeah, I think I'm nearly done," he replied gruffly, not sure whether he was talking about the garbage disposal or himself.

She nodded. "Great, thanks for this, I really mean it. You didn't have to help me out and I really appreciate it." She smiled up at him, but his eyes were following a bead of sweat that began running down her neck, onto her chest and disappeared into the valley between her lush breasts. His mouth ran dry, he didn't trust himself to speak and just turned away and started hammering at the garbage disposal again.

Chapter 12

As the week went on, Dean's temper worsened. Every day he had to watch Christy as she sauntered around in tiny, revealing outfits all designed to make him desperate to get his hands on her curvy little body. Which he obviously couldn't do. Okay, he didn't *have* to watch her, but he couldn't exactly walk around with his eyes shut all the time, could he? Each day that they arrived at the house, she greeted Beau like he was her knight in shining armor, sent forth to rescue her from the villainous renovations. And she treated Dean like Beau's dim-witted servant who smelled awful, had a weird eye and no teeth.

She continually asked for Beau's opinion on what to do on the house and ignored any suggestions Dean made which infuriated him. Why did she care so much about what Beau thought? And why was Dean's opinion not good enough? And don't even get him started on how much she and Beau continually flirted with and teased each other. They had such an easy relationship, like they had known each other for years, which although technically they had, they didn't *know* each other. She had known Dean the same amount of time and he could barely get two words out of her.

Even now she and Beau were whispering away together, and Dean could feel his anger rising. Fine it was jealousy! Although he knew getting to know her wasn't a good idea, he couldn't stop the need to know more about her from growing. He wanted to know if she forgave him for his stupid adolescent behavior, what did she think of him now, what had happened between her and her father, why did she run away, and what made her tick. He wanted to get inside her head, break it apart and bathe in the pieces until he was fully immersed in her.

Today the heat was worse than normal which made his temper even shorter. Christy said she was going out to get more supplies which he was slightly grateful for, he needed a break from drooling over her so he could actually focus on doing some work. Idiot that he was, he did offer to go with her, and when she said she didn't need his help, he had to bite his tongue to hold in a retort. His sexual frustration had been coiling inside him, looking for a way out, preferably with her in bed but that couldn't happen, so it was trying to slip out in other ways. Like nearly snapping at her, because that would have really helped them bond, not. He stood on the porch and watched her leave, round hips swaying to her own beat as Beau sidled up next to him.

"So, how long do you think it'll be before you crack and ask her out?" Beau asked, smirking.

"What?" Dean snapped, some of that frustration

easing.

Beau laughed. "Damn, she's got you worked up, that's for sure. Never seen you so tense."

"You're talking shit."

Beau fixed him with a pointed stare. "Dude, your compass has been pointing north for the last week, if you catch my drift. It's getting difficult to pretend I'm not seeing it, so just ask her out already."

Dean felt himself blush for the first time ever and he gritted his teeth. "I can't."

"I don't mind, we're totally just friends now, you have my blessing."

Dean felt guilty that he hadn't even thought about that.

"Thanks, but I can't," he repeated.

Beau frowned at him. "You can't?"

Dean shook his head, the motion clipped and watched as realization dawned on Beau.

"Shit, Taylor cock-blocked you, didn't she?"

Dean nodded again and Beau clapped him on the back, the corners of his mouth twitching, clearly fighting a smile.

"Aw, man, that's rough. So, I guess I should stop flirting with her just to piss you off then, huh?"

"You son of a-" Dean leapt at him and Beau hooted, ducking out of the way and running past him and back into the house but Dean was hot on his heels. Beating the shit out of Beau would definitely ease some of his tension. He ran after him and tackled him to the ground, fist pulled back ready to give Beau a dead arm when his phone rang.

"Saved by the bell!" Beau laughed, and Dean flipped him off, then punched him for good measure, which just made the jerk laugh harder. Dean rummaged in his pocket for his cell and answered. "Iris Motors."

"Dean, it's Christy. I've, uh, had a problem with my car again and I need your help." Her sweet voice crackled over the line.

Finally she needed him. Not Beau, *him*. For the first time all week, Dean felt his mood brighten.

*

As Dean's truck pulled up and she saw the massive grin on his face, Christy's heart sank. *Here he comes, all smug because I need him to bail me out. Why do I have to have such an old car? Oh, right because some dickhead pretended to love me and ran off with all my money so I can't afford a new one.* Her mood darkened even further at the thought of Douchebag Alfie. And why does Dean have to work at the only garage in town? Since the first day he turned up at the house and was all snappy when she asked him about the garbage disposal, she had purposefully tried to avoid him. That way she wouldn't have to deal with his hot and cold attitude anymore.

Christy may have tried to avoid speaking to him all week, but her eyes didn't get the memo. She couldn't stop staring at him. The way his muscles bunched when he moved, the way he wiped sweat off his forehead with his tanned forearms. It always seemed to happen in slow motion, like a Diet Coke ad. And let's not forget his jeans tightening against his pert ass whenever he bent over. Her eyes practically begged him to have his way with her all week.

As he got out of the truck, she looked him over. His light gray t-shirt pulling tight against his chest and biceps, he looked *gooood* in faded blue jeans too. She forced herself to look away and rearrange her features so he couldn't see the *"please touch me!"* plastered across her face. He managed to look as good in casual clothes as he had in his formal shirt and slacks the other night. He walked over to her, practically swaggering, and stopped in front of her, grinning. His dimples on display, stealing her breath.

"I'm so glad you called," he said huskily.

She looked at him confused. "You're glad I broke down?"

His smile dipped slightly as he realized what he said, and he looked sheepish.

"No, I meant I'm glad you called me when you needed help."

She stared at him, why was he glad? Because he got to swoop in and save the day and feel really good about himself? Like he didn't already. God, she hated the sexy bastard!

"So, where's your exhaust?" he asked, looking back at the road. Turns out Beau had been right the other day, it was looking a little low, because it had been hanging off. She should've checked it; she could have avoided this situation but she completely forgot about it and now she was at Dean's mercy.

She led him over to the passenger side of her car and opened the door, pointing at the seat. He stooped down, placing his hand on the roof and looking inside. His scent wafted over her and she inhaled it greedily, her stomach flipping. It was so powerful, so masculine and so...*Dean*. It nearly had her panting like a dog in heat. She took advantage of his averted gaze to really look at him. He was so tall, even stooped down, she still had to look up at him. He ran a hand through his blond hair, the sun bouncing off golden strands. He turned to face her and she quickly looked away.

"Christy, why have you put the seatbelt around it?" he asked, his tone laced with humor. She snapped her eyes back to him and saw he was clearly fighting a smile. She looked at the exhaust sitting in the passenger seat. It had fallen off not far into her journey and not knowing what to do, she picked it up. Thankfully, it hadn't been too hot to touch and she placed it on the passenger seat for safekeeping until he arrived. She stared back at him dumbfounded.

"Well, I didn't want it to fall forward," she said, like it was obvious. He burst out laughing, his laughter deep and rich. His whole face lit up with amusement and he looked gorgeous, so happy and carefree. Unfortunately, it was at her expense, once again. He laughed so hard that she could see tears forming in the corners of his eyes and he slapped his thigh. She felt her cheeks darken with embarrassment and she crossed her arms over her chest, feeling defensive.

"Are you done?" she huffed. He stood upright, taking in her expression and his laughter subsided into chuckles. He wiped his eyes.

"Sorry, darlin' but that is the funniest thing I've seen in a long time."

She felt her embarrassment rising, and tears stung the backs of her eyes. Why did this always happen around him? She spun away before he could see her, no way would she make this worse by crying in front of him. Between him and Douchebag Alfie she had enough humiliation to last a lifetime, she was so done with men making her feel stupid.

"Okay, I'll just hook her up to my truck and I'll tow her to the garage. I can fix her up while you wait, shouldn't take too long. You can go and sit in the truck out of the heat if you want."

She didn't waste her time. She went and hefted herself into the truck, instantly feeling cooler in the cabin, which smelled so deliciously like him. She stared out the passenger window, not wanting to watch him work, seeing those muscles rippling, tempting her with what she wanted but could never have would just make her feel worse. She couldn't believe she kept fantasizing about him when he thought she was just a joke, cringing again at how much he laughed at her. When he was finished, he hopped back into the truck. He looked over at her, she could feel his eyes boring into her, but she refused to meet them. He sighed deeply then started the engine, and they drove back to the garage in tense silence.

"I'm going to unload her; you can go and sit in the office where it's cooler. There's water in there if you need a drink," he said when they arrived at the garage. Christy could feel him staring at her again but still she wouldn't look at him. She nodded, got out of the truck, and headed inside. He was right, the blinds were closed to keep the sun out, keeping the room shaded and cool. She spotted the water cooler behind the door and grabbed a cup, filling it and downing the drink in one before immediately having another.

She began to cool down, smoothing her hands down her pale blue cotton jumpsuit, checking herself for sweat patches, that was the last thing she needed. She looked around the office, it was nicely decorated with minimalist style furniture. She went over to the large wooden desk, there was paperwork strewn over the top in a messy heap, an expensive looking computer, a phone, and a picture frame.

Christy walked around the desk to get a look at the picture, it was the same photo of Taylor and Dean that was in Taylor's bedroom. She picked it up and studied the image, they both looked so happy that Christy was smiling back at the image.

Dean came into the office and headed straight for the water cooler. Christy quickly put the frame down, pretending she hadn't been looking at his private things. He chugged down a cup of water then filled another and sipped from it looking around. She nervously smoothed her hands down her hips again, pulling the fabric of her outfit. She looked up to find him watching her, his eyes flaring until he closed them, shuttering his expression. He walked over to her and perched against the edge of his desk. She felt awkward just standing there next to him, the silence stretched on until she couldn't bear it.

"Thank you for fixing her, again," she said quietly. He leveled a hard stare at her. "Do you mean that?" he asked, his voice stiff.

"Of course I do," she replied, and they settled into uncomfortable silence again. She could see him watching her, his eyes roaming over her body. She began to feel paranoid; she usually only wore her summer clothes when she was alone in her apartment. She never dressed like this in public, too concerned with what people would think. However, since she was working on building her confidence and it was far too hot here, she tried not to care and wore whatever she wanted. But in that moment her old insecurities came roaring to life, and she couldn't imagine what he thought of her rounded body on display like this. She couldn't stand the idea that he thought she looked horrible. She wanted to get out of there, fast.

"How much will it cost?" she asked.

"Don't worry about it," he cut her off.

Her pride perked up. "I can afford it, you know! How much is it?"

"You can't afford it, Christy! Are you forgetting that I told you I know what that asshole did?" Dean shouted, his chest rising and falling, eyes flashing down at her in challenge. She sucked in a breath as she realized the real reason he didn't want her with Beau. *Money.*

"Is that why you tried to break me and Beau up?"

His brows dipped. "What?"

"Because you thought I was going to try and get his money? Like I'm some gold-digging whore?"

"Are you serious?" he scoffed.

"Well, you got your wish." She stormed past him and dumped her empty cup in the trash.

"No, that's not why I wanted you to break up-" he started, but she cut him off.

"Aha! So you admit it, you *did* want to break us up." She spun to face him and marched forward, her pent-up anger and hurt overflowing. "You did want us to split, you think I'm not good enough for him, don't you? Not thin enough and heaven knows I know you don't think I'm pretty enough and now I need money too? Well fuck you!" she shouted in his face, her chest heaving. He stepped forward, getting in her space.

"No, that's not why. I didn't want you with Beau because..." he started, but cut himself off and mashed his lips together. He moved back but she followed him.

"Why?"

He shook his head, shoving his hand through his hair. He wouldn't meet her eyes, but she wasn't backing down, they were long overdue a reckoning and it was happening now.

"I asked *why* Dean?"

His arm shot out and wrapped around her waist, pulling her flush against him. She gasped in surprise and grabbed hold of his broad shoulders to steady herself. He dipped his head and nuzzled down the side of her neck and inhaled deeply.

"God, you smell so good," he rumbled, licking over

her thudding pulse and she moaned, heat rushing to her core. *What is he doing? Is this actually happening?* Her mind raced with a thousand thoughts that all disappeared when he palmed her ass and pulled her flush against him. He squeezed her flesh hard then eased his grip, massaging away the sting. She gasped again when she felt his hard arousal pressing into her through his jeans. With his other hand he cupped her jaw, tilting her head to look him in the eye.

"What are you doing?" she breathed. He stared into her eyes and she was gone. His were wild, so dark and stormy with desire and she lost herself in them.

"Kissing you," he murmured, before he dipped his head and covered her mouth with his. It was the same as the last time; hot, dirty, everything she needed, but never expected to get from this man. His hand applied pressure to her jaw and she opened up, rolling her tongue into his waiting mouth. He tasted like rich wine and dark nights, a heady combination. He pulled back and stared down at her, his pupils blown wide, black gobbling up the stormy blue. Her breath caught in her throat, she didn't know why this was happening. Only that it *was* happening and she never wanted it to end.

*

She tasted like candy, the sweetest taste he had ever known and was immediately addicted. He lowered his head for another taste and she rose up on her tiptoes, lacing her arms around his neck and pressing herself into him. Their lips crashed together with burning need and fierce frenzy. She nipped at his mouth and sucked on his tongue, making his eyes roll backwards beneath the closed lids. She pulled away and he instantly mourned the loss of her.

She kissed down his neck and fit her lips over his

pounding pulse and sucked hard, pulling a groan from him. He found her mouth again, grinding his hips into her core, wringing a moan from her throat, the sweetest sound he ever heard. He ground against her, pure need driving him. He needed to hear her moan again, needed her naked in his bed, her scent surrounding him. Her body aching with desire, wet and open for him and only him. The strength of his need scared him, he had never desired someone like this before and all from a kiss.

He needed more.

He moved his hands to cover her breasts, her nipples already hard, reaching for him through the fabric. He stroked his thumbs across the hard peaks and felt her shiver, her breathing turned heavy. He pulled back from the kiss, eager to see what she looked like while he played with her. Her hands tightened on his shoulders, nails digging in and he reveled in the pleasure pain feeling. He worked the swollen tips, pinching and rolling them between his fingers. Her head tipped back, eyes closed in bliss, her tongue swiping over her swollen lips. He dipped his head and kissed along her collarbone, his hands leaving her breasts only to pull the top of her shirt to the side, exposing more of her creamy skin.

"Dean," she sighed as he pulled the material down over her shoulders, kissing the skin he was unveiling. His cock twitched hard at the sound of his name uttered in such pleasure from her lips.

As cute as her outfit was, it wasn't made for passionate moments, he had to work her arms through each sleeve so he could pull it down to her waist. When he had it down, he leaned back to look at her. Her breasts were round and spilled over the top of her strapless bra, he flicked the center clasp open and pulled the material aside.

Pale velvet flesh tipped with dusky pink nipples, hard and aching for his touch, his mouth. He palmed her breasts, shocked at the heavy weight of them and dipped his head, flicking his tongue over the tip of one, then the other. She gasped in pleasure and tangled her fingers in his hair, holding him close and arching her back to push against his mouth firmly, her hips searching for his. He feasted on them, sucking, licking, and flicking his tongue back and forth as she ground herself against his hard cock.

"So perfect," he murmured against her flesh, and began to play again, drawing more moans from her.

"Touch me, please," she begged, sobbing with need and his heart thudded in his chest. He never would have dreamed she would be so responsive, so perfect. He trailed his hand over the width of her hips, playing there and teasing her before moving his hand lower. She thrust her hips, desperate to get to him and he chuckled as she growled when he moved out of reach. He moved to her ear and licked the shell while one hand pinched her nipple and the other played with the top of her underwear.

"Are you wet, darlin'?" he rasped in her ear. She shivered again and pulled back to look at him, eyes glazed with passion.

"You tell me," she replied huskily. He groaned and kissed her again, rolling their tongues together as he tunneled his hand underneath her damp panties. Oh yes, she was wet and ready for him. He slid his finger over her swollen bud and she cried out. He rubbed once, twice, then dipped his finger lower and slid inside her.

"Oh, fuck," he groaned, as her channel gripped him tightly, so hot and wet. His cock throbbed in his jeans, desperate to replace his finger.

"More. Please, Dean, I need more," she sighed.

God, she was amazing. So sexy and wanton, wild with her passion. He slid another finger inside her and scissored them, stretching her. She met his eyes and a spark of electricity flared between them. As he moved his fingers in and out her eyelids dipped in pleasure and he felt her hand brush over his crotch. She was working on the zipper of his jeans and his breath hitched, he was desperate to feel her grip on him and worked her faster.

She tunneled her hand inside his jeans and boxers and gripped him hard. His breath hissed between his lips and he thrust into her hand. She looked down, watching herself work him as his fingers moved inside her. She pulled the skin up tight towards the tip of his cock, working a bead of desire from him. She smoothed the moisture over the head and stroked down to the base. Watching her work him so perfectly while his fingers were thrusting inside her sent him into a frenzy.

"You're killing me, darlin'," he gritted through clenched teeth. "I'm not going to last much longer."

She worked him up and down, gripping tighter and moving her hand faster as he pushed his fingers deeper inside her. The sounds of their moans and heavy breathing filled his office. He bent his head down to suck a hard nipple into his mouth and eased another finger inside her, stretching her more. He pressed the heel of his palm to her clit and moved faster.

Her eyes widened and he felt her orgasm as it barreled through her. She cried out as her muscles clamped down on his fingers and she tightened her grip on his cock. He thrust into her hand and followed her over the edge, grunting as hot seed shot out from the tip, coating her hand and his stomach. He kept thrusting into her hand, his orgasm continuing until she'd rung every last drop and she sagged against him.

His heart was pounding in his ears, their ragged pants filling the room, her breath trekking across his damp neck. A huge wave of tenderness washed over him and he pressed a long, sweet kiss to her damp forehead. He had never come so hard in his life and he hadn't even gotten inside her.

When his heart slowed to a steady pace, he separated them slightly and she turned her face away and started pulling her jumpsuit back up. He put himself away and began looking around for something to clean them up and spotted the photo of him and Taylor on his desk. Shit.

The afterglow wore off as guilt and regret flowed through him. He promised Taylor he would leave Christy alone and look at what he had done. God, he was such an idiot. He was so desperate for her he didn't even stop to consider the consequences, had only been concerned with getting them both off. He'd made a huge mistake and broken his own rules about getting with women.

He swallowed thickly. "Let me just get some paper towels," he said, his voice like gravel.

As he left the office and the full weight of what they'd done crashed down on him. How could he have been so desperate for her that he would ignore his own rules and potentially ruin his relationship with Taylor, the only true family he ever had? He'd started it as well, it wasn't like Christy had been trying it on with him, she was blameless. How could he be so stupid?

It couldn't happen again, he had to make sure of it. He grabbed some paper towels and hardened his heart as he knew what he had to do next. With a pit burning in his stomach, he headed back to Christy.

Chapter 13

Just when I was beginning to think he was a decent guy he turns back into King of all Assholes, Christy thought bitterly. She felt so stupid, how could she have let things go so far? Well, that was easy to answer, it had felt so damn good. Her body still humming with satisfaction even now. His kisses had been drugging, his touch was to die for and the way he looked at her? She felt genuinely desirable for the first time in her life, and it was an intoxicating feeling.

However, all of that had been snatched away immediately.

After their encounter she needed a moment to put herself back together, she had been vulnerable. The gentle, tender kiss he gave her afterward had shaken her, even now thinking of it she felt a strange pang in her chest she didn't want to look at too closely. It was all an illusion, because when he came back with paper towels, he was surly and distant. He refused to look at her and then kicked her out. Pulling her onto the forecourt of the garage and telling her he would drop her car by later before heading back into his office, and slamming the door shut so hard the glass panes rattled. What a fool she was to have trusted him.

"Asshole," she muttered again, as sadness hit her, tears threatening to fill her eyes. She blinked them back, refusing to cry because of him, again. What had she expected though? Why did she go along with it? He clearly pegged her as an easy mark just like Alfie had and he was right, she fell for it hook, line, and sinker. This was exactly the reason she swore off men, she couldn't trust any of them and she only had herself to blame.

Christy walked through the town, looking for Justine's office. It wasn't hard to find, being on the main strip, and as she went inside, she was instantly cooled by the blast of air conditioning. The main door led straight into the reception area. Christy gazed around taking in the fancy leather chairs, and tall, leafy plants. There was a coffee table full of magazines and a TV in the corner playing a daytime soap with the volume down low. She had never seen Justine's place of work, the small practice her friend had built from the ground up and Christy was so proud seeing what Justine had accomplished.

She was greeted by a smartly dressed woman sitting behind a neat desk, this must be Hilda, Justine's secretary. Christy heard a lot about her over the years, Justine often said she would be lost without her.

"Can I help you, dear?" Hilda asked with a gentle smile.

"Is Justine free?"

"She's with a client at the moment, she'll be done in

about half an hour if you would like to wait?"

"Is she free for the rest of the afternoon?"

Hilda scanned the screen of her sleek looking computer. "Looks like it, would you like to make an appointment?"

"No, thank you, I'm a friend. Is it possible to leave a note for her?"

Hilda nodded and passed Christy a notepad and pen. Christy scribbled that she would be at The Rusty Bucket Inn and asked Justine to swing by when she was finished so they could have lunch. She said goodbye and left the office, the stifling heat hitting her in the face as soon as she left the building.

She started walking to the bar, knowing it was going to be difficult in the heat, but there would be huge pine trees to walk under for shade. As she walked, her thoughts inevitably turned towards her encounter with Dean. She couldn't get the way he looked out of her mind. Lips swollen from their kisses, eyes stormy with passion and expression lit with pleasure. He'd given her the first orgasm she had that hadn't come from herself. It had been so intense, so consuming that her body clenched at the reminder. She shoved those thoughts to the back of her mind and instead focused on her writing. She was in the middle of a huge bout of writer's block she needed to crack soon, or she would go crazy.

She was on book four of her detective series and wasn't sure how to deal with the fallout from the end of book three. Her pen had gotten away from her and she had killed off the main character's love interest in a bold move that she now regretted; her readers were not happy with her. As she tried to brainstorm ways to get around it, aside from a sudden resurrection, she noticed a car pull up alongside her. The window rolled down and Justine smiled at her.

"Get in, it's too hot for walking!"

Christy climbed into the car, grateful to be out of the sun and distracted from her thoughts. They chatted as Justine drove and a few minutes later they pulled up outside the bar.

"Hello, my loves," Taylor called as they went inside. "Welcome to Heaven!"

"Now I know why you never leave this place, it's so cool," Justine muttered as she slipped onto a bar stool.

"I saved up for two years to get air conditioning installed here and it's already paying for itself, customers are crowding in just to get out of the heat," Taylor said proudly. Christy looked around and, for a weekday lunchtime, it was very busy.

"You should really wear less clothes, Justine," Taylor admonished, gesturing to Justine's orange knit dress and then down to her own short shorts and strapless top.

"If I dressed like you then my clients wouldn't be able to focus on their problems!" Justine shot back.

"My, my someone thinks highly of themselves," Taylor sniped at her, but there was humor in her eyes. You had to be blind not to notice how stunning Justine was and she was silly to pretend otherwise. As Christy listened to their back and forth, she felt herself relax for the first time all day. Well, second time if you count immediately after Dean made her co-

"Christy, is that beard burn on your cheek?" Justine asked slyly. Christy immediately blushed and shifted uncomfortably on her tiny bar stool as Taylor eyed her closely.

"Don't be ridiculous! It's clearly heat rash, I'm not used to this warmer climate yet," she replied, but Justine didn't take the hint.

"I thought you and Beau had called it quits?"

"Then who gave you that?" Taylor said, still staring intensely.

"Guys, it's not beard burn, okay? It's heat rash!" Christy cried. Taylor's gaze continued to bore into her like she knew exactly who's beard had burned her.

"If you say so," Justine sang shrugging her shoulders. "So, how's the house coming on?"

"It's great! Beau and Dean have been great with helping out," Christy replied, grateful for the subject change. Taylor turned away to get them some drinks.

"Mmm, all those muscles rippling and bodies getting sweaty. Is it hard having Beau around?" Justine asked, Christy shook her head.

"No, we agreed that we're better off as friends. There was no sexual chemistry, but we get on so well that we wanted to keep hanging out."

"So, you wouldn't mind if I maybe asked him out?" Justine asked her sheepishly.

Taylor dropped a glass and it shattered all over the floor. "Fuck!" she hissed, and a round of cheers echoed around the bar from the other patrons. She stepped lightly around the shards and reached for the broom that was propped at the end of the bar. She stumbled and promptly knocked it on the floor, rolling her eyes as she bent to pick it up.

"Jesus, someone's clumsy today," Christy teased.

"Yeah, you gonna chew yourself out like you would if Kayleigh had broken that glass?" Justine joked. Taylor flipped them both off and started sweeping.

"Excuse me ladies, can you tell me who the owner of this bar is?" asked a deep voice from behind them. Christy turned to see a tall, well-built man standing behind her and Justine. He removed his sunglasses to reveal a pair of slate gray eyes with thick dark lashes fanning out from them. He ran his hand through his dark wavy curls that needed a trim.

He. Was. Gorgeous.

Permanent frown lines etched across his forehead and a slight furrow in his brows gave him a haughty but brooding expression. His cheekbones were set high, his square jaw covered in dark hair, which was neatly groomed and outlined his flat unsmiling mouth. His black t-shirt was tucked into black jeans which was insane in this heat, but he didn't look like he was struggling at all. His bicep flexed as he tucked his sunglasses in the pocket of his t-shirt, and Christy noted he clearly worked out.

He oozed seriousness in spades which did not bode well for dealing with Taylor, but to Christy's surprise, she behaved herself.

"Hey, gorgeous, I'm Taylor," she said, smiling at him. Tall, dark and broody gave her a quick once over before turning his attention to look around the bar.

"Do you own this establishment?" he asked.

"Establishment makes it sound much fancier than it is but yeah, well I own half of it anyway. Who wants to know?" Taylor put her hand on her hip and raised a delicate eyebrow at him. He continued to survey the bar with such scrutiny that Christy got the vibe he catalogued every detail he saw. He knew how many people were in here, where the nearest exits were, and what could be used as a weapon if needed, *who the hell was he?*

"I'm the new deputy sheriff of Citrus Pines, Blake Miller."

Christy noticed Justine stiffen next to her and she watched as Justine turned on her barstool to face away from them.

Taylor cursed quietly. "Great, did Dean send you to

check on me? I swear that man sometimes…" she trailed off, coming out from behind the bar.

Christy frowned. "Why would Dean send him to check on you? What's going on?"

"No one sent me. I'm going to be starting soon and just wanted to familiarize myself with the town and become friendly with the local business owners, get to know them," Blake said with no hint of a smile or friendliness.

"This is you being friendly?" Taylor asked doubtfully.

"Obviously," Blake deadpanned, and Christy fought a smile. "I've not spoken to Dean but is there a reason he would ask me to check on you?"

"Excuse me," Justine muttered quietly, she slipped off her barstool and headed towards the restrooms.

Taylor sighed. "Look, I don't wanna make a big deal out of anything, but I have a teeny, tiny problem with an ex of mine. Nothing's happened yet, Dale just shows up, mouths off and tries to intimidate me, that's all." She shrugged like it was nothing.

"Taylor! What the hell? How come you never said anything? This is serious!" Christy cried, worry clouding her expression.

"This ex of yours, has he been violent in the past?" Blake asked, ignoring Christy and fixing Taylor with a hard stare.

"Um, I don't know. Not to me he hasn't, but I think he could get that way."

"Okay, who's Dean?"

"He's my brother, if you're going around meeting everyone, you'll get to him. He owns the garage in town," Taylor replied, a note of pride in her tone.

Wait, what? Dean *owned* the garage? Blake pulled out a small notebook and a pen from his back jeans pocket and took a few details down from Taylor on her ex.

"Well, I don't officially start until next month, but I'm in the area if you need me. In the meantime, stay safe and call me if you have any more trouble," Blake said, tearing off a bit of paper and giving it to Taylor. She took it from him and looked at it before thanking him. The corners of Blake's mouth twitched upwards in what Christy thought might have been an attempt at a smile, but it disappeared immediately. He put his sunglasses back on, nodded at Christy and turned around, leaving the bar.

"He seems…nice," Christy said, staring after him. Taylor nodded, then when he was out of sight, she finished sweeping up the glass and put it in the bin. Justine reappeared and sat back on her stool, sipping her drink.

"He was gorgeous, all serious and broody, did you check out his ass? That man is thicc!" Taylor said saucily.

"What did you think, Justine? I'm surprised you weren't all over him," Christy joked, nudging Justine.

"Nope, not my type, sorry," Justine replied, and sipped her drink some more.

"Are you serious?" Taylor asked loudly, her jaw dropping.

Christy remembered something. "Wait, did you say Dean *owns* the garage?" she interrupted.

"Uh huh, he owns the chain of them, hello, Iris Motors? Iris is his mom's name. Think there's about eight of them now across the state. He bought the first one for a steal, then he made enough profit to buy the second and so on. He's the one who lent me the money to buy my share of the bar. He's also one of the investors in *Beau's Bodies*," she said the last part sarcastically. Christy couldn't believe it.

"But how?" she spluttered.

"He's a hella smart businessman and he's got a great eye for profitable investments. I couldn't have done this without him." Taylor turned away to put the broom back.

Christy was shocked, she kept discovering more sides to Dean. He was clearly smart, trusting, and seriously cared about his friends to help them out in such a way. She was also confused because if Dean wanted to keep her away from Beau because he thought she wanted his money, why use himself as bait? It didn't make sense. *Unless he knew he wasn't really ever going to fall for me so there was no real concern I would get near his money?* He said that he didn't think she was a gold-digger, but she didn't believe him. The thought of him thinking she was sent a lance of hurt through her, although could she blame him for being suspicious of her? She didn't trust anyone either.

Chapter 14

When Beau turned up at the house the next day, Christy was shocked to see Dean with him. Her heart started pounding as he headed towards the house. The hot morning sun catching the blond highlights in his hair, emitting a slight glow around his head that looked remarkably like a halo. Christy snorted at the thought, he was no angel, this man was all devil. Beau came into the house and walked into the kitchen, but Dean veered off and went around the side of the house into the garden.

Christy shot out the front door, jogging around the side of the house. She found Dean bent down, rummaging in the toolbox he brought with him. Coming up behind him had been a big mistake, the way his jeans were hugging tightly across his firm ass had her regretting that she hadn't gotten her hands on it yesterday. His shirt was pulled tight across his back and shoulders, emphasizing their muscular deliciousness and again she realized she hadn't seen those yesterday either. She had been bare to him, but she hadn't seen any of his body, except for the obvious part which had been very...*stop!* Thinking of yesterday and his dismissal of her reignited her anger, and she stormed in front of him.

"What the hell are you doing here?" she demanded hotly. He stood up to his full height and ended up looming over her. She felt the balance of power shift slightly, so she lifted her chin defiantly and folded her arms across her chest. Unfortunately, this pushed her breasts higher and boy did he notice. If she weren't already still flushing from her thoughts a moment ago, she would have blushed now.

"Good morning to you too, darlin'," he replied. His southern charm flowing over her like a warm breeze, so sexy she had to fight a shiver that tried to steal over her.

"What are you doing here, Dean?" she demanded again.

"I'm helping out," he shrugged.

"I don't want you here," she said, and he flinched slightly. He reached out for her hand, but she stepped away from him.

"Look, I was going to come and talk to you before you stomped out here all in a snit. I want to apologize for yesterday. I acted like an asshole, twice. First, I took advantage of you and then second, when it was over, I treated you badly." He ducked his head and hooked his thumbs into the back pockets of his jeans.

She eyed him suspiciously. "What do you mean you took advantage of me?" she asked. He lifted his head, piercing her with his electric blues which flashed brightly in the sunshine.

"When we were in my office. I shouldn't have gotten personal in my place of business. I didn't want you thinking you had to do…that…with me to get your car fixed."

"What?!" she bellowed, and he looked at her sheepishly.

"That's not why I did…what we did! I'm not some prostitute who needs to offer sexual favors in return for services rendered!" It's just as well there weren't any close neighbors otherwise they would be hearing everything she was saying.

"Then why did you?"

"Because I wanted to! Not because it was a term of payment!"

"You wanted to?" he asked, and only then did she notice the spark of amusement in his eyes and she realized what he got her to admit.

"You…asshole!" she hissed, and he laughed.

"Hey, come on, I'm sorry, again," he said, and she took a step towards him, balling her fists. He held up his hands in surrender, laughing again. Her anger wasn't funny, she may be tiny, but she was feisty damnit.

"I'm truly sorry, darlin', I just couldn't help myself. I wanted to break the tension between us." His smile faded and his expression became serious. "I mean it though, I acted like a grade A asshole yesterday and I'm so sorry. Please let me keep helping you here, I love the work and I'm enjoying getting to know you and spending time with you." He sounded sincere and even a little shy, but she fixed him with a penetrating stare.

"You do?"

"Yes! You're important to Taylor and Justine and hell, Beau too. Which means you're important to me."

She eyed him closely, was she really important to him?

She wasn't sure, something still nagged at her, the whole situation from yesterday didn't add up. Her stomach flipped as she steeled herself to bring up the incident that lingered between them.

"Dean, I don't understand. Why did you...do what we did? I still remember what you said, in the hallway, in front of those boys all those years ago," her voice quavered at the mention of one of her most painful memories.

His face blanched, but he held her stare. "I'm so sorry for what I said back then. I didn't mean it; I was just an immature and insecure kid. I was embarrassed, hurt, and lashing out," he explained, his features softened.

"Hurt?" she asked, confusion pinching her brow. He rubbed the back of his neck, looking sheepish.

"I overheard you, Tay, and Justine talking at a sleepover one night. You called me stupid, *a lot*, and I guess it struck a nerve with me. My dad used to call me that all the time and it's true, I was struggling in school. But I was embarrassed and upset, so when the guys started talking about you I lashed out. I know that's no excuse, but it's an explanation of why I said it," he finished.

She was mortified that he overheard her bitchy comments. She thought about how she felt after what he said about her, she was so hurt and upset she would have potentially done the same thing. Jesus, she did do the same thing, with the girls. Some part of her understood why he did it and his explanation was like a soothing balm to her pride.

"I didn't really think you were stupid, I was just being idiotic and mean," she replied, and he chuckled then they fell into silence. It was impossible to stay mad at this man.

"So, you want to put this behind us and be friends?"

she asked. She thought she saw a flash of disappointment cross his face but it was gone so quickly she must have been mistaken, the heat was getting to her.

He nodded. "Friends," he said, putting his hand out and she stared at it a moment before sliding her palm into his warm grip. As they shook, his thumb gently stroked over her skin, tingles branching out from the area and her nipples tightened as she thought about what his hands had done yesterday. She pulled her hand back sharply and cleared her throat.

"Thanks for dropping my car off yesterday."

"No problem and there's honestly no charge, please consider it part of my apology?"

"Okay, thank you."

She felt tension mounting as they stared at each other, feeling awkward. The heat bearing down on them, causing a trickle of perspiration to slide down between her breasts. She nibbled her bottom lip and he dropped his gaze to her mouth and abruptly turned away.

"So, what would you like me to do today? I was going to make a start out here but it feels too hot right now," he said, grabbing his toolbox.

"I'm not sure, we better go in and check with Beau. He knows what timeline we should be following," she replied, and turned to go back to the house.

*

Man, she looks good today, although didn't she always? Dean thought as he followed her back to the house. Dressed in her little white shorts and another of those off the shoulder tops that drove him crazy. Exposing her delicate shoulders while hiding her breasts. He was desperate to rip it off and see the strapless bra underneath that would be cupping the most gorgeous breasts he had ever seen. Just the visual had his mind going crazy and his jeans tightening uncomfortably.

He was such an asshole yesterday; he was shocked at his behavior. He hadn't dealt with his emotions properly and reacted poorly which wasn't like him at all. Something about her got him all worked up like no one else had done before. The ferocity of their interaction had scared him. All he could think about was when they could do it again and how amazing it would feel.

But he had to remind himself of his goals, find his partner and start a family. Christy wasn't going to be sticking around, and with Taylor's warning ringing in his ears, he responded by pushing her away, literally dragging her out of the office. He'd lain awake last night, replaying the moment in his office over and over until he was gripping himself.

He couldn't avoid Christy, especially now he was helping her with the house and if he was honest, he didn't want to. He could spend time getting to know her, being her friend and someone she trusted was becoming very important to him. Now that they'd cleared the air properly over their past, he felt a huge weight had been lifted from his shoulders. She was a huge part of Taylor's life, which made her important to him too. The only problem was, could he try to be her friend and keep his hands off her delectable body?

They chatted as they walked back to the house, she asked him if the new deputy had come by and introduced himself yet and they were still talking about him as they went inside and found Beau.

"He seemed really keen on developing relationships in the community which I thought was really sweet," Christy was saying.

"Who's that?" Beau asked

"The new deputy sheriff, Blake," Dean replied. "I'm

glad because I worry about Taylor up at the bar on her own, especially now."

"Why, what's happened?" Beau asked, concern pinching his brow.

"Nothing yet and I wanna keep it that way. She's having some trouble with her ex," Dean said, and Beau tensed.

"What? Has he tried to hurt her? If he has, I swear to God..." he growled angrily, pacing up and down like a caged lion.

"Whoa. Calm down, Hulk!" Christy cried, staring at Dean who was covering a smile with his hand.

"Well, someone needs to look out for her," Beau grumbled, only slightly calmer.

"I've tried, but you know what she's like. She doesn't want anyone looking out for her. She guards her independence fiercely and won't appreciate anyone interfering, trust me," Dean said.

"Yes, and she's got the new sheriff's number now so if she needs him, he'll be there," Christy added.

"Exactly, and me. She knows to call me straight after him," Dean reasoned.

"We're worried too, but she doesn't want our help," Christy said, gesturing to herself and Dean and he smiled at her inclusion of him, like they were a team. She was already beginning to relax around him. Beau stopped pacing but worried a hand over his jaw.

"I'm going away for a couple of weeks on business, but when I'm back I can move into one of the cabins at the bar. That way I'm around if she needs me but not crowding her," he said.

"You don't need to do that, I'm sure Dean doesn't mind you staying with him, do you Dean?" Christy asked, looking at him pleadingly.

"Actually, I think that's a great idea, Beau," Dean said, a smug smile crossing his face. Christy narrowed her eyes at him and he winked at her. He would have loved to lean in and kiss the suspicion off her face but he had to restrain himself. *Friends. Didn't. Kiss.*

"Yeah, I can look out for her better that way." Beau nodded to himself and then all calm again, he went back out to bring in some more tools.

Christy faced Dean. "What are you up to?"

Dean tried for an innocent expression. "I'm just looking out for my baby sister, I want her to stay safe."

"Uh huh," she replied doubtfully.

"And they'll drive each other nuts which will be fun to watch." He grinned at her and she rolled her eyes and walked away, but not before he noticed the smile split her face.

But later that day, Dean was ready to lose his shit. Friendship with Christy was already proving to be very difficult. He didn't know how long he could last but he had to stick it out, for himself and for Taylor. Every time a job needed doing, Christy didn't ask Dean for his help or opinion, she only cared about Beau's, again!

"Beau, what do you think we should do about the porch railing?"

"Beau, what do you think we should do with that tree stump in the backyard?"

"Beau, would you like to go upstairs and have your wicked way with me?"

Okay, so she hadn't said the last one, but she might as well have. That's how they were acting and his jealousy was getting the better of him.

"Beau, do you think we should strip this old wallpaper off?" Christy put a hand on one hip and stared up at the walls in the living room. Dean turned to Beau, glaring at his friend once again as his input wasn't wanted or needed.

"Well, hon," Beau started, coming over and draping an arm around her dainty shoulders. It felt so wrong that it made Dean want to rip them apart.

"I think that's something the new owner can do, you don't need to worry about doing it," Beau smiled down at her and Dean muttered under his breath.

"I don't mind, I like doing it and I'm sure if the new owner knew I didn't mind and actually enjoyed it then they would be happy to let me get on with it?" she said meaningfully, Beau chuckled.

"Well, if you're sure, then I think that sounds like a good idea," he said, squeezing her into his chest.

As they broke apart, she peered up at Beau again. "What color do you think we should paint the walls?"

Dean stared back and forth between them, was he actually invisible? Enough was enough, dammit! He stepped forward.

"How about cream?" he asked through clenched teeth. Christy peered at him but didn't say anything and shifted her focus back to Beau. Beau looked over at him, smirking, like he knew exactly how much this was pissing Dean off and was loving every minute. Beau then made a huge drama over which color to pick, what would look better in daylight as opposed to night-time, what color would be better feng shui, really building up his part until finally ...

"I think cream is probably the best color for now, don't you?"

"Oh absolutely, great idea," she enthused, clapping happily. Dean threw up his arms in frustration and stormed off into the kitchen for some water and to calm the fuck down. Beau insisted on picking up the paint and as he was leaving, Dean heard him say, "I'm paying for the paint though."

Dean held his breath, smirking to himself, as he waited for Christy to start sputtering and refuse to let him pay, insisting she could afford it, like she did with Dean. But then she shocked the hell out of him by agreeing to let Beau pay. Dean's temper flared again, and he decided it was best he stay in the kitchen and have another go at fixing the stubborn garbage disposal. After a while of trying to bang his frustration away, he was getting nowhere except sweaty and angry, but for a different reason. He was ready to take a break when Christy came into the kitchen.

"Can you help me change the lightbulb in the living room?" she asked, opening the kitchen drawers and pulling out a pack of spares.

"Is Beau not around?" Dean asked petulantly.

"No, he went out to get the paint," she replied, not noticing his tone. "I can change a lightbulb myself, it's just the ceiling is really high and I'm not great on ladders. I think even if I did get on it, I might not reach. But I'll hold it steady for you, so you don't fall," she teased.

"More like tip it over with me on it," he joked.

She pretended to be hurt. "Maybe last week. Besides, I would find a much more inventive way of hurting you than a silly accident with a ladder."

"I don't doubt it," he replied, following her into the living room. The ladder was already out and in position. He made a show of checking it was locked correctly in case she had tampered with it and she giggled. He climbed halfway up the rungs and reached up to unscrew the old bulb while she held the ladder firm. He reached down to hand her the old one and get the new bulb off her, and tingles ignited where their fingers brushed against each other. He tried to ignore it and reached back up to screw the new one in, leaning his weight against the ladder, freeing both hands.

As he was doing it, he felt a warm breeze skate across his lower abdomen. He looked down and saw his shirt had ridden up, exposing some of the skin and a glimpse of his happy trail. The warm breeze he felt blowing over him was coming from Christy, and she was staring at the strip of his skin on display. Realizing it was her breath, the next time he felt it, goosebumps appeared on his skin, despite the heat.

He watched as she stared intently at his abdomen. Her breathing slightly unsteady, her eyes heating and she ran her tongue across her bottom lip, pulling it between her teeth. He felt his cock stirring in his pants, her face the perfect height to take him into her mouth. He nearly swayed off the ladder at the thought of her mouth there, he felt himself growing hard and knew he needed to distract them both before he did something stupid.

"Darlin'," he rasped, voice thick with desire. "I really need you to stop looking at me like that."

After a moment, she blinked hard and her cheeks flushed. "Sorry, my mind was on, uh, my new book that I'm due to start writing. I must have zoned out," she finished lamely.

"Glad I'm in safe hands then," he joked. He finished screwing in the bulb and got down as quickly as possible, trying to keep his pelvis turned away from her. They were saved any awkward moments by Beau coming back and distracting them with various paint tins.

*

Christy felt herself growing happier by the day. Not only was her confidence building, but she felt more and more like she had made peace with her father. She'd started to let go of everything that had happened and move on, since there was nothing she could do about it now. She spent so long letting it tear her up inside and she couldn't do this to herself anymore. Doing the house up had definitely helped. She found it therapeutic, tearing the old down and making it new again. It was like she was tearing away the bad memories and replacing them with new happy ones.

Her growing friendships with Beau and Dean were becoming really special to her. She loved their banter and relaxed nature, and they really cared for her too. Thinking about Dean still made her blush, but not in the embarrassed way of lusting after someone so far out of reach. Now it was the flush of constant arousal tainting her cheeks, a state she hadn't been able to shift since that day together in his office. The more time they spent together the more she realized he genuinely liked her, and wasn't that a boost for the old ego.

They'd discovered they had loads in common. They both loved soul music, scary movies, and reading. He promised to read her novels now he knew what she wrote, and she thought he would be great to bounce ideas off of. They talked about the crime documentaries they had watched, what they would do if they murdered someone, and how they would *totally* get away with it, which was starting to freak Beau out.

They had the same sense of humor and loved practical jokes. They had grown closer and sometimes she was convinced she could feel him watching her, but whenever her eyes sought him out, he was always looking away. She was confused about whether or not he desired her. Yes, they cleared the air and yes, they had the moment in his office, but he pushed her away and hadn't tried for anything but friendship since then.

However, yesterday when he was on the ladder she'd heard desire in his voice, had seen it etched across his face. He called her darlin' and though he tried to hide it, she saw evidence of his arousal. She knew enough about him at this point to know he was an honest person, and couldn't have been faking the times they were together. She didn't want to get involved with someone, but she felt drawn to him in a way she couldn't explain. She was so confused.

She tried to put it out of her mind as she began stripping the ancient wallpaper in the living room that had been on the walls so long, it refused to come off. She was having to use as much force as she could to chip away at it and it was taking so long she asked Dean and Beau to help her. But after ten minutes, Dean was red faced and sweating, then he cursed and stormed out of the house.

"What's the matter with him?" she asked Beau, wiping the sweat from her brow. Beau smirked at her and gestured towards her chest. She looked down and could see a rather large amount of cleavage on display and glistening from perspiration.

"Oh!" she cried, pulling her tank top up to stop her breasts from trying to escape any further. She realized Dean must have been getting an eyeful with all the jimmying and scraping she was doing. Beau chuckled and leered at her comically, she snorted and shoved him away but was secretly flattered at the attention. They did look great, she had to admit.

Dean returned to the house half an hour later with a new machine that steamed the wallpaper, loosening it, so it would peel off easily and they didn't have to scrape at it so much.

"But I like doing it this way!" Christy protested as Dean took her scraper away and shot her a dark look that resulted in heat spreading throughout her body, pooling between her legs.

"Trust me, darlin', it's better for both of us if we do it this way," he growled. "No. More. Jiggling."

They set about using the steamer despite the heat that plagued them from the soaring temperatures. Christy tried to watch Dean surreptitiously to see if he was noticing her, but he didn't look her way the rest of the day.

Chapter 15

Christy insisted they all meet at the bar to celebrate the work they had done that week. They had made some real headway with the house and she could see it starting to come together. Justine was going to be singing at the bar and it was the last night before Beau went away for two weeks. Christy knew he was tying up some business deal and he was going to clear his condo, getting it ready for the sale to close. She asked him when he was going to tell everyone he was buying the house but he still wanted to wait until it had all finalized, in case anything went wrong.

The four of them sat in a booth, Beau and Dean on one side, Justine and Christy opposite them. Taylor was working, but she managed to join the four of them, perching on the end, in between serving customers. They ate and laughed throughout the meal and Christy couldn't remember the last time she'd been this happy, surrounded by her friends, her true family. She couldn't help it, but she kept stealing glances across the table at Dean who was always ready to meet her gaze with his own and a shy smile. It suddenly hit her that Christy couldn't imagine going back to the city, back to her apartment and her life there. She shook away the feeling, she didn't need to worry about it just yet.

As they finished their meals, Justine stood up and announced, "I'm gonna go and set up, I start in a few minutes, and I want you all in the front row cheering me on."

"Yes, Ma'am," Beau mock saluted. Christy also stood up and grabbed her purse.

"I'm going to get another drink, do you both want a refill?" she asked, looking between the two men.

They both started to protest, but she shut them down. "Stop it! I can afford a couple of beers! You've earned them and saved me a fortune on manual labor," she said firmly, and stared them both down.

"Yes, thank you, same again," Beau said sheepishly, Christy turned her stern gaze on Dean, and he ducked his head and nodded reluctantly. She beamed at both of them and bounced away from the booth. Taylor smiled at her when she reached the bar and ordered the drinks.

"You look so happy, Marilyn. It's really wonderful to see," Taylor said, prepping Christy's cocktail.

Christy rolled her eyes at the nickname. "I feel happy, for the first time in so long, but please stop calling me that," she begged.

"But it's true." Taylor winked at her, and Christy huffed.

"I forget how that name started, was it you first or Justine?"

"Think it was me, but I heard it from, ah..." Taylor broke off abruptly and turned away to grab the beers for the guys.

"...I forget, Anyway is there anything in particular making you so happy?" Taylor continued, setting all three drinks down in front of Christy. Christy paid and shook her head picking up her drink and taking a sip. The fruity flavors tantalizing her tastebuds and the burn of vodka reminding her that it wasn't fruit juice.

"Romance can do that to a person," Taylor said slyly.

"Oh, no, me and Beau aren't seeing each other anymore," Christy replied, Taylor smiled at her gently.

"I meant you and Dean."

Christy felt herself flush with heat. "What? I don't know what you mean," she replied unconvincingly. Taylor rolled her eyes.

"Don't do that, not with me. I've seen the way you look at each other. But you need to know, he's looking for something serious. He wants to settle down and start a family. I know you're looking for a little distraction, which is great, but I don't want anyone getting hurt. I mean, you're not planning on staying, right?" Christy tried to ignore the hope in Taylor's last words.

"I'm not going to get hurt again," she replied, shaking her head. Taylor nodded and reached over and placed her hand on top of Christy's and gave it a tight, affectionate squeeze.

"I don't just mean you, babe," she replied, she squeezed her hand again and moved away to pick up the microphone. Christy peered over her shoulder towards the guys who looked like two mischievous teenagers. Beau's shoulders were shaking, his hand covering his mouth so stop from spitting beer out and Dean's head was thrown back in laughter. She wished it were quieter in the bar so she could hear the deep sound rumbling from him.

Taylor began to announce Justine's first song and Christy picked up her cocktail and the beers and saw the guys heading over to her. Beau took his beer, brushing her cheek with a kiss in thanks. She saw Dean frown at Beau before he took his beer from her and stared down at her, his eyes deep, intense, but full of mischief. As he smiled at her, Taylor's words started ringing in her ears and she had to remind herself, *friends only*.

They all headed over to the already packed dance floor for Justine's performance. Taylor and Christy shoving the two men forward into the front row of the crowd. Christy placed her drink on a table behind her and joined Taylor as Justine started her set with an upbeat song. The joyful music spurred the crowd on and they all danced, shimmied and laughed together.

Christy couldn't imagine all these strangers interacting in such a friendly way back in the city. Small-town life was definitely something special. Justine continued with the fast-paced songs, whipping them all into a frenzy that had the crowd shouting the lyrics back to her. The temperature in the room rose from all the energetic movement and eventually Beau begged for a break, and Taylor had to serve a couple of drinks to others who couldn't handle the heat.

Eventually, Justine took pity on the melting crowd and slowed the pace down. Christy watched as the remaining crowd began to pair off and fall into a slow dance. Feeling awkward, she turned to leave the dance floor, but a strong hand circled her wrist. Heat pressed against her back and a voice said softly in her ear,

"Where do you think you're going?" His breath trekked down the side of her neck. She shivered and turned to face him, feeling dwarfed by his height. His cheeks were flushed from the heat and his hair started to curl at the ends.

"You can't leave me here all alone," Dean said, pulling her to him. He wrapped his arms around her waist and she came up against his hot, hard body. Her heart pounding, she peered up at him through her lashes.

"Okay, just one dance though," she said, her voice husky at seeing the heat in his eyes. He nodded and they began to sway together as Justine launched into an acoustic, sultry cover of Simply Red's *It's Only Love*.

The meaning in the lyrics, the heat in the air and the feel of Dean's hard body pressed against hers, created a heady sensation. Her eyelids fluttered closed as she leaned her head against his broad chest. Dean settled his palm on the small of her back, his thumb dipping under the hem of her shirt and stroking across her heated skin, leaving a trail of goosebumps in its wake. He tightened his arm around her, and she sighed against his chest. She moved her arms up and circled his neck, listening to his heart thudding in his chest. As the music washed over them, the seductive words teased her ears. Dean's thumb continued its exploration and her body grew heavy with need.

He swayed them back and forth to the beat, their bodies falling into rhythm together and the world disappeared around them. She tried to fight it, knowing it was a mistake but she couldn't help her body's reaction. She felt herself growing desperate, the air surrounding them, thickening and after a moment, Dean dipped his head down to her ear.

"You drive me crazy," he whispered, his hot breath tickling her ear again. A soft moan escaped her and she pressed herself against him tighter, wishing they were alone. Dean placed the rest of his hand under her top and flattened his palm against her back, splaying his fingers and dabbling with her bra strap. So badly she wanted him to unhook her bra and move his hands round to cup her, stroking her nipples like he had before. She slid her hands up the back of his neck and into his hair, tugging the strands gently. He groaned and pressed his hips into her. She felt his arousal, hard, drawing another moan from her.

Suddenly, the sultry soundtrack stopped. Loud applause filled her ears and all that wonderful heat disappeared. She opened her eyes to find Dean stood a foot away from her, clapping along with the audience. She looked around, breathing heavily with awareness, the whole audience was cheering, none of them looking at her. Christy stood there a moment and then began clapping along in her dazed state, her mind elsewhere.

"I need some air," Dean rasped. He moved past her, not meeting her eyes. Christy was left on the dance floor alone, surrounded by the rest of the crowd. She looked around and saw Beau at the bar talking to a woman. Taylor stood at one end glaring down at him, but Dean was nowhere to be seen.

Did he go outside? Should she follow him? She didn't understand what just happened. He hadn't been a jerk like before, he just left without a backward glance. Did he not want to be around her after all? Before when this happened, they hadn't spoken about it. But things were different now, they had developed a friendship, which she didn't want to ruin. She wanted to make sure he was okay, so as Justine started a new song, Christy made her way towards the door in search of Dean.

*

Dean burst out of the bar, the humid air hitting him

like a wall, suffocating him, the scent from the pine trees invading his nose. He took deep breaths, trying to get enough oxygen into his lungs. He walked down the steps and around the side of the bar for some privacy while he tried to pull himself together.

Once again, he ignored his own rules, and Taylor's warning, and asked Christy to dance. Not an upbeat, friendly dance but a heated, sexy slow dance. What had he been thinking? He hadn't been, he just wanted her in his arms, wanted to bury himself deep inside her and stay there forever. The thought scared him as much as it aroused him. He leaned against the wall of the bar and sighed deeply.

Their dance started out innocent enough, his intentions had been pure. But as soon as her soft, curvy body came up against his, his intentions changed to...impure. It turned passionate and seductive with the music, the way her hips swayed to the beat, brushing against him with each movement. It had taken all his willpower not to drag her away and fuck her right then. She made him feel aggressive with need, primitive, stripped down to raw, animalistic base instinct of want and need. He pictured her hot little body rubbing against him, her sharp inhalations and moans in his ears. He gripped his erection through his jeans and squeezed hard, needing relief.

He needed to get out of here, to go home and take a long, cold shower. He pushed himself away from the wall and dug in his pocket for the keys to his truck. He was fine to drive, he only had one beer and hadn't yet drunk the one Christy had gotten him, guilt flaring at the waste of her precious money. He started to walk away but stopped when he heard footsteps.

"Dean?" Christy called, his heart pounded. He

couldn't see her when he was like this, he was too worked up and he would only do something he'd regret. He flattened himself against the wall of the bar and stayed quiet, waiting.

"Dean, are you out here?" she called again. He held his breath, hoping she would leave, her footsteps sounding fainter as she moved away.

"I know you're still here; I can see your truck," she called, sounding worried. He stayed still and quiet, and after a while he couldn't hear anything and thought she'd left. He let out the breath he had been holding.

"Dean? Were you hiding from me?" He jumped as her voice sounded right next to him. He turned and she stood in front of him. She had come around the other side of the building and doubled back, he sighed and saw a flash of hurt cross her face.

"Hey, Christy. Sorry, I just needed some air, that's all," he said. She took a step forward, the moonlight shining down on her face, her cheeks were flushed, her eyes glittering.

"Did I do something wrong?" she frowned; he shook his head.

"No, darlin'. I just needed a minute," he rasped. He could see her chest rising and falling, her skin shimmering like a pearl in the moonlight. He watched as she swiped her tongue over her bottom lip and he fought back a moan, fisting his hands to keep from reaching for her.

"Then what is it?" she asked, stepping towards him and he took a step back. Worried that if she got too close, he would grab hold of her and not let go until they were both satisfied. She looked confused and reached out to him.

"Don't touch me right now, darlin', I'm begging you."

"But, why, what's going on?" she cried. He made a

move to go back to the bar, back to being around other people, feeling it was the safest option.

"Dean! We're friends, you can talk to me, what's wrong?" she called after him, and he caved. He turned angrily and stalked back to her, grabbing her by the arms and shoving her roughly against the wall of the bar, pinning her with his pelvis. He meant to scare her a little, to make her leave him alone and then he would apologize later when he was under control. But as he pressed his arousal into her, he saw her eyes flare with heat, and she looked anything but scared.

"That's what's wrong, darlin', you wanted to know, now you know," he growled, and pushed himself away from her.

She was silent as she stared at him. "Did I do that to you?" she asked tentatively. The hope in her voice made his cock pulse hard in his jeans. He gave her a sharp nod, not trusting himself to speak.

She nibbled her plump bottom lip nervously. "The boner killer?" Her words weren't angry, just inquisitive. He felt pain lance through him at the memory of his stupid, hurtful, and ridiculously untrue words.

"You know I didn't mean it," he said fiercely. He apologized so many times, but he would keep apologizing until the day he died if that's what she needed. She nodded slowly and relief coursed through him.

"Do you want me to do something about it?"

His heart thudded in his chest as her words registered. She was offering the release he so desperately needed, the release he was craving. He closed his eyes as he fought against the tide of passion fizzing through his veins. He needed to get out of here, Taylor's words playing through his mind, he needed to leave Christy alone, now. He tried to step around her, but she moved to block his way, dammit why was she doing this to him? If he couldn't do this nicely it was time she met Mr. Bad Guy. He shoved her against the wall of the bar again, baring his teeth at her, menace layering his expression. He buried his face in her neck, inhaling deeply, licking a path from her neck to her ear lobe.

"Do you want to be fucked, Christy?" he rumbled, threat coating his words. She surprised him again though and instead of shoving him away in disgust she gripped his shoulders tight and gasped. He couldn't move, couldn't look at her, scared to see the arousal that was surely on her face. Scared she would want this as much as he did and scared because if she did, there was no way in hell he could hold back. Her grip loosened on his shoulders and she pushed him back slightly. He finally stared down into her eyes, the luminous pools clashing defiantly with his.

"Do you?" she demanded softly. He choked on the air leaving his lungs. She turned the tables on him, shocking him again. He couldn't move as he stared at her, like he was seeing her for the first time. Truly seeing her. He should've known she would be a vixen, should never have tried to play this game with her, he was out of his depth. He should have gone straight home, but as he stared down, their eyes holding each other, he realized she was dropping down to her knees. *Holy shit was she going to…he* thought he was going to explode just at the thought. No way could he let her do this. Dean opened his mouth to tell her to stop, feeling ashamed of himself and his behavior, but she rubbed her hand firmly over his aching length and his eyes rolled back into his head.

He was weak, he admitted it. She rubbed her hand over him a few more times, and he watched her, his breath sawing in and out of his lungs. She unzipped his jeans and reached inside, gripping him in her hot palm. Grasping the hot, hard length of his cock and pulling it free from his pants. He looked down at her, the seductive angel, on her knees, ready to take him into her mouth, his greatest fantasy. But, he still had some decency left. He gritted his teeth as her warm breath caressed over him.

"Christy, you don't have to do that," he huffed out, starting to pull away from her but she tightened her grip, stopping him from moving. She looked up at him, moonlight and arousal glowing in her eyes. She gripped the base tightly and she flicked her tongue over the head of his cock, watching him the whole time.

"Oh, shit…" he cursed, swaying slightly on his feet from the pleasure, not breaking eye contact with her as if his life depended on it. Watching her, watching him as she sucked his cock into her mouth was the sexiest thing he'd ever seen. He thought he was going to lose it, and he braced himself against the wall as she sucked him again.

"I don't think I'm going to last very long," he grunted out as she hollowed her cheeks. *Holy fuck, any second now.*

"Be still my beating heart," she replied dryly, chuckling as she swirled her tongue over his swollen head, taking a drop of his desire. He would have laughed at her sassiness, but he was too far gone. She sucked him into her warm, wet mouth, and his hand tunneled into her hair, cupping the back of her neck as gently as he could. She took him all the way in, down to the base and moaned deeply, the vibrations dancing along his cock making him sway forward and thrust into her mouth.

"Sorry, sorry," he mumbled, dazed. He braced himself against the wall again as she sucked him to the tip and back down again, increasing the speed. She used her hand to work him while she focused on the tip, tongue swirling, mouth sucking. The hot, wet pull making him see stars and panting as he tried his hardest not to thrust his hips. She continued to moan, the vibrations teasing him, and he thought he saw movement below him. He pulled back and looked down at her.

"Are you…touching yourself?" he choked out. She released his cock, the warm evening air tingling him. She nodded, and he saw her hand moving under her skirt.

"Show me," he commanded, her eyes flashed at him in the moonlight. She lifted her skirt up, her panties pushed to one side, and he watched her fingers dip in and out of her heat. The sound of her fingers disappearing into her wet channel brought a fresh wave of arousal and a bead of desire formed at the tip of him. He watched as she leaned forward and licked it off, he cupped the back of her head and on a moan, pushed his cock back into her mouth, she continued sucking him while working herself. Her lips tightened over him, creating a delicious, tight friction, and he couldn't help but start thrusting into her mouth. He thrust faster, clumsy in his passion and mumbling apologies. She worked herself harder, then reached up to cup his sac and he felt his release boil up. They locked eyes and she cried out around his cock, jerking as her orgasm hit. Then she hollowed her cheeks as he thrust once, twice, and threw his head back groaning as he started to come.

When he finished, he stood there, panting hard, unable to catch his breath. His whole body on fire and humming from satisfaction. He could hear her heavy breathing and looked down at her. He tucked himself back into his jeans and pulled her to her feet, a slow smile spread across her face. He placed a soft kiss across her swollen lips. Then brought her hand to his mouth, two fingers still wet from her pussy. He licked each one clean, tasting her, his shaft growing hard all over again, he should've known one orgasm wouldn't be enough. She sighed and leaned into him.

"Dean," she whispered as he pulled her into his arms and kissed his way down her damp neck and then cupped her full breasts, swiping his thumbs across her hard nipples.

"Dean, I need..." she broke off moaning, he licked the shell of her ear and nibbled the lobe.

"What do you need, darlin'?" he asked huskily, running his hand along the outside of her thigh. But before he could reach his new number one place to explore, he heard the sound of glasses smashing and loud shouts coming from inside the bar. Dean and Christy pulled apart, looking alarmed.

"Taylor!" Christy cried, and they both ran out from behind the bar, around to the entrance in time to see Beau come barreling out the door, dragging another man with him. Beau had one of the guys arms up behind his back to stop him from nailing Beau.

"You fucking bitch, Taylor!" the man screamed, enraged. "I'll fucking get you, just wait!"

"Call Blake, now!" Christy shouted as Taylor appeared behind Beau, looking pale and shaken. Beau shoved the guy to the ground and Dean ran over to help Beau flip him onto his front. The guy tried to get up, but Beau placed a knee in the small of his back, Dean squatted down to face the guy.

"I suggest you stay put if you know what's good for you," he said, a lethal edge in his voice. The playful arousal he and Christy had just shared was gone. They guarded the man that Dean assumed was her ex-boyfriend, Dale, until Blake arrived and Christy and Justine comforted a shaken Taylor. Blake spoke to Dean and Beau and cuffed Dale, who was still protesting when

Blake shoved him into the back of his cruiser. He came back to question Taylor and Beau tried to put his arm around her, but she shrugged him off.

"What happened, Taylor?" Blake asked, taking out his notebook.

"He turned up, drunk as usual, and started saying shit. He knocked over some glasses when the *bouncer* over here escorted him out," she said sarcastically, jerking her thumb at Beau.

"Cut the crap for once in your life, Taylor!" Beau snapped at her. She turned her blistering stare on him and he stared right back, angry sparks crackling between them. Blake asked a few more questions and spoke to a few people in the crowd before getting ready to leave.

"I'll hold him for tonight until he sobers up, unless you wanna press any charges?" Blake asked Taylor. Taylor shook her head and Beau turned away in frustration, kicking up dirt from the ground. Dean watched as Beau tried to get his temper under control, grateful his friend had been there and protected his sister. *Protecting her like you should have been.* He should have been watching out for Taylor, that's what big brothers did, not seducing the friend she'd told him to stay away from.

He was ashamed of himself. Family was the most important thing to him, and he turned his back on the one person who had needed him most. He felt a hand touch his back and looked down to see Christy peering up at him, concern in those wide, beautiful eyes. He moved away from her before he acted on the impulse to pull her into his arms.

"Can you stay with anyone tonight, Taylor?" Blake asked, and both Beau and Dean offered.

"I'll be fine," Taylor insisted, and Beau cursed.

"Beau, can you drop Justine and Christy home, I'll stay

here tonight," Dean said firmly, Beau nodded. Taylor tried to argue, but Dean shut her down. Satisfied with the outcome, Blake left with the promise to follow up with Taylor in the morning. The women grabbed their stuff and Taylor went back into the bar and began to sweep up the broken glass. Dean clapped Beau on the back.

"Thanks, man. Appreciate you being there, it should have been me," Dean said angrily.

"It's cool, dude. Don't beat yourself up over it," Beau replied. Dean watched as Christy said goodbye to Taylor and came over to them, but he moved away and went to help Taylor, not wanting to speak to Christy yet. It wasn't her fault, but he felt guilty about what they did when he should have been looking out for Taylor.

Beau took them home and came back to help clean up, but he and Taylor didn't speak to each other once. She didn't even thank him for helping clean up and then Beau left, saying he would be back from L.A. in two weeks.

Dean and Taylor came to an agreement that he would stay in her cabin tonight, but she didn't want him guarding her. He would do a drive by each night as she locked up to make sure she got back to her cabin and locked herself in. That way he got to make sure she was fine, but she kept her freedom. He lay on the couch in her living room that night and fell into a fitful sleep where his encounter with Christy was replayed from every wonderful angle, in high definition, over and over again until he woke up early, covered in sweat and aching for her all over again.

Chapter 16

Dean turned up ready to get to work on the house the next morning and once again Christy felt sick with nerves at the thought of seeing him. All night she lay in bed, tossing, turning, and getting tangled in the sheets thinking about what they did and how much more she wanted to do. She couldn't believe it happened, couldn't believe she brought him so much pleasure, and she couldn't believe she touched herself in front of him. She had never been that bold before. The thought of it scandalized her even now, no matter how much he seemed to enjoy it. If things hadn't gone sideways inside the bar with Dale, they would have had sex right outside, that's how crazy he made her feel.

But then he dismissed her in all the craziness that followed. She knew he was upset and worried about

Taylor and she tried to show comfort, but he walked away from her and hadn't spoken to her since. She knew he regretted what happened, his actions afterwards all the explanation she needed. Taylor's words from the night before kept playing through her head, she should have stayed away from him, should have known better but she was drawn to him. And Dean wasn't in danger of getting hurt when he was the one pushing her away. She stood at the window, coffee mug clasped tightly between her hands watching him walk up the path. She knew what she needed to do to save face and get their friendship back on track. And she had to do it before he did.

As she watched him, time seemed to slow, like it usually did whenever he came towards her, his long, lean legs eating up the distance to the house. Face tilted towards the sun, letting the rays caress those glorious features, catching the golden highlights in his hair. Weren't devils usually disguised as angels?

"Perfection," she murmured to herself, shivering slightly and turned to face the door as he came inside, he didn't bother to knock anymore.

"Hey," she called as he closed the door behind him.

"Morning, Christy," he replied, setting his toolbox on the floor. She felt a twinge of disappointment when he didn't call her darlin'. A term of endearment she would have turned her nose up at if anyone else had said it. But when he did it, his deep, southern accent rolling the syllables around, soaking them in molasses before letting them slide off his tongue, it warmed her heart. Her disappointment made her more confident that she was doing the right thing, to save herself.

"About last night-" he began, but she cut him off with a casual wave of her hand.

"A mistake obviously. We clearly had way too much to

drink and the music and closeness, et cetera…" she trailed off as if that explained everything. He pinned her with a hard stare, and she struggled to keep the nonchalant expression on her face. Her heart started pounding at all his intensity focused directly on her.

"You think it was a mistake?" he asked, she nodded vigorously.

"Yep, sure do. I mean, don't you?" she asked, her voice dipping slightly with her confidence. He just continued to stare at her and then after a beat, slowly nodded in agreement.

"Glad we cleared that up then," he said tightly, and she headed into the kitchen to make him a coffee. Luckily, he didn't follow her. She wanted to put as much distance between them as possible, otherwise he would definitely sniff out her bullshit. What she actually wanted was for him to take her into his arms and tell her that it wasn't a mistake, that *she* wasn't a mistake, and that it was the best damn decision he ever made, but it didn't happen. Wait, did she even want that? She wasn't hanging around for much longer, it was different when she thought she could have a casual fling with Beau. But this thing with Dean, it felt too intense. She didn't have much experience with men, but she knew last night wasn't enough. She had a taste and became addicted instantly, now she had to go cold turkey.

She poured his coffee adding cream and two sugars, just how he liked it and took it back to him. He was looking out the front window at the porch when she reached him. He took the drink from her, their fingers touching briefly which sent little tingles shooting up her arm.

"So, where do you want me?" he asked, his eyes darkening to a stormy blue and running over her, leaving even more tingles in their wake.

"Um, outside?" she asked, slightly breathlessly, "I'll finish stripping the walls if you want to tackle the porch?"

She watched him take a sip of coffee and close his eyes at the taste, his Adam's apple bobbing as he swallowed, and she felt thirsty herself. She turned away sharply and eyed the steamer he bought for stripping the wallpaper.

"No problem, boss," he replied, and headed back outside, the front door banging slightly. He was gone but his pine and wood scent lingered, taunting her.

He was probably grumpy because she pricked his pride, she technically got in there first to "end" whatever it was they were doing. She was sure he would be over it in a few hours, he didn't really care. It wasn't like he hadn't been with loads of other women more beautiful than...

"No!" she scolded herself. "You are beautiful and deserve just as much in life as anyone else." She felt herself relax and she finished her coffee, putting her empty mug in the kitchen sink. She glanced at the garbage disposal and flicked the switch, still nothing happened. She sighed and went back into the living room and surveyed the walls.

Out the corner of her eye, she could see Dean through the window, walking along the porch. She turned her head to watch him discreetly, his brow creased in concentration, shoulders bunched, tensing the developed muscles. She turned away before he caught her staring, and she undid all her work to appear blasé just now.

She ignored the wallpaper steamer Dean had bought. It definitely made it easier to get the old paper off, but it generated so much heat. It was already hot enough without adding to the temperature. She picked up the scraper she used previously and began to hack away at the walls, pouring every frustration into them. She stripped the walls for the next hour, putting on music to drown out her thoughts and forcing herself to dance, ignoring any movement from outside until she felt herself being watched.

She turned and saw Dean stood at the open window, looking in. He had removed his shirt in the heat and had his arms folded across his powerful chest, biceps flexed, and expression unreadable as he stared at her. She stopped mid-scrape, her eyes gobbling up the spectacular display. Her stomach clenched at the sight of those strong arms. She could picture herself laying naked beneath him, open and begging, clinging on tight to those biceps as he pounded into her.

As if he could read her mind and the direction of her thoughts, she watched as he unfolded his arms and placed his hands on his narrow hips. A bead of sweat gleamed in the sunshine, she tracked its slow journey between his pecs, dripping down the middle of his six-pack, and ending at the trail of blond hair that led down to what she was dying to get her hands on again. Her brow furrowed slightly, despite the two sexual encounters they had, sexual, not *intimate*, she reminded herself, she hadn't actually seen him naked, or even shirtless, until now. While previously she was on full, naked, fantastic display, it wasn't fair.

His pecs jumped impatiently, demanding her attention back on his chest. She noticed a light smattering of blond hair dusted across the middle, ending before it reached his small, brown nipples, which were puckered and practically begging for her tongue. He smirked at her through the window, *damn him!* She wasn't doing very well at pretending she didn't want him, was she?

"Looks good," he said nodding to the wall, she turned

her back on him before she started drooling.

"Yep, it sure does," she muttered, her tongue heavy in her mouth.

The following week was hell for Christy, the weather was getting hotter by the day and so was Dean. He turned up every morning to work on the house and whenever she saw him, she was both annoyed and ecstatic.

Annoyed because he managed to start the day fully clothed, then around midmorning his shirt always seemed to disappear and she was stuck staring at the tan, toned wall of solid muscle for the rest of the afternoon. She was sure he was trying to rile her up on purpose, everywhere she went he was always there, always shirtless and always smiling at her like the cat that got the fucking cream. He always touched himself somewhere, drawing attention to his chest, and whenever he caught her staring there was a flicker of triumph in those captivating eyes.

She was also ecstatic because, well, she loved having him around. Loved feeling his warm, masculine presence around the house, loved hearing him singing along to the radio, poorly. She enjoyed watching the way his brain worked, choosing the most practical way of getting a job done, but he didn't take short cuts. He took pride in his work and he worked hard, which was damn sexy.

As much as she loved him being here, she asked for him to take a day off, which worked out well because he was needed at the garage. She often heard him talking to his staff on the phone, he was great with them, understanding but firm when needed. He had a fantastic business mind, an unwavering faith in his employee's abilities, and it sounded like he had their respect in return.

In short, he was the whole package, goddamn perfect from head to toe and didn't that just piss her off. She was secretly relieved when they had a day apart because it meant her body could have a day off from being a throbbing, sweaty, aroused mess. It was nice. She went for a walk in the forest nearby and then she went to the bar to see Taylor and try to do some writing, needing to destroy her writer's block, but no ideas came to her. When she did finally break it, she would want to be shut away in a room to write, but by then she would have likely left town, the thought leaving a hollow feeling in her chest.

Today Dean was back, and he turned up looking sexier than ever. So obviously she had been pretty snappy with him all morning. She chalked it down to sexual frustration, but if he noticed he hadn't said a word about her mood. She went out to meet Justine for lunch, she felt bad leaving him in the house working while she socialized. He insisted it was fine, but her guilt at leaving him forced her to stop by Ruby's Diner on the way home and bring him back a burger and fries.

As she walked up the path to the house, she steeled herself against the wave of arousal that would surely plague her all afternoon. Life wasn't fair. Why couldn't she have her cake and eat him it too? She just hoped he wasn't shirtless again.

She came up the porch steps, admiring the work he'd done on it as she went. He really was great with his hands, no pun intended. She felt a sense of pride, seeing the house change and knowing that Dean, Beau, and herself had all left their mark on it.

Christy dumped her purse and keys on the coffee table in the living room and looked around. She felt a prickle of unease as she realized, they had done so much and potentially finished fixing up the downstairs already.

"Dean?" she called out.

"In here!" His reply came from the kitchen, she

headed to the door with his lunch, but she stopped dead in the doorway. He was shirtless, again, and hunched over the garbage disposal, *his nemesis*. The muscles of his back rippled with his movements, and his dipped jeans low enough that she could see the two dimples at the base of his spine. Her eyes were drawn to the valley between his shoulder blades. How she longed to wrap her arms around him from behind and rest her head against him. She shook her head; *friends didn't do that*. But they also didn't do a lot of things that she and Dean had done.

"I think I've done it!" he said triumphantly, jerking her out of her daydream. He reached over and flicked the switch with one hand. The garbage disposal roared to life, but the triumph was short lived. Dean bellowed out in pain and lurched forward as the garbage disposal made a horrible crunching sound, followed by a wet slurping noise.

"Oh my God!" she screamed, dropping his lunch and running over to him, trampling the bag as she went. She grabbed onto his shoulders and pulled him backwards as hard as she could, but he didn't budge.

"Help me, my hand!" he wailed as she kept pulling on him. *Oh my God, oh my God, oh my God, his hand! What if he loses his hand? It'll be all my fault!* Dean began shaking, no longer shouting, and she thought he was going weak from blood loss. But then the garbage disposal switched off and she could hear him laughing. She pulled away from him and looked over his shoulder but couldn't see any blood, confusion consuming her. Her confusion quickly gave way to anger as she saw no blood, bone, or flesh and noticed Dean was smothering his laughter with two perfect hands.

"Was that supposed to be funny?" she asked, her tone deadly calm as her panic and fear ebbed away.

"Um, kinda?" he asked, injecting enough boyish charm into his voice before bursting out laughing all over again. She turned on her heel and walked away, eyeing the lunch she bought him, trampled into the floor. She picked it up and stormed back to him, thrusting the bag at him, smearing it into his perfect, bare chest. Before stomping out of the room and upstairs without another word.

Chapter 17

Dean was in the doghouse, big time. But he would still do it again, he knew she loved pranks, so he thought it would be funny, which it definitely was. The look on her face had been priceless and he chuckled to himself again as he ate the smushed food she brought him. She would calm down eventually and forgive him. He grabbed a Coke from the fridge. He started leaving drinks and a snack or two around the house as he was there for so long each day, he needed his treats.

He could hear her stomping around upstairs and smiled to himself as he sipped the cold drink. He kind of liked it when she was mad, he would have enjoyed trying to coax her out of it with kisses or more, but she put a stop to any of that activity. He wanted to apologize for his behavior that night at the bar when everything went nuts, he hadn't meant to push her away again. But it stuck in his craw that she said what had happened was a mistake. Well it was the best damn mistake he ever made. One he wanted to make again and again. He went along with it to keep spending time with her. Probably a mistake on his part because all this time together only highlighted how much he wanted her.

He tried to deny it, and even though he loved Taylor and didn't want to upset her, his blood pounded for Christy, he needed her. Christy would likely leave in a few weeks anyway, his stomach clenching at the thought, so why couldn't they enjoy the time she had left? He had gone back and forth over it in his mind and decided he would rather have her for a little while than not at all. No one needed to get hurt, they were both adult enough to make their own decisions.

First, he needed to lower her guard, he figured she found him attractive otherwise she wouldn't have been intimate with him, especially not more than once. But he needed her willing and maybe even a little bit desperate for him. He'd spent so much time without a shirt on that he might as well have been modeling for a calendar. It was definitely working though, every time she came into a room, he could feel her eyes stroking over him, the intensity of her stare riling him up like nothing else. So many times, he nearly caved and reached for her only for her to move away from him. Granted his little stunt today had probably put him back a few steps, but he couldn't resist it.

He finished his lunch and tidied up the kitchen, putting away his tools, glaring at the garbage disposal, willing it never ever to break again. He went outside to make a few calls, needing to check in with his employees today. He looked up at the sky, which was fast darkening over, black clouds rolling in, turning the air thick and heavy, practically crackling with electricity.

"Storm's coming," he muttered to himself as he held his cell to his ear, waiting for the garage to answer. Took him an hour to get through his calls. He rang around all the garages he had, checking in with each manager, making sure there weren't any issues. He couldn't always be around in person in some of the locations, so he usually called every couple of days for an update. He loved being his own boss, he'd definitely paid his dues over the years and had gotten lucky with his investments, which was paying off more than ever as he was able to spend this time with Christy.

He saw a message come through from Darcy asking to go on another date. He had forgotten all about her, he had zero interest in being with her. He hoped that from his silence she would get the hint, but apparently not. He replied and let her down gently, telling her he met someone else, which was kind of true.

As he came back into the house, admiring his handiwork on the porch, he saw Christy standing in the living room and his heart stuttered in his chest. She was wearing a white t-shirt and short denim overalls, her hair kept off her face by a red bandana. She looked like a sexy 1950's pin up. *Marilyn eat your heart out,* he thought. The nickname he gave her all those years ago definitely more apt now.

"What're you doing?" he asked. She glanced sideways at him, but didn't face him.

"Getting ready to paint," she said firmly. He tried not to smile as he realized she was still in a snit, perfect.

"Great, I'll help," he said cheerily.

"No, it's fine I-" she started, but he interrupted.

"Please, I love painting."

She sighed, realizing it was pointless to fight him on this. They spent the next hour putting sheets down to protect the wooden floors, taping up any electrical sockets, stirring and distributing the paint. Then they had to pick the music which was pretty easy as they liked the same thing, Dean chose to start with Marvin Gaye. As they worked it started to rain, softly at first, but then it became darker outside, the air heavier and the raindrops fell fatter and faster.

"Looks like we're in for a big storm," he said conversationally. She turned to look out the window, and he could see she had an adorable paint smudge on her cheek.

"We've needed it, it's been too hot and humid around here."

Although she matched his conversational tone, the sparkle in her eyes made him wonder if her words had a different meaning. Before he could push her on it, she turned back to the section she was painting. As the storm continued to build outside, the day turned to night and Marvin Gaye gave way to Aretha Franklin.

Out the corner of his eye, Dean kept seeing Christy wiggle her hips in time to the music when she thought he wasn't looking. All her wiggling must have made her hot as she unsnapped the fastenings on her overalls and let them fall to her waist. He had to look away as he realized he could see her pink bra under the thin white t-shirt she was wearing, and he was suddenly dying to know if it was the same shade of pink as her lipstick.

Dean heard a rumble of thunder rolling in over the music, and the room flashed as lightning lit up the dark sky. Christy jumped next to him but tried to cover it up by pretending she was just dancing. He noticed her looking out the window every now and then, concern furrowing her brow.

"Everything okay?" he asked. She didn't speak, just nodded, and went back to painting but she no longer wiggled her hips. The thunder became louder and more frequent, and Christy began humming loudly as if trying to distract herself. When an extremely loud crack of thunder shook the house, she yelped and jumped, sloshing paint onto the drop sheets.

He sighed. "Why didn't you just say you're afraid of storms?" he asked.

"Because I'm not," she answered, too quickly, nibbling nervously on her bottom lip.

"Yeah you are," he teased, trying to take her mind off it. His experience of storms around here told him this was going to be a long one. She got this haughty look on her face and put her hand on her hip.

"No, I'm not," she huffed.

"You so are," he taunted, and she pursed her lips and stomped her foot.

"I am not, Dean!" she cried, and gestured angrily at him with her paintbrush, which sent a spray of paint splashing over his bare torso. He glanced down at his chest and then back to Christy, arching an eyebrow at her.

"Did you just throw paint on me?" he asked, trying to inject some menace into his voice.

She smothered a laugh. "Well, it was an accident and you wouldn't list-" she started, but he lunged for her and she squealed when he dabbed his brush on her face and neck. Her feet got tangled in the sheet and she began to fall backwards. He grabbed her around the waist, dropping his paintbrush and twisted them so she fell on top of him, his back taking the brunt of the fall.

In his chivalrous efforts to try and stop her from being injured, he realized he inadvertently gave her the upper hand in their paint war as he was now weapon-less and at her mercy. He saw the look of calculation cross her face as she realized the same thing and began dabbing her paintbrush all over his bare chest, stomach, and sides mercilessly. He grabbed her hands and pinned them to his chest. He looked up at her as she lay above him, panting from her efforts, grinning like a maniac and it struck him hard in his chest. She was the most beautiful woman he had ever known, and he didn't think he could resist her anymore.

She must have noticed the expression on his face change as her smile started to fade and she tried to move off him. Just then a booming crack of thunder made them both jump and she dropped back down onto him. The room was illuminated by a bolt of lightning, and as the house plunged into darkness, the music stopped.

"Well, I guess that's the power gone," he said softly in the dark. After a beat, he felt Christy move off him and then a thud followed by a muttered curse and then silence.

"Have you got any candles?" he asked.

"I don't think so," she replied, the sound of her voice coming from the kitchen. He got to his feet, side stepping the paint pots he knew were on the floor. He could hear her rummaging in drawers in the kitchen and shuffling around.

"I can't find any, what do we do?" she asked.

"Well, we could go to mine. I've got candles, a fire, and some food too. I can at least make us some sandwiches for dinner." His heart pounded in his chest at his suggestion. He *never* invited women back to his house. It was meant to be his sanctuary that he didn't parade women through, but recently he had been getting the feeling that he wouldn't mind Christy being there.

"Do you only think about food?" she joked, trying to cover up her worry, she sounded closer.

"No, darlin', I think about a lot of other things," he said, his meaning clear.

"Oh," she said quietly. "Well don't worry about me, I'll just stay here tonight," she added. A flash of lightning lit up the room, showing that she was standing by the front door.

"Really? By yourself all night in the storm with nothing to do or eat? That sounds fun," he replied sarcastically.

She sighed. "Fine, but let's go now then, quickly before it thunders again!" She threw open the front door, the sound of the rain deafening, and she ran outside.

"Wait! I need my keys first!" he called after her, but his voice was drowned out by the pelting rain and thunder. He felt his way to the kitchen as quickly as he could, and then fumbled along the worktops in the darkness for his keys. Once he grabbed them and found a second set which were hers, he stumbled back out to the open front door and outside, closing the door behind him and locking it.

The rain was hammering down, he could barely see in front of his face. He ran down the steps and in the direction of his truck. The ice-cold rain slashing his bare chest, which served him right for not wearing a shirt, again. He saw her waiting by his truck, her arms huddled around her, she looked soaked already. He ran over to her side and unlocked the door before running around to his side and getting in.

He turned the key in the ignition and the truck roared to life. He flicked his high beams on, and the bright lights lit up the road in front of them and the cabin of the truck brightened. He turned to face Christy and saw her blond hair dripping down her face, her t-shirt was so wet it was completely see-through and plastered to her chest. The sight of her damp breasts moving up and down with her breaths had his mouth running dry. Her eyes were flashing angrily, and he grinned at her, switching on the heating in the truck.

"I did tell you to wait," he started, but she interrupted him with a terse, "Just drive."

The journey to his house was, in a word, fraught. At one point his windscreen wipers were on the fastest setting and he still couldn't see the road through the rain. He also couldn't see the large puddles that formed in the road and a few times he swerved to miss a big one, making Christy yelp and grab hold of him, which he couldn't deny he enjoyed. As another tidal wave enveloped the truck, she plastered herself to his side.

"This was the stupidest idea you've ever had," she muttered, and he smiled at the slight tremor of fear in her voice.

"Come on now, darlin', you can't know that for sure," he joked.

"And you can drop the *"aw, shucks"* routine, cause I ain't buying it!" she snapped, then tightened her grip on his arm as a huge rumble of thunder shook the truck.

"We'll be fine, darlin', just trust me," he replied. After a few more minutes of driving in the worst conditions he ever experienced, he saw the turn for the road to his house, and moments later he pulled into the wide driveway and killed the engine. The lights turned off with the engine and plunged them into darkness.

"We're here," he said, stomach clenching in anticipation, he turned to look down at her. She was closer to him than he thought, her berry and candy floss scent filling his nostrils, driving him wild as her breasts plastered to him. His need for her and anxiety over showing her his home gave him an idea.

"Uh, it's a bit of a trek to the house. The ground will be solid mud so I can't get the truck close enough. Might be best to wait here for a little bit to see if the rain eases off." He felt her nod next to him, and a little thrill ran through him.

"Yes, at least it's warm in here," she replied.

"Exactly. Well, we best get comfortable then if we're going to be here for a while," he said, and reached down for the lever to adjust his seat. It slid back and he wrapped his arm around her waist and pulled her onto his lap, so she straddled his thighs.

"What are you doing?" she asked, placing her hands on his paint splattered chest to steady herself. He reached up and brushed her damp hair behind her ear, cupping her cheek and stroking his thumb across her soft skin, he heard her breath shudder.

"Giving us what we both want, no matter how much you're trying to fight it," he said fiercely.

"Dean, wait," she said, nibbling her lip and looking away. Resolve filled her eyes when they met his again. "If we do this, it's just once, purely casual. Only for tonight."

Their lips were a breath apart, air sawing in and out of them as he processed her words before deciding that having her once was better than not at all. He nodded and then pulled her down for a brutal kiss. He wrapped his arms around her and pulled her flush against him. His tongue pressing in and stroking against hers, passion burning. The days of hot tension and need boiling up inside him and igniting.

The kiss was electric, they both fought for dominance, teeth banging, tongues stroking. It wasn't enough, he would never get enough of her. He needed her body, needed to be inside her with an intensity that excited and terrified him. She pressed her damp, t-shirt covered breasts against his chest and rubbed her lower body against his hard cock. He swallowed her moans and tried to get himself under control, she was in danger of getting him so worked up that this could be over very quickly, *again*, and he couldn't have that if it was just one time with her.

He pulled back and looked up at her, the moonlight shining through the clouds, casting a glow around her. She was a goddess; plump lips swollen from his kiss, eyes hooded in arousal, cheeks flushed, and chest heaving with her breaths. She continued to stare down at him, light blue eyes shining with a sly look. She began a slow roll of her hips, rubbing herself up and down his shaft. His breath stuttered out of him at the intensity of their eye contact as she moved her body, he gripped her hips tightly, fingers digging in. God, she was killing him.

She worked herself over him, her eyelids dipping. He gripped her tightly, stopping her and then released her hips. He ran his hands up her tiny waist, then up over the front of her breasts, her hard nipples abrading his palms, he took a moment to brush the tips with his thumbs. The action had her eyes fluttering in pleasure and her head lolled back. He left her breasts to pull her damp t-shirt over her head and drop it in a wet heap on the floor of the truck. Her bra, which turned out was the same shade as her lipstick, followed her t-shirt.

He stared at the heavy weight of her breasts. Creamy, round, and perfectly tipped with those frozen berry nipples, reaching for him. He watched entranced as every inhale lifted them closer to him before they dipped away with each exhale, teasing him. When she couldn't take anymore she reached out and pulled his head to them, and his tongue flicked out to circle one of the demanding tips. She cried out and bucked against him as he whipped his tongue back and forth while his other hand reached up to pluck its twin. She pressed her breast harder into his mouth, and he couldn't get enough, sucking hard and then licking away the sting. He pulled back and blew gently over her damp breast, cool air trickling over them, before turning to do the same to its mate.

"Dean, please, I need…" she gasped out, goosebumps covering her chest and arms as he stroked his fingers over the little bumps.

"What do you need, darlin'?" he rasped. She rubbed herself back and forth in his lap and then reached down between them to stroke him through the denim. He thrust his pelvis up into her hand and sucked her nipple again.

"Inside, I need you inside me," she gasped, and leaned forward to lick the shell of his ear. "Please," she breathed into his ear and he shivered. He'd tortured her enough now. He gave her nipple a final, flat tongue lick then pulled back, working her overalls down her hips. She lifted her leg, and he managed to get one foot out the shorts and then the other until her overalls joined her bra and t-shirt on the floor. He ran his eyes over the wide curve of her hips, down to her panties and her rounded, creamy, splayed thighs. His cock throbbed in his jeans, she was perfect, made just for him.

"Touch me," she begged. His eyes went to her face, her lip pulled between her teeth. He watched her intently as he reached out and stroked over the damp center of her panties. Her head fell back, and she tried to rub against his hand, but he pulled it away. Her head shot back up and she pinned him with a sharp stare. He chuckled and then hooked a finger around the edge of her panties and slid inside her. She moaned when he added another finger, her hot, tight walls clamping down on him, he bit the inside of his cheek to keep from moaning.

He spread his fingers, stretching her and thrust them in and out faster. The wet suction filled the truck as her channel greedily swallowed his fingers. She lifted her hands to cup and play with her breasts as he filled her with a third finger. He didn't dare stop her, just wanted to watch as she found her pleasure. He loved that she knew what she wanted and wasn't afraid to take control, wild with her inhibitions.

"Oh, Dean...*fuck*," she groaned. The dark curse coming from that innocent, sensual mouth tipped him over the edge, pushing him to breaking point. He removed his fingers and yanked her panties down her legs, his urgency matched by Christy as she let go of her breasts and began fumbling at his jeans to get to him. She pulled his cock free and immediately wrapped her fingers around the thick base and pumped up his length once, twice.

"I'm on the pill, I'm clean," she rushed out.

"Same, except about the pill," he replied, and she giggled. He marveled at how they could be so worked up and yet manage to find humor in the moment. She nodded at him and pulled herself up before guiding him to her slick entrance. He felt the head of his cock nestled against her and he raised his hips to push inside. Her muscles give way around him, but the resistance was there, squeezing him tightly, making him see stars. He moved a little slower, allowing her body to adjust to him, until he was seated all the way inside her. He wrapped his arms around her waist and pulled her close to him until they were a breath apart.

He peered up at her, her hair falling in loose curls

around her face. He cupped her cheek and covered her mouth with his. They both held still, not moving as they kissed, he poured all his passion and need into her. When their tongues met, his cock throbbed inside her, but he still didn't move. They broke apart and he pulled her plump bottom lip between his teeth, nibbling gently then sucking it. He kissed down her neck to her collarbone, then to her breast, and sucked her nipple back into the hot cave of his mouth. Her sex clenched around him, and he thrust into her, earning a cry from Christy. He looked at her face, worried he hurt her, but could only see pleasure lighting her features.

He didn't have much room to maneuver himself, but Christy pushed herself back and he reclined further in his seat until he was laying nearly flat. He watched as she rose up, his sexy goddess, and impaled herself on his cock again and again. Her hot core worked him perfectly, teasing him. She leaned back further and settled into a slow grind that had his head spinning and toes curling. He wanted to pound into her, fought against the instinct and let her take control. She rolled her hips back and forth *slooooowly*, clenching and releasing him, he started sweating from the effort to not take over. She leaned back further and accidentally beeped the horn of the truck, startling them both.

"Sorry, sorry!" she mumbled, whilst working him, increasing her speed. He watched her breasts bouncing up and down and gripped her rounded hips, fantastic for holding on as she rode him so perfectly.

"It's okay, there's no one around for miles," he gritted out. The knowledge must have unleashed something inside her as she threw her head back and moaned long and loud. His control finally snapped. He tightened his grip on her hips and began thrusting up into her, pulling her down hard to meet him. The push pull sensation and suction on his shaft had his sac drawing up tight, but he wasn't ready for it to end.

He knew what he agreed to, but he already knew he couldn't have her just once. It wasn't enough, there were so many ways he wanted to take her, and have her take him. He pulled himself upright and pulled her tight against his chest, her nipples abrading his flesh and he fed her a hard kiss. His tongue sliding in and out, mimicking the motions of his cock. He left her lips and kissed her jaw, her neck, her cries of pleasure spurring him on. He trailed his tongue over her neck and fit his lips to her skin and sucked hard.

"Oh, God!" she cried, and ran her hands up his neck and into his hair, gripping his scalp hard, holding him to her. He continued to suck as he thrust up into her, faster, fucking her as hard as he could. He felt like an animal, but it wasn't enough, it would never be enough. He moved his hand between them and pressed his thumb against her clit and rubbed. She cried out again as she started to come, her muscles clenched around him, quivering from the intensity of her orgasm. As her muscles gripped his cock, he slammed into her a final time and erupted, grunting into her neck. As he came, he continued stroking her and sent her into another hard climax, the sounds of their panting filled the truck.

He pulled back to look at her. Her eyes were closed tight, a beautiful, satisfied smile lifting her lips. He kissed the corner of her mouth and buried his face in her neck, inhaling her scent, needing a moment to recover. Never had it been like that for him, he was shaking from the intensity of it.

After a few moments, Christy spoke, her voice hoarse from her climax. "It's stopped raining," she said, wiping at the steamed-up window next to her, he looked outside.

"Perfect timing then," he said, and released his hold on her so she could get off him. She quickly dressed in her damp clothes while he zipped up his jeans and got out of the truck, coming around to open her door. He held her hand as he helped her down. She smiled up at him and he dropped a quick kiss on her swollen lips. He took her hand and as they turned towards the house, he felt a knot growing in the pit of his stomach the closer they got.

Chapter 18

Oh shit, oh shit, oh shit! Christy's mind chanted over and over again as she got out of the truck. *That was mind blowing.* Admittedly, she didn't have much experience with sex, but she knew that was on a whole different level. Her thoughts were going so crazy that she didn't notice Dean was standing in front of her. She smiled up at him, trying to be normal, and he dropped a quick kiss on her lips.

He took her hand and they walked away from his truck, the moonlight shining down on the driveway, reflecting brightly off the wet surface. Gone were the rain and clouds, and the temperature had thankfully dropped. Her clothes were wet, sending a chill through her, she needed to change. They reached the front door to the house and she realized they got there quite quickly. She turned round to look how far they walked and it couldn't be more than twenty meters from the truck.

Then it hit her. "A bit of a trek, huh?" she asked, raising an eyebrow at him. He smirked at her and turned to unlock the door.

"No need to thank me, I know how much you enjoyed that."

Her cheeks heated softly at his gentle teasing. She had never been teased by a lover before. She walked into the house sputtering about him enjoying it too, desperate to hear him agree but he didn't and she felt a little disappointed. *Did he seem a bit distracted?* The house was dark inside, the moonlight shone through some of the windows, but as she heard Dean flicking a light switch it was clear the power was still out. He took her arm and steered her into the house and then to the left, through a wide arch opening and stopped her.

"Wait here while I grab some candles. Don't move, I don't want you to hurt yourself," he said. And then he was gone. She heard him banging around in another room, a muttered curse and then silence. After a beat, she heard his footsteps coming back towards her and felt his presence beside her.

"One second," he said, and she heard a clicking sound, followed by a *whoosh* and his face was illuminated. He lit a wide, square candle and she could see some more on the floor in front of him. He set about lighting them and distributing them around the room, then he knelt down in front of the fireplace and in no time, the flames were dancing and lighting up the room. There was a nervous energy about him, but when he came towards her, his features softened and her heart pounded. Now that they'd had sex, what happened next? She was in unchartered territory, she found she didn't know how to behave. What would he be expecting? What did she want? A chill swept through her, now they were out of the warm truck, her wet clothes began to feel much colder.

He frowned down at her. "I'll be right back," he said, and hurried off once again.

While he was gone, she looked around the room. The décor was nice and warm, cream walls with wooden beams running across the ceiling. The fireplace was the main focal point of the room with a soft, brown couch facing it that had a matching armchair on each side. A wooden sideboard ran along the wall under the wide window that looked out the front of the house. There were some picture frames on the sideboard and Christy went over to take a closer look. There was one of him and Beau, both bare-chested and flexing comically on a beach somewhere. Judging by the people in the background it could've been L.A.

Seeing bikini babes in the background of the photo she suddenly panicked that he saw her completely naked when they had sex in the truck. She had been so lost in the moment she hadn't thought about what he might think of the way she looked.

Old insecurities tried to overtake her, she turned her attention back to the frames, trying to shove the thoughts out of her mind. There was also one of him and his mom. He had his arms around her and they were both grinning at the camera. In between both of these photos, in a larger frame was a photograph of him and Taylor. They were both pulling funny faces at each other, Christy laughed to herself as she took it in.

"Here you go," Dean said from behind her. She turned to see him holding out a navy, fleece robe to her. He brought her something to change into, something that was clearly his. She couldn't wait to slip it on and have his scent envelope her, but…she looked around awkwardly.

The rest of the house was in complete darkness and even after what they experienced together, she felt awkward stripping off.

"I'll go make us some sandwiches; I'm starving." He must have sensed her unease, he winked at her as he left the room. She waited a moment and then stripped out of her wet clothes, leaving just her underwear on, and hung them over the back of the chair near the fireplace. Then she wrapped herself in his robe, burying her face into the soft material and inhaling his scent. It reminded her of the woods; fresh, wild and masculine.

She sat in front of the fire, legs crossed and palms to the flames. The heat felt wonderful across her skin and she could feel her hair drying already. She groaned inwardly at the thought of it drying fluffy and being unable to tame it.

After a few minutes she warmed up, so scooted back and sat on the soft cream rug covering the floor and leant her back against the couch. The room felt so warm and inviting, it was amazing how she felt right at home here. She closed her eyes, feeling herself relax.

When she opened them again, Dean was sitting down next to her, putting a plate in her lap. She looked down and saw he'd made her a cheese sandwich and cut them into four small squares, like Taylor used to make for her as kids. How did he still remember that's how she liked them? On the plate was a selection of grapes and strawberries.

"Sorry, turns out I didn't have as much as I thought," he shrugged, and his cheeks looked a little pink in the light from the flame. Her stomach chose that moment to let out a loud growl, and she cringed.

"It looks lovely, and as you can probably tell, I'm not fussy right now," she laughed.

While they ate, he told her about the house. It had been abandoned and run down, he had been looking for a project, so he put in an offer and got it. While he talked, she noticed he still seemed really tense, was it because of what they had done?

"No wonder you've been so good at fixing up my parents' house," she said, praise infusing her tone.

He nodded, not saying much more.

"I can't see the other rooms right now, but it looks like you've done an amazing job. It's beautiful, you should be so proud," she gushed.

"You really think so?" he asked shyly.

"I do."

He visibly relaxed, as if her words eased some tension inside him. Had he been worried about what she would think of his place? How cute.

"Good, I can give you a proper tour in the morning," he said, flames dancing in his eyes and just like that she felt nervous and needy for him all over again, already regretting her one-time rule.

He looked at her a moment longer and then reached up, brushing her hair back from her face and cupping her jaw in his strong hand. She leaned into his touch, it had been so long since she felt human contact, or affection, and she had forgotten how much she missed it. She couldn't help but wonder if it would be as nice if it was anyone but Dean.

He stroked her cheek with his thumb and she closed her eyes at the gentle touch. With his other hand he took her empty plate from her lap, put it to one side and pulled her into the crook of his body where she fit him like a missing puzzle piece. Her head resting on his chest as the hand that was on her cheek began stroking her hair. She heard the gentle thud of his heart through his chest and settled into him, circling her arms around his waist.

"Tell me about you and Taylor," she said with a sigh.

Chapter 19

"You know most of it," he said, moving his hand and stroking up and down her arm.

"I know it from her side, but I would like to hear about what things were like for you. Tell me more about you."

She felt him shift against her, was he nervous or uncomfortable? Did he not want to talk?

"I want to talk about you instead. What made you leave town so suddenly?" he asked gently. Her stomach flipped; she didn't know if she was ready to talk about this yet. Did she want to open herself up and be vulnerable with him? She wasn't quite ready for that, but she also couldn't expect him to share with her if she didn't open up in return. That was how trust was built and she struggled to trust anyone, having had it broken so irreparably in the past. She realized she did have a desire to tell him, to share pieces of herself with him and learn about him in return. But this was meant to be casual and if she had any hope in hell of keeping it that way, she couldn't give away those pieces of herself.

"I would rather not talk about that," she replied quietly, aware that didn't give them much to talk about now. He didn't reply at first and she wondered if she ruined everything. After a moment though he started talking, not about him and Taylor, but about his career.

He told her about his days at college, launching his first business, which happened to be an ice cream truck, and how he ended up going bankrupt. He took a part time job in a garage to keep himself busy while he had a break, reassessed, and figured out where he went wrong.

"I felt like a complete failure," he said, "I let everyone down, my employees, my mom and myself. I didn't try again for another year because my confidence took such a beating," he explained. Christy stayed quiet, just letting him tell his story. It was so nice listening to him speak, his words lilting and soothing her, relaxing her until she could feel her eyes drifting closed.

"I managed to get a deposit together, with some help from my mom, to get a loan to buy the garage. I have her to thank for everything, I couldn't have done it without her."

She smiled sleepily at his words. "I'm sure you would've done it, your determination is impressive. It just might have taken a little longer, that's all."

He kissed her forehead and she closed her eyes in tired bliss. He continued to stroke her arm and she listened to him talk about his first year as the owner. At some point, she was aware she was being lowered down to the rug and felt a blanket being placed over her. He murmured in her ear that he would be back. She reached out for him in her sleep, but he was gone.

Sometime later she came awake to the sound of the crackling fire, flames licking, embers popping. She looked around and realized she was alone.

"Dean?" She heard a shuffling outside the living room in the hallway and felt a hint of panic until he popped his head around the doorway. He smiled at her as he kicked his shoes off and came to join her on the rug.

"I just went to check on Taylor as she closed up." As he sat next to her, he nuzzled into her neck, nibbling the sensitive skin. Her eyes drifted closed and goosebumps broke out over her skin. He pulled back and met her stare; his eyes wild and alive, a hint of wickedness flirting in the depths. He dropped his gaze down and took a deep breath, nostrils flaring. She followed his stare and saw the blanket had fallen to her waist, his robe parted reveal the curve of her breast. She looked back at him, his expression serious, his eyes holding hers with an intensity that had her fighting a shiver. He arched an eyebrow as though asking her, challenging her to decide what happened next.

She was torn. They could end this now, she could leave, and they wouldn't speak of this again or she could give in to her instincts. Have the night of passion his eyes were promising and deal with the consequences in the morning. As though he sensed her dilemma, he said in a gruff voice;

"Once wasn't enough."

Her mind made up, she reached for him. Their mouths crashed together in an urgent, passionate kiss that stoked the flames of her desire. She didn't think she would ever get enough of him. His tongue played at her lips, begging to be let inside. She parted them and he rolled his tongue against hers, stroking, both of them moaning at the touch. The kiss slowed as he tilted her head for deeper contact. He pulled her against him and curled an arm around her and laid her gently on the rug.

The kiss continued; slow and sultry, his tongue meeting hers in lazy strokes, taking his time, savoring. He nipped at her mouth, so tenderly, then took her bottom lip between his teeth, nibbling softly before coming back for another soul-searing kiss. She couldn't control her body's reactions, she was a quivering mess as he continued to kiss her, not touching anywhere else, just her mouth.

When she was practically sobbing with need, he pulled back, his mouth swollen and his hair standing on end from where she plowed her fingers through the strands. His eyes were lit with arousal, his face glowing in the light from the fire. His deep breaths tickling her face, not breaking eye contact he moved his hands to the knot on the robe. She felt her old panic rear up inside and his hands stilled.

"Hey, none of that," he murmured as though sensing where her thoughts were heading. He continued undoing the knot, and she felt it give way. He opened both sides of the robe, baring her to him. He didn't break eye contact with her as he stroked his fingers across the bare skin of her waist, over her rounded stomach, her flesh pebbling under his touch. The more he explored, the calmer she became, until he began to dabble at the waistband of her panties. Her breathing grew labored as she felt her body readying for him. She grunted in disappointment as his hand moved away, his husky chuckle turning her on even more.

"Patience," he teased as he bent his head to nip her ear lobe. His hand trailed up to her breast and stroked over the sensitive skin. He pulled back to look in her eyes as he stroked his thumb over her nipple. She cried out in pleasure as he pinched the hard tip between his thumb and finger. He shifted his weight and she felt his lower half press into her side, the length of his hard cock hot like a branding iron. He stroked over her nipple again and again, taking his time, all the while holding her stare with that hot, intense gaze of his. He trailed his hand over the flare of her hip.

"You're beautiful, you know that?" he asked as he dabbled at her belly button. The sincerity in his tone, his expression so open and honest, caused a lump to rise in her throat and in that moment, she believed him. She slowly nodded, satisfaction flaring in his eyes.

"Good," he grunted, and expertly worked his hand beneath her panties and thrust two fingers inside her wet heat.

"Oh, God," she moaned, rolling her hips, trying to move against him.

"Christ," he muttered, squeezing his eyes shut. She continued working herself against him, desperate to find her release. Little moans working their way out of her throat as he thrust his fingers inside her and began to rub her clit with his thumb. He removed his hand and she started to protest, but he pulled her panties down her legs and settled his weight between her thighs.

He was going to use his mouth on her, she'd never had that before, had always wondered what it would feel like. He looked down at her, and she felt his warm breath caress her sensitive skin. He lifted his eyes to hers, gave her a delectable smirk and lowered his head. When she felt his tongue part her folds, she gasped, her hips lifting to meet him. He licked over her bud slowly, torturing her, her hands fisting the rug underneath her, her breath sawing out of her. He moved his tongue down and pressed it inside her before returning to slide over her clit. He thrust a finger inside her, working it in and out while his tongue whipped back and forth.

Her climax was suddenly upon her, and she felt her entire body tensing, ready for release. He was watching her intently, she knew he wanted to watch her fall apart, but she couldn't maintain eye contact with him while doing that. It felt like too intimate a connection to have with him when she was trying her hardest to keep this casual. She closed her eyes as her body tightened and then released, her muscles clenching on his fingers as little explosions wracked her body.

When she came back to earth, he moved up her body, dropping kisses over her chest, shoulders, and down her arms, soothing her. Despite the intense orgasm she'd just had, she wasn't ready for this to end. She placed her hand on his chest, forcing him flat onto his back and she rubbed herself against him. His body tensed as she placed hot, opened mouthed kisses across his chest, tasting the soft skin covering his hard muscles. She laved her tongue over the peak of his nipple, the muscles of his chest bunching under her touch. She wanted to commit his gorgeous body to memory, to pull out and pore over when she was back in the city and missed being in his arms.

"Christy…" he warned, but she placed her hand over his lips to silence him. She wanted to worship him without him trying to distract her. She worked her way down his chest, laving her tongue over the dips in between his abs, trailing her hand down to rub over the bulge in his pants.

"Christy," he groaned, then grabbed her hand to stop her and tried to sit up.

"No, now it's your turn," she commanded, pushing him back down and surveying the body stretched out underneath her. Her eyes started at that beautiful face of his, that made her insides turn to jelly before traveling down the wide expanse of his chest. His pecs jumped under her perusal and she arched an eyebrow at him, *show off*. He just grinned at her and she trailed her hand over his six-pack. Pressing over each of the bulging muscles before following the small trail of blond hair that stopped at the top of his pants.

She bit her lip as she remembered what it felt like when she had her lips around him, sliding him in and out of her mouth, how much he enjoyed it and the pleasure she had given him. She moved her hand inside and rubbed over him, grinning as his breath caught in his throat when she did. She dipped to cup his sac and squeezed gently, earning a dark curse from his lips. She grabbed the sides of his pants and boxers and pulled them down, he lifted his hips and then he was free.

She stared at him, thick and hard, stretching up and resting on his lower abdomen. She licked her lips teasingly and he groaned, his eyes roving over her body. She remembered she was fully naked, the thought pricking her anxiety until she saw the raw desire in his eyes as he watched her. Her breath left her at the sight of this strong, sexy man so turned on by her, and her confidence soared.

"Now who's beautiful?" she asked, her voice thick. Her nipples puckered, he growled and the next thing she knew she was on her back, his body covering hers. His weight settled on her, teasing her with its hot, hard plains and seductive scent. She parted her thighs, allowing her body to cradle his, and he settled himself against her, his cock coming up against her slick sex, both of them groaning at the sensation.

He placed his elbows either side of her shoulders, his hands cradled her face as he looked down at her. His eyes searching her as he stroked over her cheeks, forehead, eyebrows, and mouth as if memorizing her. Her throat felt thick with emotions she didn't want to be feeling, she'd never been adored like this. She lifted her head to kiss him, to break the spell, but he dropped his head lower and licked across her nipple then sucked hard.

He thrust his hips at the same time, entering her slowly. He thrust gently, pushing himself inside, nearly to the hilt then withdrawing at the last moment. The delicious friction and sensations it created had her eyes rolling back into her head. The next time he tried to withdraw, her muscles clenched around him tightly. A strangled sound left his throat and whatever control he had been exhibiting, snapped.

He bared his teeth and started pounding into her with hard, fast thrusts. She wrapped her legs around him, holding on for the wild ride, latching onto his firm biceps, just as she had imagined. But this was better than any fantasy.

He was wild, a beast, grunting and snarling with every pound of his hips. When they had sex in his truck she was on top, she controlled the tempo, she was in charge of the way he moved and what he felt. Now he was in control and a force to be reckoned with. He controlled and dominated her body, what sensations she felt and when. She surrendered to him and took what he gave, relishing it. She knew she would have scrapes on her back in the morning, but she didn't care. Seeing him so savage in his need heightened her own arousal like nothing she ever experienced.

She dug her nails into his back and tilted her hips, so

he hit her deeper. When she trailed her hands down and sunk her nails into his firm ass, he cursed and tangled his fingers in her hair, pulling her closer for a brutal kiss. She tasted herself on his tongue and she felt her orgasm building but was taken aback by the intensity of it. She buried her face in his neck as she cried out, her grip on his ass tightening, a cry tearing from her throat. He grunted as her muscles contracted around him, squeezing him so tight before he cursed again and followed her over the edge into bliss. He shuddered and she felt him inside of her, hot and wet.

They stayed locked together, her face buried in his neck and she could feel his pulse pounding, the beat matching hers. When their breathing calmed, he pressed a gentle kiss to the tip of her nose, then her lips and they both moaned as he slid out of her. He didn't move off her, just stayed there covering her body, her soft skin pressed to his. She ran her hand up and down his back and they settled into silence.

"I'm sorry, I was too rough," he said, his voice gravelly. She opened her eyes and looked up at his concerned expression with disbelief. *What?* That had been perfect, he'd lost control, owned her body and she loved every moment of it. She was still humming and throbbing with satisfaction.

"Are you serious? That was amazing!" she gushed, feeling herself blush under his scrutiny. "No apology necessary," she added and lifted her lips in a lazy, satisfied grin. He looked down at her, shocked, but didn't say anything. Instead, he tried to roll off her, but she latched onto his shoulders and snuggled into his chest, feeling his arms go around her. She knew snuggling was a no-no for keeping this casual, but if this was the only time she would have with him she was going to do what she wanted. She was exhausted and as she drifted into her dreams, she realized this was the happiest she had felt in a very long time.

*

She woke in the morning, snug and warm in her blanket burrito, the smell of the fire still lingering in the air hours after the embers burnt out. Her muscles burning deliciously, she burrowed in and smiled as she inhaled Dean's lingering scent. The smell evoking memories of their night together. Turns out once wasn't enough, neither was twice. Third time's the charm? Still not enough. He woke her in the early hours trailing hot, wet kisses down her spine, his palm squeezing her ass. He got her so worked up that she begged him, honest to God *begged*. Of course, he had been happy to oblige, he was a gentleman like that.

But today was a new day, the antics from last night were a one off, a casual fling. They flung and got it out of their systems or at least tried to, she wasn't sure she had him out of her system yet. She never experienced anything like that with her previous partners, all two of them. Dean made her feel alive, sexy, desirable, and confident. The way she felt when he looked at her? Unparalleled.

It also worried her, she couldn't become attached to him and she was fast learning that Dean was the kind of man that a woman could get attached to. She would be leaving town once the house was done, they'd had some fun and now it was back to reality. With a deep sigh she threw the blanket back and sat up, looking around the brightly lit room. Even during the day with the bright sunshine streaming in the wide windows, it still felt cozy.

She wrapped his bathrobe around herself and decided to explore the house since she hadn't gotten to see any of it last night due to the blackout. She left the living room and went across the hall, through the open archway opposite and found herself in the kitchen. It was an open plan room, brightly lit from a wall of full-length windows with a door facing out onto the terrace. Outside was a corner sofa curving around a glass table with a firepit in the center, a pair of armchairs, and against the wall was a barbecue grill.

She could just picture Dean standing at the grill, flipping burgers laughing over his shoulder at Beau and Taylor's back and forth, then Justine and Christy would come out through the doors with a pitcher of cocktails and snacks for everyone. She smiled at the visual and then realized what she was doing. Where had that come from? It unsettled her how easily the scenario had come into her mind and how right it felt. She turned her focus to the rest of the kitchen, trying to ignore her thoughts.

The kitchen itself was gorgeous; wooden counter units ran along the walls and an island sat in the middle with wooden stools that had pale yellow and blue cushions. There were bottles of various oils and dressings clustered together, a spice rack, cookbooks, and a fruit bowl decorated the counters and island. It seemed more like a country style kitchen perfect for a family than somewhere a bachelor would meal prep.

The whole house felt like it was designed for a family rather than just one man. And like the living room, it was cozy and inviting. She could sit at the island and chat to him while he cooked; there was nothing sexier than watching a man in the kitchen. She sighed at her imagination again, getting frustrated and left the room. The hallway carpet was a soft, plush cream color which ran up the wide staircase. She flexed her bare toes, loving the feel of the material squishing between them.

When she reached the top of the stairs there were four doors leading off the landing, she could hear the sound of running water coming from behind one of them. Dean must be in the shower, she longed to join him, clearly she couldn't get enough of him after all. If she were his girlfriend, she could slip inside quietly, let the robe fall to the floor and step inside the steamy – *argh!* What was wrong with her?

She moved away and went to the first room on the right. It was a spare room with just a bed, dresser and TV so she moved to the next one, opened the door, and stepped inside. The room was brightly lit from the huge windows along the south wall, sunshine flooded in, Dean was clearly a fan of natural lighting. As she looked around, she realized this was his study.

There was a worn, wine colored couch with a black throw casually draped over the back. A bookcase was on the wall opposite and she went over, scouring the titles, intrigued to see what he had. She found a mixture of crime novels, mainly Scandinavian authors, but a few American authors she recognized, "how to" guides on running a business, DIY books, and a couple of biographies. She even spotted a sneaky romance here and there. She ran her fingertips along the broken spines, some of them deeply cracked from multiple reads.

Next to the bookcase was a small filing cabinet and a rubber tree plant that looked a little neglected. There was a map of the world mounted on the wall above with pins in a few countries, like he was marking where he had traveled. She had never been out of the States herself. She turned toward the wide window that had a wooden writing desk in front of it with a leather chair tucked underneath. She could picture Dean sitting there going over his accounts and then getting distracted and looking out the window.

She ran her hands over the wooden desk, loving the feel of the grain beneath her fingertips, wanting to touch the things he touched, his possessions. There was a fancy looking computer, a small wilted bonsai tree, a notepad with "Iris Motors" stamped across the top and a pen pot. Beside this was a photo frame of Dean with his mother, Iris. As she studied the photo, she could see that there were similarities between the two. They had the same mischievous, sparkling blue eyes with matching dimples.

She looked out the window and gasped. She was looking down over the back of the property which had another small terraced area with a stone path that led to a large pond. The pond had a miniature concrete water fountain in the center of it. Small birds were lining up along it, dipping their heads under the streams running off the fountain, and flapping their little wings, enjoying their bath. The pond had flowering lilies scattered across the calm water. Behind the pond were two rows of orange and apple trees, with collections of both fruits dotting the ground surrounding them.

It was beautiful, so bright and colorful and alive with nature. It was perfect and so evocative she could imagine sitting at the desk and writing, looking out the window for inspiration and at that moment she wanted nothing more. She felt her mind stirring with thoughts of her next novel. The bubbling from the fountain, the birds singing, the sun shining, and the breeze ruffling the trees all sparked her creative instincts, flaring them to life. Suddenly ideas started bombarding her, thick and fast, too many to keep up with. Like the dam of writer's block had been cleared and the thoughts that had been mounting up rushed out.

She cried out in excitement and grabbed for the

notepad and pen on the desk and began scribbling furiously, stopping now and then to ponder and watch the birds. She didn't know how long she was writing before she realized she wasn't alone in the room. She glanced up from her scribbling to see Dean leaning against the doorway, his arms folded across his chest. Her stomach clenched, God he was gorgeous, although he had an odd expression on his face, was he annoyed she snooped through his house?

"Oh, hi," she said, feeling a little guilty at being caught in his study, pen and paper in hand.

"Hi yourself," he replied smoothly.

"I didn't mean to snoop, I was looking for you when I came in here, and then I looked out the window and needed to…your house is lovely," she finished lamely.

"I'm glad you think so," he continued to stare at her in that way that made her feel very hot and aware of herself but left her with no idea what he was thinking.

She shifted uncomfortably on the spot. "Dean-"

"I thought I would drive you home, you must want to get some clean clothes on after last night."

She watched him, studying his face for a sense of what he felt. Unable to work out if he was giving her the brush off or trying to muddle through the complexity of what they had done together.

"Yes, that would be nice thank you."

He nodded and stepped back to let her leave the room. She glanced at the notepad in her hand and tore off her notes, folding them up and gripping them tightly in the palm of her hand. As she walked past him, she caught a hint of his scent and had to stop herself from reaching for him. She went downstairs and grabbed her clothes from the back of the chair by the fireplace. Then took off his robe, laying it over the arm of the couch and put her dried clothes on. When she was dressed, she found him in the kitchen looking out onto the terrace.

"Ready," she said, and watched his shoulders tense, muscles bunching under his thin t-shirt. He nodded before striding across the kitchen, grabbing his keys from the island, and only flicking his eyes over her briefly before heading for the front door.

Her heart sank, he was giving her the brush off, which she had to remind herself was *fine*, because this was just casual. They couldn't be together, she lived in another part of the country, and she didn't think she could ever trust someone enough to settle down anyway. It was better this way. But she couldn't deny it hurt a little to think last night was the best night of her life, and she would never experience it again.

Chapter 20

The drive back to Christy's was steeped in tension with Dean calling himself every name under the sun. He glanced over at Christy, the sunlight shining down on her, highlighting her golden curls as she looked out the window, her body turned away from him. Last night had been...he didn't have words. Nothing and no one had ever felt as right as she did when she was in his arms, he hadn't wanted it to end. His body couldn't get enough of her, *he* couldn't get enough of her and he didn't think he ever would.

He watched her sleeping this morning, so beautiful and serene in her dreamworld. He tore himself away figuring that when she woke up, she wouldn't appreciate his morning breath or him staring at her. After his shower, his body primed for round four, he went to find her to see if she was interested in stretching out this casual one-time fling. She hadn't been where he left her, so he had gone looking for her and found her in his study and that's when his world tilted on its axis.

He watched her, in his robe with her hair all disheveled, the sun bathing her in its golden rays as she jotted down notes, mumbling to herself and pacing. At one point she started arguing with herself but he just stayed silent and watched her. He knew she had been struggling with writer's block, she must have had a breakthrough and he didn't want to interrupt. He loved watching her mind work, sorting through the detailed intricacies of the story she was planning.

The feeling he got watching her, the sense of rightness of her being there, in his house and in his clothes hit him right in the chest. He just knew she would be at home in his place, it was one of the reasons he'd brought her here. Only he wasn't prepared for how he would feel seeing her, so comfortable in his world. It was something he didn't want to look at too closely.

She was clear she only wanted casual, that she wasn't staying in town, she was leaving soon and going back to her life. He could feel himself beginning to get attached and he didn't want to get even more so for her to rip his heart out when she drove off into the sunset. He was looking for forever and that wasn't what he and Christy would have.

Fuck, he was an idiot. He shouldn't have gotten involved with her, but it was too late now. He couldn't change what happened, wouldn't want to change it for the world but he could protect himself.

When she finally spotted him, smiling shyly, his heart clenched in his chest. Her sweetness, her sexiness, it drew him in like no other, but now he had to reset the boundaries. His thoughts distracted him the entire drive and too soon they arrived at her father's house. He turned off the engine and faced her, clearing his throat.

"I need to go to the garage today, I've got another friend of Beau's dropping their Ferrari off and I need to be there. Bear could accidentally mangle something if I don't supervise."

She turned to face him, her eyes searching his face and trying to read him, but he kept his features carefully blank. A curl fell across her cheek, he clenched his hands tightly on the steering wheel to keep from reaching over and tucking it behind her ear.

"Okay," was all she said.

"But I'll come back tomorrow, we've got lots of painting still to do," he added, not wanting her to think that now he had gotten her into bed, he didn't care about her. They had developed a strong friendship prior to last night and he wanted to be around her as much as possible, even if he couldn't touch her how he wanted.

She smiled. "Great."

He reached into his pocket and held out her keys to her. She stared blankly at them before realizing what they were.

"Thanks for dropping me back," she said, taking them and holding them in the same hand that held the notes she made on his notepad. He wondered if she was going to write today now she had broken through her block, did she have somewhere set up to do that?

"No problem, see you tomorrow." He smiled at her, she nodded and stared at him again before getting out of the truck and going into the house. He drove to the garage, greeting Bear with a grunt before shutting himself in the office, going through his emails on autopilot.

Beau's friend, Will, turned up on time with his Ferrari.

Will was a businessman himself, something of a celebrity, he had one of those entrepreneur reality shows, like Shark Tank. He knew that Will had a reputation for being a ruthless hard ass but Dean thought he was actually a pretty nice guy. They chatted while Dean worked, talking about their companies, telling each other stories and sharing advice. Will promised to bring his car back for detailing later in the year and both of them exchanged business cards when he left.

Dean stayed late at the garage, trying to bury himself in work before getting a late dinner at Ruby's Diner. When he finally went home and stepped inside his house, it felt empty and quiet. He walked into the kitchen, grabbing a beer from the fridge before heading out onto the terrace. He tried to think about other things, distracting himself from his thoughts. He rang Beau for a quick chat, the guy would be back soon, thank God. Dean was already used to having him around and knew he would miss him like mad when he finally returned to L.A. for good.

When they hung up it was time for him to do his drive by at Taylor's. It didn't take long and he was soon back home again. He went into the living room and spotted his robe draped over the arm of the couch. He grabbed it, fighting the urge to bring it to his nose and inhale Christy's lingering scent. He decided to end the day and went to bed. Tossing his robe over the end of the bed, he stripped down to his boxers and slipped between the sheets.

He lay there, his mind tired, but not letting him sleep, instead playing a reel of his night with Christy. The images of them together, the sound of her moans in his ears had his cock hardening. He bit his cheek and put his hands behind his head to keep from reaching for himself. The memories continued to plague him, making him increasingly frustrated and angry. He could smell her scent in his room, had she come in here during the day or was it just drifting from his robe?

After fighting it as long as he could, he gave in and grabbed his robe, burying his face in the material and inhaling her scent, groaning. One hand reached under the duvet to grip himself tight, his mind played through all the things he wanted to do to her. What he wanted her to do to him, until he was panting and moaning her name as he climaxed. He removed his boxers and used the material to clean himself up, then lay there willing sleep to come.

By 4 am he'd given up, got out of bed, and was padding around the house wrapped in his robe. He found himself in the study, he didn't really use it much, but tonight it was drawing him. He surveyed the room and then started rearranging his desk, moving his computer, picture frame, and troublesome bonsai to one side, and arranging more notepads and pens across the top of the desk. *That way she would have plenty of space and writing material.* He didn't know where the thought came from or why he needed to rearrange his desk the way he had when he knew she wouldn't be coming by again. He only knew that if he didn't do it, he wouldn't have been able to sleep at all.

*

Christy's mind was cluttered with thoughts. More thoughts than she had in a long time and it was wonderful. The only problem was, she had nowhere to put them. When Dean dropped her off in the morning, she was eager to start writing and get some of those thoughts down on paper. She had gone inside, grabbed her notebook and sat on the porch, ready for the inspiration she experienced earlier to take over. She waited, pen poised, sun shining down on her. But no. After an hour she hadn't written a word, she forced the nib of her pen onto the paper, leaving a mark, but she couldn't move her hand to draw letters.

"It's fine, I just need a change of scenery."

She went inside, grabbed her purse and keys, and went to her battered car. She drove to The Rusty Bucket Inn and went in. The place was pretty quiet for once, perfect for writing. She waved to Taylor and got comfortable in a booth. She loved her friend, but right now she wanted to avoid an in-depth conversation with her. Otherwise, Christy would end up blurting out that she spent the night banging Taylor's brother and telling her how amazing it was when he made her come apart, *awkward*. Taylor was busy showing Kayleigh how to make cocktails which, thankfully, meant she wasn't free to talk.

Christy pulled her notebook and pens out and lined them up on the table in front of her. Now she was ready, ready to end this writer's block and start writing.

Just write.

Write.

Any second now...

After two hours, three coffees, and one trip to the bathroom which resulted in memories of her and Dean's first kiss, she still had nothing. A knot was forming in her chest, her frustration palpable. After a little while, a defeated Christy packed up her stuff. Maybe she was too relaxed, maybe being in a more formal setting like an office would help her focus. With a hurried wave to Taylor, she was out the door and driving into the town, parking outside Justine's office, and avoiding looking down the road at Iris Motors. She rushed inside the building, accidentally slamming the door against the wall, and came face to face with Hilda. Hilda frowned at her for a moment before a smile lit her face.

"Hello dear, can I help you?"

"No, I, uh…" Christy stammered, her eyes wide before spotting the leather chairs in the waiting room. Hilda's face remained perfectly friendly, her smile not flickering at all at Christy's odd behavior. *She's probably used to it, no wonder Justine loves her.*

"I just need to sit." Christy said, backing away into the waiting room until she bumped into one of the chairs and sank down into it, not breaking eye contact with Hilda. She forced herself to smile at the nice lady, a normal smile, not a serial killer smile, before turning away and rummaging in her bag for her notebook. She crossed her legs, looking out the window and saw Dean on the forecourt of the garage down the street, talking to a gorgeous man and gesturing to the sports car in front of them. Her heart did a weird little flip in her chest and a wave of longing hit her.

Get a hold of yourself, you saw him this morning.

She realized he had been telling the truth this morning when he said he was needed at the garage. Part of her had assumed he was lying to get away from the awkward morning after chat. She really needed to start trusting people more. Dean hadn't given her a reason not to trust him so far, and he deserved the benefit of the doubt. She watched as he threw back his head and laughed. She found herself smiling and with great difficulty, she turned back to her notebook.

Two hours later.

"Sweet baby Jesus!" she cried. This was ridiculous, how was it possible that after trying, literally, all day she couldn't write anything when she was so inspired in the morning? She dropped her head into her hands and sighed, the knot in her chest tightening. She rubbed her palm against the area, trying to ease it. She looked up and caught Hilda's eye.

"Sorry for the outburst," she mumbled. Hilda stood up and came out from behind her desk and sat next to Christy.

"Anything I can help with?" she asked kindly.

"I have writer's block. I had a breakthrough this morning, but now that I'm trying to sit and write I can't do it and I don't understand why!" she whined, and Hilda laughed gently. "I thought coming here and being around someone familiar and in a more suitable environment would help but it hasn't."

Hilda tsked. "Well, where were you this morning when you had your breakthrough?"

"I was at Dea -uh- a friend's house."

"Was it the first time you had been to Dean's?" Christy's eyes flicked to Hilda, *is she a mind reader?*

"You've been staring at the garage every ten minutes, dear, it's not hard to figure out." Hilda laughed. Christy instantly felt stupid, clearly paranoia had joined hysteria to have a little party in her brain.

"Sounds to me like you need to go back there if that's what triggered your inspiration," Hilda continued, but before Christy could respond, Justine came out from her office saying goodbye to a client.

"What are you doing here?" she asked, when she spotted Christy, flopping into a chair opposite her. Christy looked at Hilda who smiled and squeezed her hand before moving back to her desk.

"Just thought I would stop by and see if you had dinner plans?"

"I do now," Justine replied. "Shall I meet you at the bar?"

Christy wanted to avoid the bar if possible, not

wanting to see Taylor or Dean right now.

"How about we go to yours instead, you can either poison me with your cooking or we can grab takeout, just the two of us?"

"How dare you, I've a mind to cook for you now!" Justine joked.

"Perfect," Christy smiled. Justine went back into her office to grab her stuff and came back out.

"Let's go. Hilda are you heading off now too?" she asked, Hilda was switching off her computer and grabbing her purse.

"I sure am, I'll lock up, have fun you two."

"Great, see you in the morning." Justine replied. Hilda nodded and Justine left first with Christy trailing behind her. As she was leaving, Christy turned back and mouthed a "thank you" to Hilda who waved her off.

Justine didn't poison her, or if she did it was taking a while to kick in. They chatted while they ate, mainly about Justine's hunt for Mr. Right, which was not going well, she was getting very frustrated.

"Are we still going to pretend your beard burn and love bites are sun related?" Justine said as she cleared their dishes away. *Busted.*

Christy felt a smile spread across her face, "I guess not."

"Dean?" Justine asked. Christy nodded and Justine squealed.

"I noticed you couldn't take your eyes off each other at the bar the other night. Does that mean you're going to stay now? Taylor will be so gassed if you're staying!"

As fast as it appeared, Christy's smile faded. "No, it was just a one-time casual thing, nothing more."

"*Chula,*" Justine began, fixing her with a hard stare. "You're more suited than any couple I've seen. That man doesn't do casual, and he hasn't for a very, very long time."

"What do you mean? He was hooking up with some woman the night I came back to town. I saw them the next morning leaving one of the cabins."

Justine shook her head. "No sweetie, he takes the women there so he can get to know them without the whole town listening in. Everyone knows he only talks to them, the poor man is practically celibate. He's looking for something serious so he can settle down and start a family. He uses the cabin because he doesn't want to take anyone but the right woman back to his house," Justine finished, turning back to the sink and filling it with water. Christy felt shocked, did she even know him at all? He took *her* to his house, had been intimate with her there, multiple times.

"How long has he been…saving himself?" Christy croaked out.

"Not sure, quite a while though," Justine dried her hands and turned to face Christy. "I take it he's not anymore though?"

Christy shook her head. "No, he took me to his place last night and we, well, you know…" she trailed off, dropping her head into her hands and groaning. "Taylor."

"Did she say something?"

"She tried to warn me. She's going to kill me."

"No, she won't. She just doesn't want either of you getting hurt. She loves you both so much," Justine paused, "and so do I." Something about the way Justine said the last part made Christy lift her head and look at her, she swallowed thickly.

"I know you do, I love you too. You know I'm sorry, don't you? I feel sick when I think about the fact that I left and didn't say goodbye to you." Christy felt tears well in her eyes. Justine was studying her nails intently, sniffing occasionally.

"I know you do, and I've forgiven you, I really have. I just remember it every now and then and it hurts." Christy went over to Justine and put her arms around her.

"I know, it hurts me too. Especially as I know I can't undo what I did. But I'll never leave like that again without saying goodbye, I swear it," she said emphatically. Justine pulled away and held up her hand, pinkie finger extended.

"Promise?" she asked.

Christy laughed and linked their pinkies. "I promise."

They hugged again and the tension eased. Justine played with Christy's curls. "Of course, if you keep seeing Dean you might not want to leave again," she teased.

"I told you it was a one-time thing, no matter how amazing it was." Christy sighed.

Justine smirked at her. "Well, I was there, the night you danced remember? Your eyes were burning into each other so intently you damn near set the bar on fire. I nearly forgot the lyrics! Whatever it is between you, it's not a one and done, trust me *mamacita*," she patted Christy's hair and turned back to the dishes, leaving Christy to her thoughts.

That night she lay in bed tossing and turning, frustrated at not being able to write, frustrated at herself for her hurtful actions all those years ago. But most of all she was frustrated that Dean wasn't in bed with her. She missed his heat, his scent, his voice. His groans in her ear, his touch. The sheets tangled around her and she wondered what he was doing, was he thinking of her? Probably not, he made it clear that he wanted to get back to being friends. She valued their friendship so much already that she didn't want to lose it either. She wasn't interested in having a relationship, so she would have to put aside her desire for him and continue to be friends. She finally drifted off to sleep, her brain obviously not getting the message because all she dreamt about was being back in his arms.

Christy was a bundle of nerves the next morning, both excited and nervous to see Dean again. She knew it was crazy, but she couldn't wait to be around him. He made her feel happy and shiny, brand new, and so full of life, he lifted her up. She watched for him out the living room window, peeking from behind the curtains like the desperate stalker she was.

When his truck pulled up, a smile split her face and her heart began to pound. She tore herself away from the window and ran into the kitchen, pretending she hadn't been waiting for him because she was far too busy scrubbing the phantom dirt off the kitchen tiles. When he came into the kitchen she looked up, fake surprised he was here. He had two coffees in one hand and a bag of treats from Ruby's in the other.

"Morning, Tiger," he said, and flinched. "Sorry, that sounded better in my head." He set the bag on the counter and held out a coffee to her. She practically snatched the cup from him and took a long sip.

"Mmm…" She tipped her head back, moaning at the glorious taste. When she looked at him again, she noticed his coffee cup had stalled halfway to his mouth, his eyes locked on her. She looked away, embarrassed. *Note to self, stop making sex noises around men.*

"Nutritious breakfast?" she joked, poking in the bag on the counter.

He took a sip of his coffee. "Of course, it is the most important meal of the day, it needs to be done right."

She looked him over, white t-shirt, faded denim jeans,

and blond stubble dusting his chiseled jaw. *James Dean eat your heart out!*

"Unfortunately, although that looks delicious, I'll have to stick to fruit. I need to keep an eye on my figure," she replied, patting her rounded stomach.

"It looked pretty good to me," he said softly, his eyes trained on her intently. "Felt pretty good too," he added, and heat flared between them, tension crackling. Her hands twitched, desperate to reach for him. His jaw clenched as his eyes traveled over her body, slowly. Then he turned away abruptly, breaking the spell and shoved his hand into the bag, snagging a donut.

"More for me then," he said, taking a bite before moving past her and heading out onto the back porch to assess what needed doing there. She swallowed thickly against the desire pulsing through her and went into the living room to continue painting, making a note to Google any convents she could join when she went back to NYC.

As she painted, her mind drifted back to her brief conversation yesterday with Hilda. Seeing Dean this morning had eased the knot of tension in her chest. She had been inspired in his house, was this her body's way of telling her where she needed to write? She wanted to dismiss the thought but couldn't, she needed to at least test the theory, her writing career could depend on it. But she couldn't get into his house without him knowing, that was kind of illegal, right? She needed to think about it.

They chatted on and off throughout the day but kept their distance from one another physically. She couldn't look at him without picturing him gloriously naked like the dirty girl she was and wondered if he did the same. Picturing her obviously, not himself. That was when the idea came to her and she knew how to get into his house.

"Dean, can I borrow the keys to your house? I just need to pop round," she asked innocently, coming up behind him which she still hadn't learned was a mistake. He always looked so good from behind.

He turned to face her, confused. "What for?"

"This is kind of embarrassing, but I think I left my panties there yesterday morning," she said, her cheeks flushing. He choked on a breath and pounded himself on the back.

"You think, what?" he croaked.

"My panties. Obviously, they came off and I don't remember putting them back on."

"I think I would have noticed them." He smirked at her in such a roguish way that she nearly combusted on the spot.

"They might have fallen behind some furniture?" she squeaked.

"Okay, well I'll have a look tonight for them and bring them with me tomorrow," he shrugged, turning back to the railing.

"But I really need them now!" she burst out, desperation fusing her tone. She forced herself to calm down. "They're my favorite pair."

He turned back and stared at her like she'd lost her mind and in that moment, she would struggle to disagree with him. "Besides, they're dirty and need washing so you shouldn't have to touch them."

He fixed her with another scorching look. "Darlin'," he started, and God, her body *felt* things when he said that. "I've had my hands all over you, including the parts of you that these "dirty" panties covered." She fought a shiver at the memories that tried to fill her mind. "I'm not bothered about touching them, but if you really need them right now, then be my guest." He reached into his pocket and pulled out his keys, handing them to her. She snatched them, sighing with relief, and thanked him.

"And Christy?" he called as she walked away. She turned back to face him, a gleam in his eye and that damn smirk tugging at his lips.

"They're my favorite pair, too."

She couldn't speak, just left as quickly as possible, his dark chuckle following her.

When she got to his house, she unlocked the door and went inside. Once she closed it she leaned against it, her heart pounding. She took in the surroundings, the feel of the house and his scent enveloped her, and she instantly felt herself calm. She knew she couldn't be long, she was only meant to be looking for fictitious panties, so she headed straight upstairs to his study.

She had to know if it was this house that inspired her. She didn't want to snoop in the other rooms, she already felt guilty enough that she had lied to gain access to his sanctuary, especially now that she knew from Justine that he didn't bring women here. She wondered what made him bring her here that night? A small flicker of hope lit in her stomach before she crushed it. *Gah, I don't have time for this!*

She opened the door to his study, went inside and instantly froze.

It was different. His computer had moved and the items on the desk had been shifted to one side, allowing more space on the surface and a better view of the garden below. She went over and studied the surroundings, she could feel the knot in her chest unfurling, the creativity taking over. She spotted that more notepads and pens had been added to the desk. Why would he add more, but move his computer away? Had he done this for her? He'd found her in here writing, maybe he had. A wave of tenderness consumed her, what a wonderful man. Why would he do that for her? She felt tears come to her eyes, the gesture was so sweet, so touching, so…

"*Ridiculous*," she muttered. "You're an idiot, he didn't do this for you, what's the matter with you?" she chastised herself. She looked out the window, the birds were back, flinging water over their backs, ruffling their feathers. It started as a slow drip feed of images into her mind, then all at once the ideas flooded her. She dropped down into the leather chair and placed her hands on the desk. Was it a coincidence that the chair was set to the perfect height for her? *Yes, stop being silly!* She grabbed a pen and a notepad and began jotting down notes and ideas that came to her.

They flooded her, her excitement growing, her nerve endings sizzling. She couldn't write fast enough, barely finishing one sentence before another zinged into her mind. She gasped when she glanced at the time and realized it had been nearly an hour. She ripped the pages out of the notepad, folded them up and put them in the back pocket of her shorts. She straightened the notepad and pens, trying to hide evidence she was there.

As she left, she wondered what she was going to do when she needed to write again, like tomorrow and the day after? She would think of something else. She locked up, reluctant to leave the house, but keen to get back to Dean. So she could make sure he was okay and hadn't hurt himself DIYing…that's all.

When she got back, she found him on the back porch, sanding down the railings, shirtless. His muscles flexing with each forceful stroke, tan body shimmering in the sun from the sheen of sweat coating him. She never really had *urges* before, until now. That's what he did, he gave her urges and needs, both of which she had to ignore.

"I'm back," she called, tearing her eyes away from him. He stood up and turned to face her, wiping the back of his hand across his forehead.

"Did you find them?" he asked, holding out his hand and she dropped the keys into his palm.

"Find what?"

"Your panties?" He gave her a funny look.

Shit, you idiot, try and keep your lies straight! "Oh, yeah I did!"

He looked at her empty hands. "Where are they?"

Very good question, she really hadn't thought this through. "Uh, I put them on."

He leaned against the railing, folding his arms across his wide chest and arched a brow at her.

"Over the pair you were already wearing? You're now wearing two pairs of panties?"

"No, just one pair," she said, unconvincingly.

"So, you weren't wearing any panties earlier then?"

"I, uh, guess not."

He walked towards her, slowly, meaningfully and she swallowed thickly. *Busted, he knows I'm lying, I'm dead.* When he reached her, he bent down to her ear and she got hit with the scent of him, pine, sweat, and dangerous man. The sensation so heady it took all her willpower not to grab him and drag her tongue across his chest.

"I always knew you were a naughty minx," he whispered, and her breath caught in her throat, his damn sexy chuckle drifting over her. Then his heat was gone, and she watched him go into the house. She groaned and slumped against the porch, feeling like the biggest idiot in the world. Also fighting the urge to charge in after him and demand he take her to bed and make her come alive again.

Chapter 21

Dean came home that night and once inside, he released a deep sigh. He could smell her sweet, candy floss scent lingering from when she was here earlier.

Today had been torture, so many times he'd nearly given in and reached for her. But he hadn't, he made it a full day without grabbing Christy and slamming her up against the nearest wall. *Just call me Mr. Restraint.* He had never struggled to keep his hands off a woman this much in his life, he had to keep reminding himself they were friends only, no funny business. He sent up another silent thanks that Beau would be back in a few days to supervise them.

He hadn't believed her for a second about needing to come to his house because she couldn't find her panties. But for some reason she needed to come here and he had his suspicions about why. He ran up the stairs, taking them two at a time, excited like a kid at Christmas. He burst into his study and her scent still hovered in the air, stronger in here. Oh, she had been in here alright. He went over to the desk, the pens and notepads were still where he left them, the chair tucked under the desk. Maybe she had just looked in here for her *missing* panties. Then he noticed the notepad, he grabbed it and brought it closer to his face to inspect it. There were indents in the paper from her writing and he felt a flare of satisfaction unlike anything he'd felt before.

She came back here to write, the knowledge that she needed to come here to do that filled his chest. He ran his hand over the indentations on the paper, trying to figure out what she had written. He grabbed a pen and flicked to the page underneath and scrawled across it. She would be back, as he hoped, anticipation flooding his veins. His little writer needed to write and she could only do it here.

So when she came up to him the next day with another excuse, he didn't ask any questions. She stared up at him, nibbling her plump lower lip and shifting on the spot nervously, she was goddamn adorable. He also found it super cute – uh – reassuring that she was a shit liar. This time, she said something about dropping earrings in the house yesterday. Earrings he knew she hadn't been wearing, but he just smiled and handed his keys over. She snatched them and scurried away, leaving him laughing to himself.

While she was gone, he worked on sanding down the old wood on the rest of the porch. It was another scorching day, although there was a slight breeze, the humidity had taken a break after the storm the other night. He removed his damp shirt and wondered if the scratches she'd left on his back had faded yet. He loved that she marked him, that he brought out that kind of passion and wildness in her. She marked him like he was hers and everyone needed to know it.

Except he wasn't, and it was really starting to rub him up the wrong way. He wanted her back in his bed but knew he was getting too attached. He knew it couldn't work between them and she made it clear that she wasn't interested in repeating the performance. He scowled, putting his anger into his work. He loved this kind of physical labor; it was the same feeling he got when he worked on a car and vowed to spend more time doing manual work at the garage and less time with his head buried in the books.

He was so lost in his thoughts that he didn't realize Christy had come back. He turned to find her standing behind him, her expression unreadable.

"Hey, did you find your earrings?"

She didn't answer, just stared at him. Then she came forward and flung herself into his arms. She plastered herself against his damp, bare chest and buried her face in his neck. His arms circled her, and he rested his cheek against the cloud of her hair, breathing in the sweet scent. She felt right, she felt like *home*, damn she was twisting him up inside. She pulled back slightly, their faces close together, mouths a breath apart. Her eyes were shining with emotion as he cupped her jaw and stroked over her cheek, catching a tear on the pad of his thumb.

"Thank you," she croaked, her voice thick. He smiled down at her, she must have found his note which meant she had definitely gone to write again. A fierce possessiveness overtook him, and he squeezed her tight to him. The atmosphere around them changed, tension thickening the air. Breathing shallowly, he stroked her cheek again and her eyes dipped to his mouth, her lips parted slightly in invitation. He could feel the beat of her heart pounding against him. He wanted her, *needed* her but he couldn't do this to himself, couldn't have her only to lose her again. Resignation filling him, he squeezed her again and then set her away from him, putting space between them. A look of hurt flashed across her features before she quickly masked it.

"You're welcome," he replied gruffly. "You can go anytime, there's a spare key in one of the rocks on the terrace." She nodded and then handed back his keys.

"I better go inside and paint," she said quietly. He stared at the porch and nodded, not trusting himself to speak. She went inside, banging the kitchen door and he closed his eyes tightly, clenching his fists to stop from going after her. It was better this way, he told himself, even if it didn't feel like it. He grabbed a hammer and started fixing the wooden slats of the porch, using more force than was necessary.

*

I'm going to kill him! Christy glared out the window at Dean, banging around on the porch. He had been in a foul mood for days, ever since she came back from "looking for her earrings" and frankly she'd had enough of it. She tried ignoring him which made him angry, she tried talking to him which just made him angrier. Then she asked him if he'd gotten his period which *really* didn't help, she just couldn't win.

Beau had messaged her this morning, he would be here any minute and she was glad he was back today, they needed a buffer. She went into the living room, inhaling the smell of fresh paint as she moved over to look out the window for him. She thought back to when she went to "search for her earrings". She had gone straight to Dean's study to write, after filling a page of notes she flipped to start a new one and had stopped dead. Her eyes gliding over his neat, cursive writing –

Believe in yourself like I believe in you. Don't ever stop writing your masterpieces.

– Your number one fan.

Tears had sprung to her eyes, he knew exactly what she was doing and *had* moved his study around for her. He made allowances for her in his home when he didn't bring any other women here. He changed his desk to accommodate her before she even came back the first time, like he knew she would need the space. Not only that, he *trusted* her enough that he was happy for her to go there whenever she needed. She couldn't put into words what that meant to her, what it could mean for *them*.

His words branded themselves in her heart and soul. No one had ever said they believed in her before. They touched her deep inside and she needed to see him immediately and rushed back. She'd needed to be in his arms, and when she was finally in them, she needed him to take her body again. But he hadn't, he'd rejected her subtle offer.

She's the one who should be banging around all sullen and angry, not him. She was distracted from her thoughts by Beau's car pulling up. She was ridiculously pleased to see him, she had spent so much time with him that to have him gone felt like she was missing a part of her family, like her big brother. He came inside the house and she jumped on him, hugging him tight.

He laughed and spun her around. "Great to see you too, Christy."

They pulled apart and Beau's eyes moved to the doorway and he smiled. "Hey buddy, long time no see!"

She turned, letting go of Beau's shoulders and saw Dean leaning against the doorway, arms folded across his chest, watching them.

"Christy sure seems glad you're back, have I been that bad?" he asked, his eyes boring into her. She knew he was kidding, but there was a bite to his tone. *Wait, was he jealous?*

"I like the grumpy, broody thing you've got going on. It really makes me just wanna mess with you some more," Beau said, lacing an arm around Christy's shoulders and hugging her tightly to him. Tension seemed to crackle in the air as the men looked at each other and she looked between them, *what's going on?* Then Dean smiled and came over to clap Beau on the back.

"Nice to have you back, bro," he said, and they bumped fists before Dean headed up the stairs. She watched him until he disappeared from view, then the bathroom door slammed shut and Beau chuckled next to her.

"Wow, look what you've done with the place!" he gushed

She suddenly panicked. "Is it okay? Do you like it?"

"It looks great!"

"Thank you, we've nearly finished downstairs now. Dean's just finishing the back porch off, the garden is nearly done too, it's all come together so quickly."

"How do you feel about that?" he asked, furrowing his brow and she thought for a moment.

"Surprisingly okay, it's been quite therapeutic actually, but I think upstairs will be harder." He nodded in understanding, and then she heard heavy footsteps coming down the stairs.

"We need an electrician, the bathroom light has been on the fritz since the storm knocked the power out,"

Dean said.

"Really? Ugh, perfect I can't afford an electrician."

"I'll pay for it," Beau offered, giving her a pointed stare.

"No one needs to pay for it," Dean glared at him, "I've got a guy who owes me a favor, I'll go and call him."

"Thank you, Dean," she said gratefully. He winked at her before heading outside to call his buddy. She and Beau chatted some more, catching up, then started teasing each other like siblings. Dean came back and confirmed the electrician would swing by tomorrow before stomping off again, and Beau went to join him to check out the porch.

She needed to break Dean out of his mood. She glanced around thinking and her eyes landed on the stairs, an evil grin playing at her lips as she decided it was time for a prank payback. She tiptoed to the top of the stairs and waited there until she heard him moving around in the kitchen. She let out a loud scream and then pounded down the stairs, ensuring she rebounded off the walls to make it sound like a realistic "fall". She threw herself on the ground, twisting her leg backwards and moving an arm up behind her back at an awkward angle.

"Christy?!" His voice sounded panicked, and he came running. She had just enough time to wipe the smile off her face and twist her expression to one of pain as he found her.

"Holy shit!" he shouted, dropping to his knees beside her.

"My leg Dean, my leg, I think it's broken!" she screamed, and smiled internally. *Where do I go to collect my Oscar?*

"It's okay, darlin', you're going to be okay. *Oh my God*

that looks so bad, but you're going to be okay!" he chanted, panic flaring in his eyes as he took in her arm and her leg. "Beau, get in here now!" he shouted and tried to slide his arm under her to pick her up, but she let out a pained moan and he dropped her. She didn't want Beau getting caught up in their prank war, so she dropped the façade and started laughing. He reared back and stared down at her. After a moment, realization dawned on him, relief then annoyance playing across his face.

"Very funny," he pouted, his pillowy bottom lip sticking out and it made her laugh harder.

"As funny as you pretending you lost your hand to the garbage disposal?" she countered, a smile tugging at his lips.

"Okay, we're even," he muttered before seriousness clouded his features, he gripped her tightly and tucked a strand of hair behind her ear, she leaned into his touch.

"You scared me."

"Well, you scared me too," she retorted, and held his stare, placing her palm on his chest over his heart, it was pounding furiously. He covered her hand with his and held it gently, his grip warm. As they stared at each other, heat soared between them and this time there was no question, they both knew. He scooped her into his arms and headed for the stairs, urgency gripping them.

"No! Not here, can we go home?" she asked, then realized she referred to his place as home. Before she could correct herself, he nodded and immediately turned and headed for the front door.

"Wait, my purse!"

Just then, Beau came into the living room and took in the fact that she was in Dean's arms and they were heading for the door. Dean grabbed her purse and flung the front door open.

"We're done for the day, see you tomorrow!" she called to Beau over Dean's shoulder, and Beau shouted, "I've only been here five minutes!" The sound of his laughter following them out the door.

The drive to Dean's felt like a lifetime, the cabin of the truck steeped in silence and white-hot tension. They didn't speak, didn't touch each other. When they pulled up outside his house, they both jumped out and ran up to the front door. When they were inside, she reached for him, but he picked her up again, swinging an arm under her legs.

"I want you in my bed, *now*," he growled, and her stomach clenched in anticipation. He carried her upstairs to his room and laid her down across his bed. She tore at his clothes and he tore at hers, their movements frenzied and uncoordinated.

When they were both naked, Christy moved to cover herself, but hesitated and changed her mind. He had seen her naked already and she knew he wanted her. His eyes drifted over her curves, lingering, heating before coming to her face. She lifted her chin defiantly, finding power in her confidence, the chains of insecurity broken, and it was exhilarating. He gripped her chin and stared into her eyes.

"You're exquisite," he murmured. He bent down and pressed his lips softly to hers, sipping at her with gentle, seductive kisses. He played at her mouth, easing it open to accept him inside. When their tongues touched, they both moaned, and the sweet kiss changed into a frenzied mating. Biting, sucking until she was writhing on the bed, her hands roving over his hard flesh.

They pulled apart panting, his lips swollen, eyes glazed with arousal, and her heart stuttered in her chest. He bent his head and kissed down her chest, holding her closely to him. He pressed his face between her breasts, closing his eyes and enjoying the intimacy they found. He nuzzled his way across to her breast and kissed her nipple. She tangled her hands in his hair, and he moved to her other breast to give it the same attention. His hand stroked over her hips, then brushed across her sex, but moved away to stroke her stomach. She tried not to let her frustration show, but she needed him to touch her, like, *now*.

She arched her hips and the message was received as he slid his hand down between her damp folds and brushed over her bundle of nerves. She moaned loudly, and he released her nipple to watch her. He rubbed small circles around her clit, his slick fingers creating wonderful sensations. He moved down and pushed a finger inside her and cursed as her muscles tightened around him.

"You feel so good, *always*," he grunted, his eyes closing. She arched into his hand and he pressed another finger inside her, curling them both. He opened his eyes and met her stare as he thrust them in and out of her. He used his palm to press against her clit, she moaned again at the feeling. His jaw clenched and sweat beaded across his brow. She was so close, she knew he wanted to watch her like before. Last time she hadn't been able to meet his stare, it felt too intimate. Now, she reveled in the intensity of it, wanting to show him exactly how he made her feel. She held his gaze, he moved his fingers faster and put more pressure on her clit. Her breathing deepened and she felt her orgasm coiling, it would be explosive. Her eyelids fluttering closed in pleasure, she couldn't fight the reaction.

"Look at me." His words, a command and a plea and she was helpless to resist. She swung her eyes back to his as her sex started quivering. Her climax ripped through her, her core clenching tightly and she cried out, maintaining eye contact with Dean the whole time. Her body quaked with aftershocks, and she felt herself shaking with emotion. She was stripped bare to him, raw and sensitive like a wound. She clapped her hands over her eyes to try and stop the tears from forming. He pulled her hands away, showering her face with kisses and murmuring gentle words to soothe her. He told her how beautiful she was, how amazing they were together and how much he desired her.

She pulled away and looked at him, desire sharp in those fiery blue eyes of his. He pulled her onto her side, grabbed her leg and slung it over his hip. He lined them up and slid inside her to the hilt. She cried out as she felt him thick and hard inside her. He pulled out and slammed in again, her eyes flew open as she gasped. Her eyes found his as he slammed into her again and again, and before long a second orgasm was building. His hand gripped her ass tightly, pulling her against him as he thrust. He groaned, dipping down to take her mouth, he thrust his tongue in time with his hips until she couldn't hold out any longer. She came, hard, and he swallowed the moan that wrenched from her throat. Her core clenched around his cock, gripping it tightly and she felt him thicken inside her before he grunted and followed her over the edge.

Their ragged breathing filled the room as they tried to catch their breath. She felt amazing, she looked at him out the corner of her eye and saw he was already watching her. He wrapped an arm around her, grinning wickedly and pulled her on top of him. She squealed and sat up, so she straddled his thighs.

He looked at her through lowered eyelids. "Fuck, you're sexy."

"Oh yeah?" she replied, planting her hands on her

rounded hips.

"Yeah, my little Marilyn," he said softly.

Her pulse thudded. "What did you call me?" she asked, she can't have heard him right.

His cheeks flushed. "Uh, it's just a silly nickname I had for you years ago."

"You started that?"

"Yeah," he said sheepishly, and a wave of tenderness rushed through her. She couldn't believe it had come from him. She always assumed Taylor started it, but she must have heard it from Dean. He had always found her attractive, just as she always wanted him and tried to hide it.

She looked down at this amazing man she lov-*liked*. The word tried to form but she brushed it aside. She watched his eyes roving over her and felt wanted and desired. She felt him hardening against her thigh and a wicked smile played over her lips and she bent down, finding his mouth with hers.

A long time and lots of orgasms later they were exhausted. She lay half on him, her head resting on his chest, and staring up at him while he watched her, running his fingers through her hair. They laid like this for a while, just watching, taking in the details, and memorizing each other. She had never felt like this before and never had this kind of connection. It was intoxicating, she wanted to burrow into him, become one with him, but it would never feel enough. He opened his mouth to say something but then closed it, frowning.

"What?" she asked, drawing patterns across his chest with her fingers, he thought for a moment.

"I need to know. I need to know what happened and why you left. I need to know that he didn't…hurt you," he said raggedly. She held her breath, this wasn't something she talked about with anyone, even Taylor. She didn't like to be vulnerable ever, but Dean was different. He had been there for her, supported her in so many ways in such a short space of time. There was no one she was more vulnerable with and she realized that he had earned her trust, something very few people had done.

"I'm not going anywhere," he said, brushing his thumb over her lips, her eyes fluttered closed at the feel of him. So, she told him. She told him all of it, held nothing back. It was hard, he tensed at certain parts, and she knew he was struggling to hold back his emotions. She couldn't hold back hers, she stopped occasionally when it was too much. He let her take breaks, didn't push her, and just listened all the while stroking her hair, keeping them connected. When she finished, he pulled her tight against him and buried his face in her hair and murmured comforting words in her ear. About how brave she was, how amazing she was, and how lucky he was to know her. Yet, she felt she was the one who was lucky.

He then told her about his father, how he abandoned Dean and his mom, and although it hurt, Dean was happy, it meant he didn't get hit anymore. She felt sick at the thought of him as a young boy being hit by someone who was meant to love and protect him. He told her about his relationship with Taylor, how she had shown him love and the importance of family. They talked until their lips found each other again, and then he was showing her how he felt with his body, and they poured themselves into each other.

Chapter 22

When Dean woke up the next morning, he instinctively reached out for Christy but the bed was empty, the top sheet was missing too. He smiled to himself at the thought of those sexy curves draped in the thin sheet, the image making him harden as he pictured her berry nipples playing peekaboo through the cotton.

They shared an amazing night together; he'd never experienced this kind of consuming lust before. Even now, he was astonished that his body was begging to sink into her wet heat again, remembering how it felt. He needed to find her and bring her back to bed, *now*.

He wrapped his naked body in his duvet before searching for her. She wasn't downstairs or in the shower so he went to his study and when he looked inside his heart burned in his chest. She was sitting at his desk, writing, the bedsheet wrapped around her and tucked under her arms. The smooth, creamy skin of her bare shoulders on display, teasing and taunting him.

He watched her for a while with a smile on his face then he got dressed and made some coffee and toast. He brought it back upstairs and placed the mug and plate on the desk beside her, bending to kiss the sensitive spot between her neck and shoulder. He had the satisfaction of watching goosebumps break out over her skin. She turned to capture his lips, and he gave her a brief kiss before pulling away.

"I refuse to be your distraction. The electrician will be at yours soon."

"Okay, I'll go and change."

"No, you stay here, I'll go," he offered.

"Are you sure?"

"Yes, stay. Write. Miss me," he joked, kissing her again and she laughed against his mouth. Damn, that laugh made him so happy. With a reluctant sigh, he pulled away from her.

He met his friend, Karl, at the house. He had helped Karl hide a dent in his wife's car a few years back free of charge and now he was collecting on the favor. As they went inside, Dean was pleased to find that Beau had locked up for them yesterday. He smiled and made a mental note to thank his friend later. He showed Karl upstairs to the bathroom light. Karl got out some tools and began poking around the fixture and the socket.

"These old houses have got some dodgy wiring. Builders used to run them all over the place, through the walls into different rooms. Looks like this is a wiring issue but it's not here, let me track the cable and see where it goes." Karl started roving the walls with some handheld gadget and Dean followed him as he left the bathroom and went down the hall. He was too busy thinking about what he was going to do to Christy when he got home that he didn't realize until it was too late that Karl was going into her father's room. He cursed under his breath and went after him.

"Uh, Karl, this room is off limits."

Karl gave him a funny look. "I think the loose connection may be coming from in here, but I need to see, do you want me to fix it or not?"

Dean stood in the doorway, unsure of what to do. He knew Christy didn't want people coming in this room, but they also needed to fix the electrics. It was a safety issue for her while she was still in the house, and they couldn't hand it over to the new owners with faulty electrics.

Dean sighed. "Okay, just tell me what to look for and I'll find it." When Karl looked at him like he was crazy, he added, "you want me to tell Darlene what you did to her Tesla?" Karl groused but agreed in the end. He left the room and Dean went inside, he tried not to look at any of the surroundings, just wanting to get in and out as soon as possible. He listened to Karl's instructions and ended up rummaging in a small walk-in closet, he moved some items to one side trying to get to the back of it.

"Can you see it?" Karl called out.

"I can't see shit!" Dean shouted back. "Can you get me a flashlight?

He heard a distant rattling, then a muffled curse. "The battery just died."

"I've got a toolbox in the kitchen; you can grab my flashlight from there."

A few moments later, Karl was back and rolling the flashlight into the room. Dean grabbed it and went back to investigate the closet. He found the socket at the bottom of the closet on the back wall, it was extremely old and hanging partially off with exposed wires. Karl managed to talk him through what to do without electrocuting himself, and Dean felt a sense of satisfaction at fixing the socket and wiring.

As he tried to duck back out, he tripped over a box and knocked it onto the floor, the contents spilling out. He dropped to his knees, placing his flashlight beside the box and started scooping up the contents. As he did, he saw it was lots of envelopes, his eyes caught the name on them. They were addressed to Christy to her place in New York. There was no stamp fixed to any of them as though they hadn't been mailed, and Dean realized that Christy's dad must have written them but never sent them.

The understanding of what he held in his hands made him feel sick. How long had these been here? Did Christy know? Of course she didn't, she never came in here. He wondered what they said, and although curious, he couldn't bring himself to open any of them, that would be a huge betrayal. It was bad enough that he came in here anyway. Guilt punched him in the gut and he hurriedly put the letters back in the box.

There had to be at least fifty letters, his hands were shaking. What did he do? He needed to tell her. He shoved the box back and practically ran out of the room, slamming the door. He said goodbye and thanked Karl, declaring the debt paid.

Dean drove home, thinking about what to say to Christy. Because she'd opened up to him, he knew the full extent of what happened, how it had scarred her and how she had only just made peace with it. He didn't want to ruin that for her, didn't want to be the one to cause her so much pain and shatter her hard won happiness. How did he even start that conversation? Why did this have to happen? Why couldn't they just continue on as they were?

It wouldn't be long now until they started working on the upstairs of the house, she would find them soon anyway. He could just be there for her when she did and support her, but the idea of her experiencing any pain hurt him too. His thoughts continued spinning until he came into the study, expecting her to be there still writing, draped in his sheet.

"Oh, God," he groaned. The sheet had fallen and she was bare to the waist. Although her back was to him, he could see her reflection in the window. His cock hardened instantly at his goddess, naked in her element. She met his eyes in the window and half turned, baring herself to him. His need was a powerful force inside him, driving him to her. He stormed over and grabbed her around the waist, hefting her up, and laid her across his desk.

He bent his head, sucking a hard nipple into the wet warmth of his mouth and she moaned, arching into his touch like she always did. He kissed down her stomach, dipping his tongue into her navel before shoving the sheet away and burying his face in her triangle of short, blond curls. He slid his tongue into the heart of her, her hands flew into his hair as she began babbling. She writhed against his face, chasing every sensation and he brought his hands into play, thrusting two fingers in and out of her while he licked, sucked, and nibbled at her center. When he thought she was close, he pulled back. She lifted her head, her lips swollen from biting them in pleasure.

"No!" she moaned as he disengaged. He moved his hands to the front of his jeans and unfastened them, springing his hard cock free.

"Yesss," she hissed, eyeing him eagerly and he couldn't hold back his laughter, his woman was perfect. He grabbed her thighs and spread them as wide as they could go.

"Shirt off," she commanded before he could enter her. His cock twitched at her dominating tone. He gripped himself, stroking up and down lazily watching her. Her eyes heating and following the motion, she licked her lips.

"What are you going to do if I don't?" he teased. She struggled to tear her gaze away from his hand.

"I'll…um…"

"Christy, I'm waiting…"

She turned her fiery gaze on him. "If you don't remove your shirt, then I think we're done here." She sniffed primly and tried to close her legs.

"Oh no you don't," he released himself, and tore his shirt off, much to her amusement. Her laugh turned into a moan as he thrust himself inside her. She arched her back again, and he bent down to suck her nipple as he pounded into her. She went wild, moaning loudly, not caring who heard and fuck if that didn't turn him on even more. To hear how good he made her feel, it turned him into a beast, and he rubbed her clit as he fucked her on his desk. She came, hot, hard, and loud as her walls clamped down around him, squeezing him tight. He could barely push through, but he powered on, sweat dripping off him. He felt his climax boiling up, his face screwed up in intense pleasure, and he came with a shout.

After an impossibly long time he collapsed onto her, his head resting on her chest listening to the beat of her heart. Her arms came round him, and she quivered against him as aftershocks teased her body. He carried her to the couch and draped the blanket over them as they fell asleep.

When he awoke, she was writing again. He lay there watching her for a while, thoughts going crazy. He decided he would wait for the right moment to tell her about the letters, he didn't want to ruin her joy. It was selfish, he knew this, but she was writing again and happy. He didn't want to ruin that just yet, she needed this peace. He would tell her when the time was right. He got up and grabbed his book from his room, he didn't think she had spotted it before, but it was one of hers. He'd ordered all of them once he learned the titles. He came back into the study and lay there, alternating between reading her impressive work, and watching her write her heart out.

*

Christy's body ached all over, but she didn't care. It was a reminder she had been thoroughly satisfied by a man who couldn't get enough of her. She watched, a coy smile playing at her lips, as Dean and Beau lifted the battered old couch and carried it outside, putting it in the bed of Dean's truck. She was fully aware she was ogling Dean's muscles, watching them flex and ripple and didn't even try to hide it. He caught her watching him and gifted her with a knowing smile, his dimples teasing his cheeks. It was a smile reserved just for her and she reveled in it. Beau witnessed the interaction and rolled his eyes before jumping into the passenger side of the truck. Dean came over to her, lifting his hand and tucking a strand of hair behind her ear, she leaned into his touch.

"We're gonna go and drop this off then get some food so I'll grab you something greasy and fattening," he said, then dipped his head to whisper in her ear, warm breath trekking over her. "You're going to need to keep your strength up for when I get back." She shivered and he kissed her slowly, lingering until Beau leaned on the horn of the truck.

Dean reluctantly pulled away and stared down at her, concern shining in his eyes before it was gone and kissed the palm of her hand before leaving. She noticed that a few times this last week, he seemed concerned or worried, but she couldn't work out what was wrong. Maybe he was just conscious she would be leaving soon, it was definitely playing on her mind a lot. She'd felt their connection growing and deepening, it wasn't casual anymore and they didn't bother trying to hide it. She tried not to think about what it meant and the fact that she was still leaving and with a sigh, went back into the house.

It was nearly empty now and freshly decorated, looking as good as new. They'd pretty much finished downstairs this week, now it was time to start clearing out upstairs. She didn't think it needed as much work, there weren't really any repairs needed, just to clear the furniture and maybe freshen up the paintwork. She stood in the doorway of her old room thinking she could start there, but she didn't really want to go through any of the stuff, it wasn't anything she wanted to keep. Whereas there could be things in her father's old room she might want to hold onto as a keepsake.

Christy turned to the room in question and stared at the door, she knew she needed to tackle this one soon. She was in a good place emotionally, she'd actually never felt better. She wanted to do it on her own and with the guys being out for a little while there was no better time, especially if she got upset as she didn't want them to worry. She steeled herself and grabbed the door handle, taking a breath before turning it and opening the door.

She was immediately hit by the scent of her father, it elicited a range of feelings and memories, some good and some bad. Good ones from when they were a happy family of three and bad ones from where it was just the two of them and he began to spiral. She pushed the memories away, they had tortured her enough over the years and she wouldn't give them power anymore.

She looked around the room; deep green curtains and bedding accentuated the dark wood furniture of the room. There was a dresser opposite the bed which had photos and knick knacks sitting on top of it. She glanced at the photos; one of the three of them as a family, one of her mother and father laughing, wrapped in each other's arms, and then one of herself from when she was about fifteen, just before her mother died. She ran her hands over them and then gathered them up, she didn't really have any photos, so these were important to her.

There were nightstands on either side of the bed, she went over to the one that used to be her mothers and saw an old mirrored jewelry box on top. She opened it and gasped as she found her mother's wedding ring inside. She picked it up carefully as though it were the greatest treasure, which to her, it was. A lump formed in her throat as she slid the gold band onto her finger. It fit perfectly, the light playing off the row of small diamonds. She stared at it for the longest time before she finally turned away and continued her assessment of the room.

Her eyes landed on an armchair in the corner of the room and she went over to it. She had a flash of memory of her father sitting in it reading, and her mom perched on his lap. She smiled at the happy memory even though it was painful. She wandered over to the small, walk-in closet and opened the door, her father's scent stronger in here where it lingered on his clothes.

She flipped through the hangers, glancing at the different shirts he had, trying to imagine him in them, running her hands over the fabric. She snagged herself on one of them, knocking it off the hanger and onto the floor and she bent to pick it up where it was draped over an old box. When she grabbed it, it caught the corner of the box, knocking it over. She muttered to herself about her clumsiness and started putting the contents back inside it.

She paused as she saw her name and address on several bits of paper. She grabbed one, looking at it more closely and realized it was a letter addressed to her. There were loads of them, but they didn't look like they had been sent. She felt a prickle travel down her spine as she turned one over, confused and opened it. The paper was faded, like it was old but still crisp as it unfolded. She ran her eyes over the words on the page before her, and her world began to spin, a sob tearing from her throat.

*

Dean practically skipped up the path to the house, he'd sent Beau home after they grabbed lunch knowing that when he got back, all he wanted to do was ravage the blond, curvy vixen waiting for him. He was thrilled at the prospect that soon she would be underneath him, naked and begging. God, he loved it when she begged. His step faltered slightly when he thought about the fact that he still hadn't told her about the letters.

It had been a week since he accidentally discovered them. He felt so guilty keeping it quiet, he promised himself he would tell her and see if she wanted him to sit with her while she read them, if she needed the support. He'd put off telling her, worried she wouldn't forgive him for finding them and not telling her about them straight away. His selfishness disappointed him, which is why he was going to tell her tonight.

"Christy? I hope you've removed all clothing as instructed," he called, peering into the kitchen. He'd messaged her on his way back with his demands. There was no answer, and he couldn't see her. He placed the food on the counter and looked out onto the back porch but no sign of her there either.

"Christy?" he called again from the foot of the stairs. Maybe if she were naked, she wouldn't come and find him, he would have to find her. Anticipation fired his blood and he took the stairs two at a time, but when he reached the top, he saw the door to her father's room was open and his stomach dipped. He braced himself as he headed inside, he spotted her sitting on the floor in the closet, surrounded by the letters, she had some clutched in her fist. She looked up at him and the sight of her broke his heart.

Tears streamed from her eyes, her cheeks flushed from crying, and she started hyperventilating when she saw him, shaking her head. Then she stopped suddenly, opened her mouth and wailed. The sound of her cry pierced his soul, full of so much anguish, grief, and heartbreak and he knew he would never forget it. He rushed over, sat on the floor beside her, and pulled her onto his lap. She sobbed hysterically and he tried to soothe her, running his hands over her face and hair. He squeezed his eyes shut as he tried to calm her and failed, tears filling his own eyes.

How could he have kept this from her, it surely would have been less painful if he told her before. They could have built up to reading them, so it wasn't such a shock. He didn't think he could ever forgive himself for his selfishness.

They stayed like that for over an hour, him murmuring in her ear, stroking his hands over her back. She pulled back and looked at him, her eyes wide and watery, blue pools of devastation. Her mouth opened and closed as she tried to find words, but they failed her. She just raised her fist that had the letters clenched in it and closed her eyes. His heart ached for her. She quieted after a while, exhaustion taking over.

"He found me," she croaked, her voice hoarse from her tears. "He found me, but he didn't approach me because he didn't think I could ever forgive him. He said I looked so happy that he didn't want to ruin it. He was just glad I was happy." She choked on the last words and began crying again. It devastated Dean to think they could have reconciled before he died, he couldn't imagine how she was feeling and he'd made it worse by not warning her.

She lifted her head from his chest and looked back at the box. She crawled off his lap, he didn't want to let her go, but he held himself back. She started rummaging through the letters and then stopped. He watched her stiffen in front of him before she swung those soulful eyes to him, but this time her baby blues were cold and hard. She grabbed something and held it up in front of him; his flashlight. He felt cold all over and swallowed thickly as he tried to think of what to say but there was no denying it was his, she saw him with it enough times.

"Did you know about these?" she asked, gesturing to the letters and her voice cracking.

He couldn't lie to her, he wouldn't. "Yes," he answered simply. She closed her eyes and nausea churned his stomach. He reached for her, but she batted him away.

"How could you not tell me?"

"I wanted to tell you; I just didn't know how. You've been in such a good place and I couldn't bear the thought of ruining that for you," he began explaining, desperation fusing his tone.

She held up a hand to stop him from talking. "You need to leave," she stated, her tone void of any emotion now.

He reached for her again. "Please just let me-"

"Don't touch me!" she yelled. He jumped, surprised at her outburst. He took a step back, he didn't want to leave, couldn't stand to leave her like this. She turned away from him, dismissing him, and he knew she wasn't in a place where he could reach her. He resigned himself to the fact that he needed to give her some space.

"Okay, I'll go, but I'll be back in the morning."

She didn't respond.

She picked up the box of letters and carried them over to the armchair in the corner of the room, not looking at him. She was in shock and needed some time to process her feelings.

"I'll come back," he said again, but she didn't respond, just stared at the box of letters in her lap.

It killed him to leave her, but he did. He sat in his truck for an hour outside the house before he drove home, then he sat in his study all night thinking about her. It shredded his insides when he thought about the woman he loved hurting so badly.

Wait, loved? Did he love her? It hit him with such sharp clarity he could have laughed if things weren't so grim. But he felt it, like fire coursing through his veins. He'd never felt like this about anyone before, the strength of his feelings terrifying him. That she was hurting so unbearably and to know he could've prevented it or eased it, clawed at his heart.

He betrayed her, just as she was starting to trust him and he'd destroyed that precious gift. He needed her to forgive him, he needed to tell her how he felt, and he prayed she would feel the same. She was the family he needed, she was the missing piece of him that he had been searching for; he just hoped it wasn't too late and that she could forgive him.

After a long, sleepless night, Dean headed back to Christy's in the morning, his sense of urgency driving every step he took. He let himself into the house, calling out to her. He checked downstairs first and the food he brought yesterday still sat on the counter. He tossed it in the trash before it attracted wildlife.

Worried, he went upstairs and found her still sitting in the armchair where he left her yesterday. She was wearing the same clothes as the day before, her eyes red and swollen, a glassy sheen to them. She looked heartbroken and exhausted, and still she was the most beautiful woman in the world. She slid her gaze to him when he came in, her eyes appeared so emotionless they scared him. She didn't move other than that, so he wrapped his arms around her, carried her to the bathroom and sat her on the lid of the toilet. He turned the shower on, stripped her, then himself, and helped her into the stall. He sat her on the lip of the bath while he washed her hair and body.

She didn't say anything, didn't react, so he talked. He told her how sorry he was, how much he cared for her, how he planned to make it up to her and how he would never do anything to hurt her again, desperation lining his words. He switched off the shower, dried and dressed them both, and carried her into the room she was staying in and put her into bed, tucking the duvet around her, hoping she would just drift off. He kissed her forehead and left, returning to her father's room.

He picked up the letters that were scattered around the floor, tucked them back into envelopes, and put them back in the box. He didn't read any of them, refused to unless she wanted him to. He placed the box back on the armchair so she could find them if she needed them and then went back to check on her. He found her out of bed and pacing around the room.

"Christy, I'm so sorry I kept this from you. I'll do whatever it takes to make it up to you. I didn't read any of them, not that it makes a difference, but I just wanted you to know. I didn't know how to tell you. You were so happy, and I couldn't ruin that, I was selfish because I lov-"

"I need Beau," she interrupted.

His heart thudded in his chest at her words. "What?"

"Beau. I want Beau, now," she repeated, her tone hardening. A roaring sound filled his ears as he tried to understand what she was saying.

"You *want* Beau? You *need* Beau?" he demanded, voice rising with his hurt. As she nodded, his chest started tightening, how could he have been so blind? He should have seen it, the way they interacted with each other and their closeness, he had assumed it was just a platonic love. Could she have wanted Beau all along? Was it never really Dean she wanted? She tried to tell him she didn't want anything serious, only wanted casual, but he didn't listen and he lost his stupid, soft heart.

The determination in her eyes cemented his thoughts; he said he would do whatever it took to make this right, he could at least give her what she asked for. With a heavy heart, he made the call. Ten minutes later, Beau burst into the house and Dean met him at the top of the stairs.

"What's going on?" he demanded, concern pinching his features. Dean couldn't talk, just gestured into the room. Beau brushed passed him and into the room, when Christy saw him relief flooded her face and she threw her arms around him. Dean's heart cracked in his chest as his suspicions were confirmed. He didn't know what to do, was this it for them? When they broke apart she sat Beau on the bed and then came over to Dean.

"You can leave now," she said, and shut the door in his face.

His mind exploded with images of what she and Beau would do in that room. His chest split open, acid poured inside and he couldn't catch his breath. Taylor had been right; he was a fool.

Dean left the house, his heart breaking with each step he took. He had never loved anyone like he loved her, the pain like nothing he'd ever felt before. He didn't know what to do or where to go. He couldn't stand the thought of going to his house without her. This was why he had never taken a woman there, because now all he would think of when he was there, was Christy.

He couldn't take the pain, he needed to numb the way she made him feel and to forget he loved her, until it stopped hurting.

He got in his truck and headed straight for the bar.

Chapter 23

Christy waited until she heard the front door slam, she couldn't stomach the thought of Dean witnessing what she was about to do.

"What the hell is going on?" Beau demanded, and she told him everything. About finding those heart-breaking letters filled with love, regret, and honesty that came too little too late. Her father loved her, it was all over the pages, but he couldn't find the courage to send them. He begged for her forgiveness, begged for her love and now she was about to beg too.

"I can't sell this house Beau. I know it's too late now, but I'll buy it back from you, no matter what it costs."

"What are you talking about?"

"I need to buy the house back, I can't let it go now." Her voice cracked with emotion, she was barely holding it together. He looked at her like she was crazy.

"Please Beau, I'll beg. I'll get on my knees and beg you if I have to. I can't let it go, my father..." she trailed off. Beau shook his head and tried to place his hands on her shoulders.

She dropped to her knees, tears spilling from her eyes. "I will give you everything I have, whatever you want. Please don't take this from me, I can't leave him Beau, I can't leave him here. It's the last piece of him I have, don't take it from me, I'm begging you!"

Huge gut-wrenching sobs tore from her throat as she stared up at him, his eyes wide and shocked. The more she repeated herself, the harder his expression became. She was humiliating herself, but she didn't care what he thought, she just didn't want Dean to witness her mortification. Beau grabbed her under the arms, hauled her up, and sat her on his lap on the bed. He tried to soothe her, but broken pleas fell from her lips, and she was powerless to stop them.

"Christy, please stop, this is killing me. You don't need to beg. I would hand it back to you in a heartbeat, please tell me you know that?" his voice wavering slightly. She pulled back to look at him, wiping her eyes. "But I want you to think about it carefully, I'll give you all the time in the world to think about it. Do you want the house that's caused you so much pain? There are so many bad memories here. The letters can erase some of the hurt, but they can't change what happened here." He spoke gently now, she knew he wasn't trying to hurt her, just as Dean hadn't when he kept his knowledge of the letters from her. She tried to take a step back and think about it. She knew Beau was right, the memories weren't good and finding those letters wouldn't change that.

"I think it's time for you to let this place go, end the torment and move forward free to create new memories with those of us that love you. It doesn't mean you lose the last piece of your father; he'll always be in your heart."

Her mind was reeling. Beau was right, she needed time to think. She and Beau spoke a little longer before he hugged her and left. She needed sleep, she was exhausted, but there was only one place she wanted to be. She grabbed her purse, got in her clapped out car and drove to Dean's. He wasn't there so she let herself in using the spare key, and got straight into his bed, feeling her mind calm. Tucked under his duvet, shrouded in his scent, in his home, it was like he was there with her and she was able to sort through her thoughts. Her eyes drifted closed and the last thing she thought was that she couldn't wait to see him when she woke up.

*

"Are you worried you're gonna run out? Pour me another goddamn shot!" Dean slurred at Kayleigh who reluctantly poured him another shot of whiskey.

"To getting kicked in the guts by love!" he shouted, and tipped his head back, downing the amber liquid, nearly falling off his stool as he did. *Damn, these things are a safety hazard.* He slammed the glass back down on the bar and gestured for a refill, he was well and truly on his way to numbing the pain. He wanted to keep going until he was ready to black out, so he didn't have to think about her anymore. How much he'd hurt her and how she didn't love him. How he would have to be happy for her and Beau because they both deserved so much happiness.

"I really don't think you should have any more, sir," Kayleigh said tentatively.

"Sir?" he barked out. "I ain't my father and I don't remember asking your opinion, so pour me a fucking drink!" he shouted, a look of fear passed over her face and penetrated his drunken state.

"*Shit*, I'm sorry Kayleigh," he said. "Maybe I am my father," he muttered to himself. He decided it was time to go, the warm floaty feeling was kicking in, but the thought of going back to his empty house, that smelled like Christy, was too painful to contemplate.

He tried to smile at Kayleigh, but he didn't think it was one of his best.

"Can I have my usual room, please?" He remembered to add in a please so he didn't seem like a complete asshole, she bobbed at him and went into the office. *Did she just curtsy?* At least Taylor was out on a date this evening, she would have cut him off immediately.

A prickly sensation traveled down his spine, and moments later a cold hand settled on the nape of his neck. "*Baby!*" A shrill voice squealed. "There you are, I've missed you!"

He turned, his vision swimming from the alcohol and saw Darcy standing there. She planted a kiss on his lips, he tried to duck away, but the alcohol slowed his reflexes.

"What do you mean, *there you are*? I told you I wasn't interested." He was so not in the mood for this, she placed her hand on her hip and popped it to one side.

"I know you didn't mean it, you were just playing hard to get, and it *totally* worked," she pouted, her botoxed lips puckering grotesquely. God, what had he seen in her? Thankfully, Kayleigh came back and handed him the key. Dean thanked her, reminding himself he must apologize in the morning when he was sober.

"Oh goody, round two!" Darcy clapped.

"No thanks, I'm leaving, *alone*." He fell off his stool but managed to get himself back up without too much trouble.

"Let me help you." She grabbed at him, plastering herself to his body under the guise of trying to keep him upright.

"I'm not interested, Darcy. I told you I belong to someone else." *Even if she doesn't want me back.*

"Okay fine, I get it. At least let me help you though? No funny business, I swear." She held up two fingers in scout's honor.

"Bye, Darcy," he said, tripping his way over to the door. He made it outside but fell down the steps, eventually picking himself up and trudging around the back to his cabin. It took five attempts to get the door unlocked, but he finally made it inside and when he tried to kick the door shut behind him, a stilettoed foot blocked it, he cursed.

"I just want to make sure you're okay," Darcy said, barging into the room.

"Darcy, I don't know how to make this any clearer. I don't want you, I never did and I never will, now get out."

He needed to fall into oblivion, he could feel it beckoning. He pulled his shirt over his head and collapsed onto the bed, trying to sit up to take his jeans off. Darcy marched over and jumped on the bed straddling his hips and giggling loudly.

"What are you doing?" he shouted, reaching up and grabbing her arms, trying to shove her off him. That only made her writhe against him, he felt sick, alcohol sloshing in his stomach. Sleep trying to pull him under, his eyelids starting to close.

"Oh my God, Dean?"

He would recognize that voice anywhere. He turned his head to the side and saw Marilyn Monroe standing in the doorway to the cabin. Eyes wide and pretty pink mouth open in horror as she took in Darcy rubbing herself on his half naked body. No, not Marilyn Monroe,

Christy. Then she was gone, panic clawed at him.

"No, wait!" he called out, but his limbs wouldn't move. The numbing darkness he was begging for only moments earlier finally descended and he passed out.

*

Dean came awake spluttering, cold water dripping down his face. His head pounding at his sudden movement, like someone had taken a sledgehammer to it. His stomach roiled and he turned to the side just in case he vomited but found himself face to face with Darcy.

"What the fuck!"

"Exactly, Dean. What the *fuck*!" He turned to the other side and saw Taylor and Beau stood near the bed, Taylor had an empty glass dangling from her fingers, her expression deadly. Darcy stirred beside him and sat up.

"Get rid of the angry redhead, she makes my head hurt," she pouted.

"Oh, I'll make more than your head hurt, you skank!" Taylor growled, and lunged for her, spitting fire. Beau was quicker though, slinging an arm around Taylor's waist, he hauled her away.

"Okay, calm down, Tyson Fury," Beau grunted as her flailing limbs connected with his. Taylor shoved him off and moved to stand on the other side of the room.

"You need to leave," Dean said to Darcy, his tone leaving no room for argument. Seeing she was outnumbered and unwanted she grabbed her stuff and slunk out of the room.

"Dude, what the hell?" Beau asked, looking at him with such disappointment. Dean felt his temper flare remembering how things were left yesterday.

"You tell me, buddy," he spat.

"What?"

"You. Christy. Her bedroom. Even I'm smart enough

to put that one together."

"Wow, and here I thought you were such a nice boy, Beau. I'm a little disappointed in you," Taylor's tone dripped with sarcasm.

Beau sent her a withering look, then turned back to Dean. "You clearly aren't that smart after all. I don't know what you think is going on but it's nothing like that," Beau exclaimed, Dean scoffed at him. "It's true! Look, I'm the one buying her house."

"Congratu-*fucking*-lations," Taylor deadpanned. Despite the situation Dean felt a smile almost form at her sass, almost.

"So, you're moving back to town?" he asked.

"Yes, I wanted it to be a surprise. She knows it's me who's buying the house, she's known all along, and she wanted to ask to buy it back. You should've seen her Dean; she was so distraught she got on her knees and begged me, actually begged. I guess that's why she sent you away, she didn't want you to see it."

This was too much information for Dean's hangover fueled brain to comprehend, but he knew one thing, he was a fucking idiot. He groaned loudly and laid back on the bed.

"I told her she could have it, it doesn't bother me, but I don't think she really wants it. I think she just panicked after finding the letters." Beau added.

"What letters?" Taylor asked. As Beau filled her in on what happened, Taylor was shocked into silence.

"I need to find her," Dean said, standing up slowly. When he didn't vomit, he headed towards the doorway when his memory decided to finish downloading. Christy had already found him last night, with Darcy.

"Oh shit, she saw me...with Darcy. Except I wasn't doing anything, Darcy wouldn't get off me and leave, and then I must have passed out," Dean explained, and Taylor cursed.

"Dean, I swear to God, I told you not to hurt her!" she shouted.

"I know, I'm sorry Taylor, but I'm not messing around, okay? I need her, she's it for me."

"Let's go find her, now, before I beat the shit out of you for being so stupid," Taylor grunted. All three of them made their way to the door when it burst open and Justine charged in.

"*Qué hiciste?*" she shouted at Dean, storming over to him and jabbing her finger into his chest. "She's gone, she left town!"

Dean cursed. "When?"

"She's driving home, she left about half an hour ago," she said to Taylor, a watery smile on her face. "At least she came and said goodbye this time."

Taylor turned to face Dean, a fierce expression on her face. "Fix it, now." she said, her tone cold and deadly.

"I will, I swear."

"No, don't go after her, not unless you really care about her. You can't mess around with her anymore," Justine said.

"I do care about her, I tried to tell her I love her yesterday, dammit!" he shouted, frustration and panic clawing at him.

"Come on, she can't have gotten far," Beau said, clapping a hand on his shoulder. Dean's mind was whirring away; what was he going to do if he lost her, if he couldn't reach her? *Wait a minute.*

"Did you say she's driving home? To New York?" he asked Justine.

"I guess so?"

A smile spread across his face as he stood there for a

moment, thinking.

"Come on, let's go!" Beau yelled.

Dean shook his head, "No."

"No?" Taylor and Justine chorused.

"I've got an idea." They all looked at him skeptically. *"Trust me."*

He sent the others back to the bar to wait and he made a few calls on his cell. When he was done, he went and joined them. They were sitting in a booth, the mood somber with tension filling the air. Justine and Taylor kept shooting him death glares at his apparent lack of action, and Beau and Taylor kept sniping at each other. After five hours he started to panic, what if he had played this all wrong?

"Dean, if this doesn't have a happy ending, I will never forgive you," Taylor said quietly.

"It will, trust me," he replied fiercely.

After another two anxious hours, he got the call he was waiting for.

Chapter 24

Could this day get any worse, actually not this day, this freaking year? Christy watched as smoke billowed from under the hood of her car as she rolled to a stop on the side of the road. She sighed and hiccupped, tears still streaming unchecked down her cheeks. Of course she'd broken down, why would she catch a break? She switched off the engine and folded her arms across the steering wheel, burying her face as sobs overtook her.

She cried for herself, for her mom and dad, the home she had decided to give up and for the man who'd broken her heart, the final nail in the coffin. The image of him half naked and writhing on the bed with that gorgeous woman was seared into her brain and she saw it every time she closed her eyes, hurt piercing her heart each time. She was shocked she still had tears left to cry. She had woken up in his bed the night before, feeling refreshed from her sleep and clear headed. She decided she didn't want to keep the house, it wasn't a home to her and Beau was right, she wanted a clean break. But she also wanted to stay in town, she was ready to try and make the small town her home again. She didn't have many ties in the city, her closest friends were here and she could write anywhere.

And then there was Dean. At first, she was hurt when she found out he knew about the letters and didn't tell her. But when he explained, she completely understood, she probably would have done the same thing. No one wants to hurt someone they care about, him especially. And after everything that happened with her father, she'd learned not to hold grudges, time was far too precious. She trusted Dean, something she was never able to do before, having had it broken so many times in the past. But she cared about him, knew he cared about her and would never try to hurt her. Until last night.

When he didn't come home, she went in search of him, worried that he thought she was angry with him. She checked the garage, went to the diner, and then she went to the bar and saw his truck in the parking lot. She went inside, eager to see him. When Kayleigh told her he was in one of the cabins, she went to find him, to bring him *home*. Then she saw him with *that* woman and her heart and trust had broken all over again. He had already moved on; he thought so little of her that he was able to jump into bed with the next random woman that came along. Christy had been deluding herself that they'd had something, she had hoped they could be something special to each other but not anymore.

She drove back to her parent's house, packed up her belongings and shoved them in the car. She then grabbed the box of letters, the picture frames, and a few other trinkets that were of sentimental value. She left the house, there was nothing else inside she wanted so she would pay someone to come in and clear the rest of it. She was so done with this town. His betrayal had tipped her over the edge and made it so she would never want to step foot in this town again. She couldn't leave just yet though, there was something she needed to do first. She slept in the house for the last time and said her goodbyes in the morning. She might have felt relieved if she wasn't so numb.

She drove to Justine's; she couldn't leave again without saying goodbye. She would call Taylor, she couldn't bear the thought of going to the bar to see her and potentially running into Dean and his woman. Taylor would forgive her, but she didn't think Justine would if she left her for a second time with no explanation.

Justine opened the door and took one look at her and she knew. "Please don't go," she pleaded.

"I have to, I can't stay here," Christy said, her voice broke at the look on Justine's face.

"But, what about Dean?"

Christy laughed humorlessly. "He won't care."

"Then stay for me and Taylor. We'll be so happy just the three of us, I know it."

"I'm sorry, I can't. I'll call you when I get back and maybe you can come for another visit soon?" Justine gripped her in a fierce hug, squeezing her so damn tight. Christy was going to miss her so much, she'd enjoyed spending so much time with them, it felt like they were kids again and they reconnected in a way that she didn't realize she had been missing. They broke away and Justine implored her again to stay, but Christy just shook her head and got in her car. She drove away from her friend, both of them crying. She made it an hour before she heard a loud bang, and then the smoke appeared.

She sat in her vehicle, cursing the death trap that had clearly wheezed its last breath. She needed to call for a tow, but she couldn't, she was still too close to the town. It would be Dean's garage and if he knew it was her then he might turn up. She knew from listening to him on the phone there was a twenty-four-hour towing service, and it was someone else who went out at night so she would have to wait.

So, she sat and waited, cursing the car, the town, and her stupid heart. She felt such longing to be back in his arms, her heart hurt and her stomach ached. Was it possible to get homesick from missing a person? He twisted her world upside down, he was unexpected, that was for sure. If someone told her when she arrived home that first night and bumped into him in the bar that she would end up getting so close, so intimate with him, she would have accused them of having too many of Taylor's cocktails.

But he made sense. It felt right, she had never been this happy with someone before, had never cared this much.

She *loved* him.

She didn't know when it happened, but it had. She was foolish and dammit Taylor had been right to tell her not to get involved with him, she had ended up getting hurt, when would she learn?

She wouldn't change it though, not for the world. Dean made her laugh, made her angry, frustrated, happy, and he had shown her true love. He'd made her a better person and had helped her become a better writer. He wanted to nurture her creativity and had made changes in his life to support her.

Tears ran silently down her cheeks at the thought of

never seeing him again, it wasn't a choice she'd made though, his actions spoke loudly. She loved him, but he didn't love her.

She watched the sun set, drowning in her misery. Then when it was officially late evening, she grabbed her cell and dialed the number she knew practically by heart, ignoring all the missed calls she had received. She sighed in relief when a woman she didn't recognize answered and took some details from her. Christy requested to be taken to the next town over, not wanting to risk seeing Dean, the woman agreed before promising someone would be by within the hour.

Christy got out of the car and stretched her legs, not wanting to roam too far in the dark. After an hour of wandering around and around the car in misery, she watched as a set of headlights approached. She flagged the truck down, the lights so bright they blinded her. When the truck stopped, someone got out of the cabin and came towards her.

"Hello?" she called out, holding her hand up to block the bright lights. Her heart thudded in her chest, hopeful and painful, as she realized who had come for her. He stopped two feet in front of her, his arms folded over his chest and smiled, those damn dimples appearing. Her knees threatened to go weak at the sight of them before she pulled herself together.

"Am I gonna find that exhaust of yours buckled up in the passenger seat again?" he asked, his southern drawl warming her skin, teasing her with memories of all the sweet nothings he had whispered to her. She swallowed thickly against the pain and shook her head, not trusting herself to speak. His smile fell and he fixed her with a hard stare, taking a step forward.

"Where are you going, darlin'?"

"H...home," she stammered. He took another step forward until he was right in front of her, and she had to crane her neck to look up at him. She knew she looked a mess, betrayal and heartbreak did that to a person. She studied him, he smelled clean and fresh, but he looked tired and his eyes were bloodshot. His jaw was dusted with stubble, his hair sticking out in spikes, like he'd plowed his hand through it one too many times. His features were pulled tight, lines of strain bracketed his eyes and mouth.

He shook his head at her. "New York isn't your home."

He was right, but she wouldn't admit it, even if she did feel like she was running away and abandoning her family. On the other hand, it was because of his actions. She found her backbone and straightened her spine.

"So glad you managed to pull yourself away from your lover long enough to come and help out poor little me," she spat sarcastically.

"She means absolutely nothing to me, and it wasn't what it looked like."

"Said every man ever caught cheating!" she scoffed and turned to leave before she lashed out even more. She didn't want to turn into the person she used to be with him. She had matured out of that, but if he kept needling her, she would sink back into her old behavior. As she walked away, he grabbed her hand and spun her around, holding her tightly against him.

"I was wasted last night after I thought you had thrown *me* over for Beau. I went to drown my sorrows at the bar, trying to forget how much I was hurting," he said intensely.

"What? I didn't choose Beau, don't try to blame your actions on me!"

"I know that now and I know why, for the house, but I didn't last night. So, I drank a lot, I wanted to pass out. I left the bar *alone*, it's important you know that." He stroked his fingers over her cheek, she was torn between leaning into his touch and trying to pull away. In the end her anger won out. She tried to wiggle out of his grasp, but he held her too tightly, not letting her get away.

"So, what? She turned up later for a quickie and you thought, yeah, why not?"

"No," he said through clenched teeth. "Darcy followed me, she practically attacked me, and forced herself on me after I *repeatedly* asked her to leave. If anything, I should be mad at you for leaving me in her evil clutches, I barely escaped with my honor intact."

Her eyes flashed angrily. "You seemed like you were enjoying it enough!"

"Darlin', can you stop? I'm trying to tell you something very important," he sighed. She was fast running out of steam, but she still wasn't sure if she believed him. When he called her darlin' like that it made her insides melt which wasn't helping. "Also, if you paid attention during all the times we made love, you would know how I look when I'm enjoying myself," he pouted.

"If I paid attention? How dare you!" she spluttered. He tweaked her nose, clearly relishing how much of a snit she was in. "Don't do that!"

"Anyway, after you left, I passed out. Darcy and I did nothing. I haven't done anything with anyone but you for years. I don't want anyone except you, I've never wanted anyone as much as I want you."

"Wait, did you say '*made love*'?" she whispered, staring up into his brilliant blue eyes. He nodded and as she took in his words, she felt tears welling up in her eyes. He kissed them away as they spilled over onto her cheeks.

"You'll never know how sorry I am that I didn't tell you about the letters. I found them by accident about a week ago and I didn't know how to bring it up, but that's not an excuse because when you love someone, you don't hurt them. That's what I did, I broke your trust and I just hope one day you can forgive me," he said, sincerity coating his words.

"You love me?" she uttered softly, almost scared to ask him to clarify. He just smiled and nodded. "I forgave you immediately, I know you wouldn't have done it on purpose. Since I came back home you've done nothing but care for me, help me, and support me. But when I saw you with Darcy, that hurt," she said, sad eyes peeking up at him through her lashes.

He closed his eyes and sighed, resting his forehead to hers. "I don't know how I can make it up to you."

There was a pause as she replayed his words, letting them sink in.

"You can start by towing my car home," she murmured. His eyes flew open and met hers, hope shining in their depths.

"I'm not towing it home, I'm sending it for scrap and buying you a new one," he joked, and she laughed before he cupped her cheeks, seriousness taking over.

"I love you so much, I promise I'll never hurt you again." He dipped his head and hovered just above her mouth, a breath away, waiting patiently and allowing her to make the choice. She met his lips, pressing their mouths together in a tender kiss.

"You really love me?" she asked gently when they pulled apart.

A smile lit his face. "Very much, tell me you love me too?" he asked hopefully. She bit her lip hesitantly, unsure if she could let go of her issues and give herself over to him completely.

He bent down to her ear. "Tell me you love me, darlin', I know you do. It's only love, you don't need to be afraid anymore, I've got you," he murmured. His breath tickling her ear, sending her pulse skittering.

She wavered. "This is crazy! We've never even been on a date!"

"A date?!" he whooped with laughter. God, she loved his laugh. "I don't need to take you on a date to know I want to spend the rest of my life with you! We might never have been on a date together, but I've spent my whole life learning about you. I know everything I need to know, and I can't wait to find out anything else. But if this is a sticking point, then I guess I'll have to take you on a date."

She threw her arms around him and plastered kisses all over his face.

"Does this mean you want a date?" he asked.

She smiled at him. "No, you fool, it means I love you."

He pulled her tighter to him and kissed her again before setting her back down. He ran to her car, grabbed the box of letters and her luggage from the back seat, throwing it into the bed of his truck. Then grabbed her purse before coming back to her and sweeping her off her feet and into his arms.

"What're you doing?" she gasped as he hefted her up and marched back towards his truck.

"I'm taking you home, Marilyn." He put her in his truck and they drove off. On the way back to town she called Taylor, Justine and Beau. She told them she was staying and would see them tomorrow morning at the bar to celebrate.

"Good," he growled. "Tonight, you're mine."

He spent the night showing her how much he loved

her, and she showed him right back.

Two months later...

Dean waited outside his study, his ear pressed to the door, his heart pounding in his chest. *Honestly the first time ever she goes in there and doesn't immediately start writing, just typical!* He thought with a smile. Although it wasn't *his* study anymore, it was hers since she moved in with him. Who would have thought fifteen years ago that he and Christy Lee would be head over heels in love and shacked up together, not him that's for sure! The last two months had been the most amazing time of his life, all thanks to her.

The second he'd brought her back to town, she declared his home was now hers. He chuckled at the memory, although she declared it, there had been worry in her eyes that he wouldn't feel the same. Hell, this place only felt like a true home when she was here, he had been ecstatic that she wanted to move in straight away, and he spent the rest of the night...and morning...showing her how happy he was.

They only left the bedroom to show up at the bar the next morning to see everyone. He felt so proud walking in there, with her on his arm. She was his. His forever. Taylor had thrown herself at them both the second she saw them, sobbing. The first time he'd ever seen her actually cry. She was so happy Christy was staying, so grateful to him that he made it happen and that they were going to be one big, happy family.

Beau came over and hugged them both, equally pleased, especially now he was moving back to the town, something Dean was also ecstatic about, could life get any better? As Christy moved away to speak to Taylor and

Justine, squeezing his hand gently before letting it go, he and Beau started talking.

"So, I guess I'll officially have to stop flirting with her now, huh?" Beau asked, a shit-eating grin on his face.

Dean punched him on the arm. "Bitch, please. You were never a threat."

Beau nodded. "That is true, although how does it feel knowing I kissed her first?"

Dean's smile fell off his face. Beau turned to face Christy, folding his arms over his chest and tapping his chin in contemplation.

"I mean, you have her now, and forever, blah blah blah, but technically, I had her first..." Beau trailed off and fixed him with a stare.

"Run..." Dean growled, Beau barked out a laugh and ran outside, Dean following close behind. They had made it to the children's play area before Dean tackled him to the ground, and gave him a dead arm, and a dead leg for good measure. Dean chuckled at the memory, *served the bastard right*. The women had come outside to watch them wrestling and, eventually, Christy begged them to stop, not wanting Beau to damage Dean's pretty face. They both laughed and came over to where the women were standing.

"Hey, Blake," Taylor called, waving as the new deputy headed into the bar. All of a sudden, Justine grabbed Beau and pulled him to her for a kiss. Beau stumbled and slammed into her, pinning her to the wall of the bar, obscuring her from view.

As they kissed, Dean flicked his eyes to Christy, *when did this happen?* Christy just shrugged and he moved his eyes to Taylor, whose lips thinned and eyes narrowed as she watched them. As soon as the door to the bar banged shut behind Blake, Justine pulled away from Beau.

"Sorry, Beau, I don't think it's going to work," she said, patting his shoulder and turning to speak to Christy. Beau looked as confused as the rest of them.

The sound of Christy's mumbling brought him back to the present, she was working on the first draft of her new book. He wasn't allowed to read it until it was finished, but he couldn't wait. He loved curling up with her on the couch in her study and having her bounce ideas off him. She was so talented and he was so thrilled that he got to be part of her process.

"*Oh my God...*" she cried from inside her study. Dean smiled to himself, *showtime*. He took a deep breath, tried to stop himself from shaking and opened the door. He walked into the room and she stood up from her desk, her notepad in her hand, still reading what was on the page. She turned to face him, shock lining her features and watched as he slowly got down on one knee and produced a small box. Her hands went to her face and he opened the box.

"Christy, will you-" he started, his voice shaking slightly from his nerves, but that was as far as he got. She screamed and flung herself at him, tackling him to the floor, showering him with kisses.

"Yes," *kiss, kiss,* "of course," *kiss, kiss, kiss,* "I'll marry you!"

He chuckled and rolled on top of her, pinning her with his weight, kissing her lips, tilting her head to dive deeper, and she sighed into his mouth. When they pulled apart, he took her hand and placed the ring on her finger. She looked at the ring, then at him and promptly burst into tears. He laughed and pulled her to him, swallowing the lump that formed in his throat.

*

That night, when their friends came around for a

barbecue, Christy showed everyone the ring. There was screaming, applause, tears, and hugs all round. Even Beau got a little choked up, which Christy thought was super sweet. The girls took her to one side to start talking wedding dresses and venues, while Beau and Dean were at the grill talking bachelor parties.

"No strippers!" she shouted over to them, and Dean laughed.

"I don't wanna see anyone naked but you, darlin'," he replied. Justine sighed dreamily, Beau chuckled, and Taylor muttered, "Gross."

"Let me go and get some drinks," Christy said, getting up and heading into the kitchen, leaving Taylor and Justine to talk flower arrangements. As she made her way back out onto the terrace with a pitcher of margaritas, Christy paused. Dean and Beau were at the grill, Beau and Taylor sniping at each other, and Justine was sitting watching them and laughing. Her heart squeezed in her chest. This was it, what she imagined but even better because it had come true.

She was so full of love and surrounded by her family that she felt her heart would burst with happiness. Who would've thought a few months ago, when she returned home with such dread, that this would be the outcome? Not her that was for sure.

She went back outside and sat down with Taylor and Justine, not really listening to what they were saying, instead she was eyeing up the sexy blond at the grill. The way he threw back his head with laughter, his biceps flexing when he moved his arms, his back muscles rippling through his shirt. She shivered and couldn't wait to get her hands on him later. As though he read her mind, he turned and their eyes met. He smiled at her, those gorgeous dimples of his making an appearance and he winked, his smile promising a night to remember.

"-I just don't understand, that's all," Taylor cried out, pulling Christy's attention away from her future *husband*.

"Understand what?" Christy asked.

"Why Justine isn't interested in asking out Blake," Taylor replied.

"The new sheriff?" Dean called over his shoulder.

"He's just not my type, how many times do I have to tell you?" Justine replied, exasperation in her tone. As they bickered back and forth, Christy watched Justine closely, Justine avoiding her stare. She didn't believe for a second he wasn't her type, there was definitely something more there. But then Dean came over and dropped a kiss on her mouth, distracting her.

Later that night when everyone had gone home, Christy was back in her study. She was looking at the pictures on her desk; one of her and the girls, one of her and Dean, and the one of her parents. Now when she thought of them, she felt nothing but love. She had chosen to let go of the past and embrace her future. She looked at the photo frame she added to the collection this afternoon. A black wooden frame with a slip of paper inside. She had been furiously writing away earlier today when she turned to the next page in her notebook, and her heart had stopped dead.

Will you marry me?

Four simple words. The promise of forever. The best thing anyone had ever written and the easiest decision she ever had to make. She felt him come up behind her now, wrapping his arms around her and trailing kisses down her neck.

"It's time for bed, my future wife," he murmured

against her skin.

"Mrs. Campbell...has a nice ring to it doesn't it?" she replied.

He moaned against her skin. "Say it again."

She laughed, dropping her voice seductively, "Mrs. Campbell."

"That's it!" he shouted and lifted her into his arms. She shrieked with laughter as he ran out of the study and into the bedroom where he gently placed her on the bed and then began loving her in that way of his that promised her forever.

THE END

Turn the page for a sneak peek at Justine and Blake's story coming Autumn 2021!

Lila Dawes

Chapter 1

*Any second now I'm in danger of being able to talk about myself...*Justine Valentina Rodríguez-Hamilton thought, fighting an eye roll. The man sitting opposite her was so engrossed in talking about himself that he hadn't even noticed her boredom. She ran her eyes over his rust-colored hair, then took in his ruddy complexion and pale blue eyes. He was very attractive, smartly dressed and had nice manners, but his conversation skills were definitely lacking. She tried to remain attentive but if she had to listen to him talk about tractors one more time, she was gonna lose it.

She was *sick* of dating. There were slim pickings in her small town so any new bachelors she heard about through the gossip grapevine she pounced on immediately, investigating them for any potential to become Mr. Justine Valentina Rodríguez-Hamilton. She tried not to come across like she woke up every morning and spritzed herself head to toe with *Desperation* by Calvin Klein, but she felt like Charlotte in that episode of *Sex and the City* where she was ranting that she was exhausted from dating.

Her current date Tommy was from the next town. He had recently bought a farm and he was looking for a ~~farmhand~~ wife to help him run it. Although Justine was looking to settle down, a farm was not where she wanted or needed to be. No, thank you. Not that there was anything wrong with farming, it just wasn't her thing. For starters, she wouldn't be able to do her actual job, which she loved.

She was a psychologist, she loved her work, relished delving into the complexities of people's thoughts and feelings, learning the way their brains worked. She loved that her job combined academics and patient care, and that every day was different. Her drive to help people was what kept her motivated to continually grow and develop her skills. In her spare time, she liked to flex her creative muscles by writing music and performing occasionally here at The Rusty Bucket Inn. Her life was well-rounded, it was as full as it could be, but there was something missing. Something that couldn't be filled by working on a farm, darn it.

She didn't exactly have lofty ambitions for life. It's not like she wanted to be a millionaire married to Chris Evans...*drool*...or even become a world-famous musician. She just wanted a normal life, a strong career and marriage to a wonderful man followed by the typical two point four children. It wasn't very forward-thinking of her, but she was traditional at heart, raised in a traditional household. She could almost feel Susan B. Anthony turning in her grave.

Justine had done the other stuff. She had a successful

career, owned her own home and had been fully independent since she was eighteen years old. She had ticked off all the items on her 'Checklist of Life' except the man and the kids. *So, thanks for everything Susan, truly, but I'll take it from here.* She sighed deeply, she just needed to keep going and to believe that these things were coming, but damn she was tired.

"Do you have much experience with udders?" Tommy asked her, interrupting her deep thoughts.

She offered him a smile, "I'm afraid not, I'd be udder-ly useless."

"Not a problem, you can always learn," he replied, her lame joke going straight over his head, banging the final nail in the potential romance coffin. *Dios mio.* She sighed inwardly and reached for her glass of rosé, downing it. Tommy was good-looking but far too serious for her. She definitely had a type: the men she went for tended to be preppy businessman types, smart, mature, funny, emotionally available family men. A bit like her father actually. *Ooh don't open that door.*

Her parents had met when they were in their senior year of high school. Justine's grandparents had just immigrated from Mexico. Her mother, Valentina, didn't speak very much English at the time. One afternoon after school, some of the local boys were trying to take advantage of her naivety when Justine's father, James, swooped in and saved the day. He was besotted with the Mexican beauty, and they had been together ever since, true high school sweethearts.

It was a fairy-tale, and Justine wanted the fairy-tale too and wouldn't settle for anything less. She wanted that perfect, easy, all-consuming love that you only read about. The kind of love her parents shared, that her brothers had with their wives, and that her friends Christy and Dean had recently found. When she was around them, she could see it, feel it, in everything they did, it lifted them up. She sometimes found it hard to be around them, on days when she struggled to keep up the happy-go-lucky *I'm not gonna die alone!* façade. So, when would it be *her* turn?

Justine's lungs constricted in mild panic; her parents had been nearly twenty years younger than she was when they met. When would she catch a break? She'd begun to panic that she would be alone forever. She was thirty-four and time was running out if she wanted to find her true love and start a family.

"Oh, look, I need another drink," Justine said, leaping to her feet, then her manners kicked in. "Would you like another beer?" she asked. Her date nodded, and she tottered over to the bar, her heels clicking on the wooden floor. She placed her empty glass on top of the bar, sighing again.

"Hey babe! What are you doing here tonight?" Taylor, one of her best friends and part owner of The Rusty Bucket Inn, cooed at her, coming out of her office. Justine hiked her thumb over her shoulder towards her date.

"Ooh he's cute, what do you think?" Taylor asked, but Justine shook her head sadly. "Aw I'm sorry hon, another rosé?"

"Yes please, a large one, and a beer too."

Taylor turned away to get the drinks. "You're looking mighty fine tonight, FYI. You're even giving me feels!" she called over her shoulder. Taylor always complimented everyone; she was such a sweetheart under all her sass. Justine ran her hands over her orange satin dress.

"Thanks, Tay. You know exactly what to say to cheer me up," she laughed.

She felt her mood lifting, not only was she feeling down about the whole single thing, but she was stressing about work. Well, about a new client in particular. Blake Miller, the town's new deputy sheriff. She had successfully managed to avoid him so far, not wanting to meet him before their first session tomorrow. She didn't like having personal relationships with her clients, she felt that they came to their sessions with preconceived notions of her and behaved differently, and how else could she help them if they weren't authentic with her?

She would start from scratch with Blake so he would come to his session open-minded, fresh and raw. She wanted to delve into his psyche, immerse herself in his thoughts and feelings until she understood what made him tick. He was intriguing, something about him drew her. Maybe it was because he had a list of problems as long as her arm.

He was a widower, ex-military, suffering from PTSD, insomnia, anxiety, depression *and* he was hard-faced and emotionally stunted...*come to mama!* He presented her with a true professional challenge. She'd never had a client like him before and she was eager to get inside his head, even if she was a little scared she might be out of her depth.

Her mind scoffed at the thought of him, how this gorgeous man had been sent to her town, as though the universe were mocking her. He was definitely the most attractive man in Citrus Pines, and the most serious. Although she preferred men who didn't act like the world would end if they smiled, watching Blake Miller frown around town these last few weeks had made her seriously reconsider her type. *Goodbye comedians, hello Mr. Broody.*

But it didn't matter, she couldn't have him. As his new psychologist she was bound by her ethics, to treat him and not develop any personal attachments to him. Which was fine because Blake wasn't her type, he was too *messy*, and Justine didn't do messy. She was a perfectionist. When she met her one true love, he wouldn't have any emotional baggage, he wouldn't have been married before, he wouldn't be emotionally stunted and unable to connect to others. She would be his only love; they would be soulmates and live happily ever after.

Justine was pulled out of her thoughts by a loud, high-pitched giggle. She turned to see her friend, Beau, entering the bar with a cheeky-looking blond woman on his arm. He gestured to a booth in the corner, the blond giggled again and went to take a seat. Beau headed towards the bar, smiling when he saw Justine.

"Evening Justine, don't you look beautiful. Who's the lucky guy?" he asked, friendly charm coating his words. She nodded in the direction of her date and Beau peered over her shoulder.

"Not bad!" he exclaimed as Taylor put Justine's glass of rosé on the bar.

"Then why don't you date him?" Taylor drawled sarcastically. Justine rolled her eyes, *Lord, here we go.* She hated getting caught in the middle of their spats. Christy wasn't the only one of their original friendship group who had recently moved back to town. Beau had returned to Citrus Pines after living in L.A. for the last fourteen years. They had all been friends as kids, he and Taylor at one point had been best friends. Then they had a falling out and shortly after, he had moved away. She was so glad he and Christy were home, their group was back together, and everything felt right again. Well, despite Beau and Taylor's obvious hatred for each other, but you can't have everything.

"Hello Taylor, I see your sunny disposition is brightening up the bar this evening as usual," he drawled.

Taylor shot him a withering look and moved away to fetch Tommy's beer.

"You're not usually one for dating on a school night," Beau teased Justine.

"Desperate times and all that," she shrugged. He was right, normally she wouldn't be on a date during the week but with tomorrow being her first session with Blake, she needed something to take her mind off her nerves.

"Well, let me know if you need rescuing at all," Beau said, and Justine gestured towards his date, who currently had her hand in her bra trying to get her cleavage to really *pop*.

"You too."

Beau glanced at his date and chuckled, "I think I'll be fine, she's a little handsy but I like that," he replied loudly, his gaze flickering to Taylor's back before moving away again and Justine thought she heard Taylor snort.

"Two beers Taylor, hold the arsenic. Bring them over to us whenever you're ready," he said, then winked at Justine and sauntered away.

"Thank you!" Taylor called after him sarcastically.

"You're welcome!" He threw back over his shoulder and Justine watched as rage reddened Taylor's cheeks.

"You brought that on yourself, *chica*," she said, and Taylor turned her glare on Justine.

"Card or cash?" Taylor seethed through clenched teeth. Justine laughed and handed over her credit card. As Taylor walked off to grab the card reader, Justine felt heat envelope her, followed by the heady scent of spice and sin. She recognized the scent, it was already ingrained in her. She turned and found herself face to face with a pair of silver eyes that had haunted her dreams for months.

Her new client had entered the bar...

Acknowledgements

I want to thank my mum for showing me how this is all done, like she has with everything else in life, it never would have happened without her. She's been saying for years that I should write, and I wish I'd listened sooner.

I also want to thank Anna, Andrea and Carly for all your support and feedback, I'm so lucky to have met you wonderfully talented writers through this community. Thank you for befriending me, encouraging me and for being the first people to ever read something I'd written and not telling me it was crap!

Thank you to all my amazing BETA and ARC readers and reviewers, your feedback and comments helped me shape this story and get the best out of it and I'm so grateful for you all!

About the Author

Lila is a thirtysomething writer living in Derbyshire, England with her *cough* parents *cough*, elderly tortoiseshell cat and perpetually dying bonsai tree, Benny. She loves romance, sharks, cats and has an ~~un~~healthy obsession with Henry Cavill.

It's Only Love is her debut novel and the first in the Citrus Pines series. Lila is a huge fan of the romance reading and writing community so why not say hello, she can be found on Instagram, Facebook, Goodreads, Tiktok and website: https://linktr.ee/liladawes

Printed in Great Britain
by Amazon